Praise for Shelley Munro's
The Bottom Line

"The Bottom Line was such a fun and sexy read. There is a scene where the group of friends decide to try speed dating and Maggie starts off each meeting with "How do you feel about spanking?" I could recommend this book based on that scene alone but, luckily, I don't have to. I thoroughly enjoyed it from beginning to end. Another keeper from Shelley Munro!"
~ *I Do Not Want To Wait, I Want The Book Now.*

"Ms. Munro has created an erotic story with The Bottom Line which will keep your thoughts heated while you read about Connor warming certain parts of Maggie's anatomy!"
~ *Fallen Angel Reviews.*

"The Bottom Line is a delightful tale with an interesting twist with the blog. I found it laugh out loud funny and hypnotizing at the same time. The story draws you in immediately and makes it very difficult to put down, waiting to see what happens next. Shelley Munro scribes a superb story that I completely enjoyed."
~ *Sensual Reads.com.*

"This book took me by surprise. I went in thinking it would be a quick fluffy read but, as it turns out, this story was a great read full of emotion and depth... Shelley Munro does a wonderful job of catching the reader's attention and keeping it all the way to the end."
~ *Whipped Cream*

Look for these titles by
Shelley Munro

Now Available:

Tea for Two
Seeking Kokopelli

The Bottom Line

Shelley Munro

Samhain Publishing, Ltd.
577 Mulberry Street, Suite 1520
Macon, GA 31201
www.samhainpublishing.com

The Bottom Line
Copyright © 2011 by Shelley Munro
Print ISBN: 978-1-60928-020-8
Digital ISBN: 978-1-60504-985-4

Editing by Linda Ingmanson
Cover by Scott Carpenter

This book is a work of fiction. The names, characters, places, and incidents are products of the writer's imagination or have been used fictitiously and are not to be construed as real. Any resemblance to persons, living or dead, actual events, locale or organizations is entirely coincidental.

All Rights Are Reserved. No part of this book may be used or reproduced in any manner whatsoever without written permission, except in the case of brief quotations embodied in critical articles and reviews.

First Samhain Publishing, Ltd. electronic publication: April 2010
First Samhain Publishing, Ltd. print publication: March 2011

Dedication

Thank you to Jina Bacarr for your enthusiasm and help with The Bottom Line during the initial stages. Your advice and input was invaluable.

Thanks to Fedora for reading this story and giving me such great feedback. I appreciate your help more than I can say.

For my editor Linda Ingmanson. Thanks so much. This story is much better after your editorial eye.

And last, but definitely not least, thanks to Paul, my original sounding board. You're the best.

Chapter One

"Your turn, Maggie." Julia's eyes sparkled with devilment.

"Already?" *Yikes.* Maggie Drummond grabbed her margarita off the table and took a fortifying sip. The tart, icy liquid did nothing to quell her jitters.

It was time—*Tell a Secret* to the gang from work. The Tight Five, they called themselves, the name taken from a rugby term where five players bound in a tight formation to face the opposition team. They were like that. Five friends who worked in close proximity at an accountancy firm and who maintained the friendship away from the job. The good and the bad—they knew each other well.

Julia had spilled the beans about her latest boyfriend on a night much like this over margaritas. A blow-by-blow description of the seduction. The red crotchless panties. The blue pubic hair. Soon their love of gossip grew into a weekly ritual at the Cock and Bull, a "You tell me yours, I'll tell you mine" kind of thing.

The crowded pub rocked with music and erotic promise. Maggie squirmed, avoiding catching the gazes of her three friends. She never had anything worth telling.

Until today.

Fidgeting with her drink, scratching at an imaginary zit, clearing her throat a dozen times wasn't helping. She was losing her nerve and losing it fast.

"C'mon, Maggie. Tell us your secret," Julia shouted.

Maggie slouched in her seat as several heads turned her way, giving her the once-over. *Why did Julia have to yell?* Okay, so the men sitting at the next table wouldn't hear her over the pounding throb of guitars, saxophone and the male vocalist headlining in the packed bar. She hoped.

Susan and Christina nodded with enthusiasm, grinning, their attention focused on her. Maggie hated the limelight, always had since a childhood filled with her mother's antics and histrionics. The big *event* that had sent her scurrying north to hide in Auckland had helped cement Maggie's resolution to stay away from the glare of publicity. Sighing, she forced her thoughts from the past and wondered if this was a good idea. It wasn't too late to stop, yet gut instinct forced her on, telling her she was an adult. Free to make choices and deal with the consequences. She wasn't her mother, despite her father and stepmother's harsh words.

The fine tremor of nerves slipping down her arm confirmed her disquiet. The slushy ice in her margarita tinkled against the edges of the glass, jogged by the quiver of her hands. She set her drink on the table and sucked in a deep breath, steeling herself to blurt out her secret. Not a feeble confession, like it usually was. Today she had a real secret.

Get it out.

She opened her mouth and closed it again. She couldn't. Sure, it was a game they played when there were a few drinks involved—margaritas usually. But this time was different. It was her innermost desire she was about to reveal. The others had taken their turns and giggled like schoolgirls instead of employees of the staid Barker & Johnson, one of Auckland's premier accounting firms. They'd released their inhibitions—a side effect of Friday night drinks and the promise of a long holiday weekend.

Now the floor belonged to her.

She licked her bottom lip, stress bubbling in the pit of her stomach. Time to produce a secret.

"What are you waiting for, Maggie?" Susan asked in a sing-song voice. "We've told you ours."

"*Secret. Secret. Secret.*" Christina banged her palms on the edge of the table. Julia and Susan joined in the beat, their eyes gleaming with challenge in the dim light of the booth.

Maggie picked up her margarita and gulped to moisten her

dry mouth. "Okay. *Okay.*"

Placing her glass on a coaster, she glanced around the bar. No doubt about it. People were starting to stare. Time to spill her secret before things turned ugly. After another deep breath, she dropped her gaze to her clasped hands. "I've started a website called BigBadAss.com." She spoke so quickly the words ran together. Once finished, she scanned each of her friends in turn, anxious now for their reactions.

"Big bad ass?" Christina's watchful eyes held curiosity while her lips curved in an approving smile. She pushed her frameless glasses up her nose with perfectly manicured copper fingernails. "Isn't that pretty racy for you?"

"What's the big deal?" Julia scoffed and tossed her head before Maggie could answer. Her blonde hair stirred and settled in sexy curls around her almost bare shoulders. Shoestring straps held her low-cut black top in place. "It's just a website."

"Who's a bad ass?" Susan smirked. "Don't say Greg has gone and found some balls?"

"Bother, I have a smear." Christina rifled through her handbag for a tissue to clean her glasses. "Anyway, I want to hear more about this website."

Questions. Maggie had expected them, but the comments and queries didn't put her at ease. Her stomach vibrated like one of her younger brother's toys—over-wound and about to fly apart. She wiped sweaty palms on her sensible navy skirt, swallowed and said, "It's more of a blog."

"A blog about what?" Julia asked, rolling her eyes. "Desperados? Bandits? What's a bad ass?"

Maggie closed her eyes briefly to summon courage. This next part was worse. Her teeth clacked when she closed her mouth. The longer her hesitation, the worse the mental strain would become. Big bad ass, she wasn't. More like a marshmallow, burnt on the outside with a gooey interior.

"I explore...um...my adventures in spanking," Maggie said, forcing a smile. "Does anyone want another drink?"

"Spanking," Susan cried out as the band ended their song and the haunting notes of a sax faded. Everyone in the vicinity heard her shocked shriek. Heads turned, customers surveying them with distinct interest. Two men at a nearby table leered.

Their dark suits suggested they worked at the lawyer's office next door, but their toothy smirks told Maggie their minds crawled in the gutter, armed with floggers and paddles.

"Shush," she muttered, aware of the two plum-sized patches heating her cheeks. "It's a secret. I don't want everyone to know."

Christina picked up her drink, golden bracelets jingling with musical grace. "Since when were you interested in spanking, Maggie?"

"Yeah," Julia demanded. "How long has this been going on?"

Susan smirked, her gaze darting from Christina to Julia and back to Maggie. "Does Greg spank you?"

"Um..." Oh, heck. She'd known they'd have lots of questions. Greg was her boyfriend. Solid, dependable and boring. How was she going to tell him? True, she was still a spanking novice, but Maggie was determined not to chicken out. She would explore spanking. It wouldn't be like the fad diets she tried and failed.

Her spanking interest—or sickness, depending on how a girl looked at it—began with a book and some in-depth soul-searching along with a bottle of wine. She'd hauled her drunken self off to bed and, after reading more of the erotic romance, she'd had the best orgasm ever. Yeah, if she could scale those heights by herself, a real extravaganza lay ahead with a male lover. Right there, she decided to explore her wild side and the naughty spike of pleasure that jolted her right to the core every time she considered a swat on the ass. The fiery heat...

She could see the curiosity filling Susan's blue eyes, the nosy interest mirrored in Christina and Julia's faces. "You asked for *one* secret. I've given you one and you have to promise not to tell anyone." Maggie had no idea where this new bravery had come from. It reminded her of her teenage years, and she liked its return. The inner Maggie cheered, enjoying the nonplussed expressions on her friends' faces.

"What about Connor? We can tell him, right?" Julia toyed with her straw, cocking her head to the side as she studied Maggie. "He would have been here if his rugby coach hadn't called an extra training session."

"No!" Color climbed into Maggie's cheeks. "Not unless you're going to tell him your secrets as well." A glower through narrowed eyes served as a warning, an attempt to enforce her will.

She closed her eyes briefly. Her recent behavior would appall her father and stepmother who still reeled over the scandal of Penisgate. More gossip about their daughter would send them over the edge. What had come over her lately? Maybe a vitamin deficiency or something. In addition to thinking about spanking and researching kink, her fantasies had sprung into full sexy Technicolor. They featured Connor, and it wasn't his cooking skills that interested her.

It was wrong.

"You can't tell Connor." Her friends would kill her if they learned about her fascination with Connor, especially since they'd all agreed over a year ago he was off limits. His friendship and insight into the male mind was more valuable than momentary pleasure. None of them had experienced male friendship on this level before. Besides, the inevitable breakup would tear the Tight Five apart. Connor's relationships didn't last long.

Her crush on him was wrong on so many levels because she was still involved with Greg. But a bad girl struggled beneath her skin, trying to kick her way out in a bid for freedom. Her pointy boots were like sharp weapons, pricking at Maggie's conscience.

"You can't spill a delicious secret like this and not give us a little more. Please, I'm begging you," Christina said. "I'll give you a free makeover in exchange for details."

"And I'll contribute to the cost of the makeover." Julia lifted her glass and toasted Christina. "Your fledgling business can't take the entire cost of a freebie."

"I'll contribute too. See? That's how bad we need the juicy details." Susan lifted her glass, empty except for one ice cube. Frowning, she tipped the ice into her mouth and crunched it loudly. She swallowed without taking her attention off Maggie. "We need more drinks. Wait right there, Maggie, and don't say another word until I get back."

Susan grabbed a tray from under the table, stacked the

empties on it and pushed through the throng of customers to get to the bar. Julia and Christina stared at Maggie in fascination. They gawked for so long she raised her hand to check for an extra nose.

"Stop staring at me. I feel like a specimen on a microscope slide." Maggie shot to her feet. "I'll go help Susan with the drinks. It's my turn to buy, anyway."

"You're not going anywhere until you answer our questions." Julia grabbed her arm, her blonde brows scrunched together. "By the way, where's Greg tonight?"

"He's at rugby training with Connor," Maggie said, sitting back down. "They're on the same team, remember?"

"Does he know about the spanking? Heck, I can't imagine him with a flogger or a paddle—" Christina broke off, her eyes widening. "Does that mean you're—" Part of a chortle escaped before she slapped a hand over her mouth to block the rest.

"You're not spanking Greg, are you?" Julia asked, finishing her friend's sentence.

"No one's spanking anyone yet," Maggie snapped, wriggling a little on her seat as arousal sped through her body. The merest thought of a perfectly placed thwack brought a rush of excitement. Not with Greg, though. Imagining Greg and spanking in the same sentence made her head ache. A big time problem, since he was her boyfriend. How did a girl broach the subject with her guy? *Honey, I want you to spank me.* Nope, it wasn't something that came up in normal everyday conversation.

Susan arrived back with the tray of drinks in time to overhear Maggie's reply. "Why not?" Her friend shunted a margarita across the pitted wooden tabletop and tossed two bags of peanuts and a bag of crisps at them. "Tell us why, Maggie, and don't leave out a thing."

Her friends' expressions told Maggie escape would be impossible until they received an explanation. In detail. She dragged in another breath, which did nothing to still her skittish nerves. Best to spit it out so they could move on in conversation.

"When I flew to Wellington to visit my father and stepmother two weeks ago, I forgot to take a book with me. I was running late and grabbed the first one I saw with an interesting cover." She grinned, remembering the hunky guy on the book jacket. "I didn't realize I'd purchased an erotic romance until I'd boarded the plane."

"You read romances in a public place?" Julia demanded, shocked.

Maggie shrugged. "The cover wasn't graphic. Quite tasteful with a naked back and a sexy tattoo. Besides, I don't care what anyone thinks about my reading material. I'm not apologizing for enjoying genre fiction."

Not even to Greg, she finished silently. His snide remarks pissed her off. These days she kept her erotic books out of Greg's sight. It was easier than listening to a lecture about literary fiction.

"Don't forget we know you," Christina said, wagging a bejeweled finger in Maggie's direction. "You don't like talking to strangers, and shoving your nose in a book is a way to ignore people."

"So I'm shy. Shoot me." The truth was strangers who paid her attention scared her. There was always the chance it was a reporter who recognized her and wanted to dissect the past. Heck, recollections of Penisgate still gave her nightmares. Only when she came to know people did the wariness fade to manageable portions.

"Don't change the subject." Susan licked the salt off the rim of her glass, her long, straight hair falling forward to cover her cheek. Impatiently, she brushed it back, tucking the annoying strand behind her ear. "Get back to the spanking." The foil packaging of the peanut packet rustled when she opened it. "Carry on."

Maggie's nose wrinkled in acknowledgment. Seemed prevarication wouldn't do the trick. Her friends knew her too well.

"The romance novel was about a couple who used spanking as part of their sex lives. It..." She paused to lave her lips again, the resulting soreness telling her it was time to quit with the licking. "It turned me on," she finished on a rush, her gaze dropping to her drink. Her quick sip gave her friends a convenient pause to slip in questions. They didn't take advantage, remaining silent, waiting for her to speak again. *Bother.*

"It...ah, made me curious," Maggie continued. "So I did some research and decided spanking sounded interesting, something I wanted to try." And she still couldn't believe she'd ignored her past experience and done something that might attract attention from others. She scanned her friend's faces, waiting for them to say something, anything. "I suppose you think I'm some sort of freak."

Susan's hand covered Maggie's. "Of course we don't, sweetie. It's what you think that's important. What does Greg say?"

"I...I haven't mentioned it to him yet. I thought I'd do it tonight or some time during the weekend."

"Bigbadass dot com," Christina mused. "What sort of things do you write about?"

"Stuff," Maggie said, keeping her answer purposefully vague. Was it hot in here or what? She slid the top button of her cream shirt open and picked up a cardboard coaster to fan her face. She couldn't help but smile. Her blog stats were going to rise. It didn't take a genius to realize her friends would check out her guilty secret.

"You know we're gonna look," Julia said.

"That's okay," Maggie replied. *Liar. Liar. Pants on fire.* "But if any of you tell anyone I'm Big Bad Ass, I'll...I'll smother you with my breasts." Raised brows and a broad grin signaled her triumph. She bounced on the padded seat, making her generous breasts jiggle. "It won't be a pleasant way to go. And don't think I couldn't hold you down, because I could. I've been going to the gym with Connor." A flex of her right arm showed off her new muscle tone.

"Ooh," Susan cooed. "Armed and dangerous."

"Yeah. And don't forget it," Maggie said, firm and sure of herself.

Julia giggled. "Connor said he'd dragged you off to the gym, but I didn't believe him."

"He felt sorry for me because Greg was so busy with his clients," Maggie said. "He caught me crying one day, and before I knew it, he had me sweating my way through a boxing class."

"And you're still going to the gym?" Christina asked.

Maggie nodded. "I whined a lot during the first visit, and I still complain for form's sake, but I enjoy it. And don't tell Connor. I'll deny everything."

She'd die if the gang knew her other secret. Watching Connor work out at the gym. A sigh whistled past her teeth. He looked mighty fine with the sheen of sweat coating his skin. They didn't exactly work out together, since, as a newbie, she couldn't keep up with him, but they arrived and left together.

Maggie valued the time spent with Connor. They laughed and talked about things—lots of things that had nothing to do with work or the weather. It had been so easy to let him slip into her fantasies. The bad girl inside Maggie hadn't put up much of a fight, happy to daydream about Connor and lots of delicious kink at the same time.

Another change she'd have to make in her future. Connor had a girlfriend, one of many in a long line of leggy blondes. She had Greg, and there was her agreement with Julia, Christina and Susan, not that Connor would be sexually interested in her voluptuous curves.

"Are you sure we can't tell Connor?" Julia asked with a faint pleading tone.

"Not unless you want me to tell him about your blue pubic hair," Maggie retorted. The others laughed, albeit a trifle uneasily. Their secrets were hers to tell as well.

"I did it for a dare," Julia snapped.

Maggie's brows rose. "Doesn't matter. A juicy secret is a juicy secret."

"Oh, all right." Julia's shoulders slumped in defeat. "I won't tell. Mine is a girls' only secret."

"Your current lover will know," Christina said with a chuckle. "What does he think about the blue heart?"

"He likes it," Julia retorted, unfazed by their laughter. "He thinks I'm adventurous." Her grin brought a host of giggles.

Maggie glanced at her watch. After ten. Definitely time to head home. "I should go, otherwise Greg will arrive at the apartment before me."

She stood and lurched to the side. *Problem.* On the second attempt, her legs trembled, her balance not the best. A tight grasp of the tabletop prevented an embarrassing fall on her butt. Bother, the last drink had been a mistake. She should have eaten some peanuts. Diets and cocktails weren't a good mix.

"Greg doesn't need you to hold his hand," Susan said.

Julia winked. "Maggie might want to discuss spanking with him."

"Not tonight," Maggie said in a wry tone. "I'll need all my wits about me when I start that discussion."

Besides, her stomach hurt each time the topic of Greg and spanking combined in the same thought. Call her a pessimist, but her present anxiety didn't bode well for the future.

The cabbie dropped Maggie at her door. She paid the driver, then stumbled from the cab and up the three steps leading to her apartment building. She took the lift to the second floor and pulled out her keys. A curse squeezed past her tight lips when the keyhole moved from side to side. Muttering another string of naughty words under her breath, she aimed her key at the lock. Without warning, the door opened. She lurched forward, her nose colliding with a masculine chest. *Oops.*

"Hey, G-G-Greg!" A wave of alcoholic fumes exited with her warble. It must have been worse than she thought, because Greg took a step back, holding the door open. He smiled, except it didn't reach his eyes. Even in her relaxed state, his chilly attitude registered, and her stomach plunged with apprehension. Great. The last thing she wanted was a fight.

"You're drunk."

"They kept forcing margaritas on me." Maggie smirked, admitting to herself her friends hadn't exactly twisted her arm.

"Those girls are a bad influence on you." Disdain shone in his eyes. "I don't know why you hang out with them."

"They're my friends. I like them." *Same old. Same old.* Maggie put her hand to her forehead, but the pounding continued. Well-meaning people, including her parents, always told her how to behave. Why did she put up with it?

"Maggie..." Greg began, his tone telling her he had more to say.

"Can we change the subject?" she asked, trying to smile. "We always fight about my friends."

Maggie flicked on the light. If her unsteady steps made her bump into something, she'd prefer reality over imagination. Objects developed creepy crawly legs in the dark, but that didn't prepare her for what she saw—Greg sporting a black eye.

"What happened to your eye?"

"It's nothing," Greg said, trying to make light of his injury.

"Yes, it is. Who hit you?"

"Connor."

"What?" Disbelief colored her voice. "Why?"

"He jabbed me in the eye during a maul at rugby practice."

That revelation put Maggie on the defensive. "I'm sure he didn't mean to hurt you." Too late she realized she shouldn't have stood up for him. After all, Greg was her boyfriend, not Connor. She sighed. Connor didn't like Greg and all she could get out of him was that it involved a girl.

Maggie shrugged. Boys will be boys. Didn't everyone have stuff in their pasts they'd rather forget? She sure did.

"It hurts like hell." He raised his hand to his puffy cheek, and she could see he was in pain. "I'd like to stay, but I'll head back to my place. I'll put some ice on it when I get home."

"Are you sure?"

"Yeah, I have an appointment with a big client in the morning. Besides, I didn't bring a change of clothes."

"Oh?" She narrowed her eyes. What was with Greg, treating her like a commodity? Her inner bad girl wanted to let rip with a few well-chosen words. Instead she buttoned her lips. She'd hold her tongue until she was in control again. Two deep breaths did the trick. "Thanks for waiting for me. I'll see you tomorrow night."

Greg smiled and all the starch seeped out of her. She always was a sucker for a sexy smile. The flash of his dimples made her heart go pitter-patter. Her breasts prickled. "Are you sure I can't entice you to stay the night?" Her sultry tone hinted he might receive a reward.

"No." His voice was firm. "I'll see you tomorrow night for dinner."

The fizz went out of her good mood. The abrasive way he spoke to her irritated her. Maybe it wasn't spanking they needed to talk about, but the future of their relationship. At first, his take-charge manner had charmed her, although the bossy attitude had grown old fast. Why couldn't he see her side? Compromise a little? Sure, dominance in the bedroom worked for her, except Greg tried to extend the power into all facets of their lives.

Maggie marched to the door, yanked it open and waited, proud of her lurch-free walk. She considered tapping her foot, but didn't think her balance would stand the challenge. "See you tomorrow."

He sidled past her, hesitated and stooped to brush a kiss on her cheek. Then, without another word, he left. She closed the door, leaning against it. A hollow sensation dropped into the pit of her stomach. Their relationship—what there was to it—wasn't working for her anymore, but she wasn't so sure breaking up with Greg would help.

The idea of having to go on another man-hunt cleared the alcohol-induced fuzziness from her head. Good men were hard to find. With a quiet chubby girl like her, it was practically impossible. Maybe it wasn't such a good idea to throw her fish back into the sea.

Deep in thought she wove a crooked path down the hall to her bedroom and shed her shoes and clothes, leaving them in an untidy pile on the middle of the beige carpet. She thought about picking them up—her conscience made her—then shrugged. Nah, they needed to go into the wash anyway. Naked, she hit the shower, emerging five minutes later, encased in her favorite scruffy blue robe and smelling like a field of lavender. The shower had helped clear her head. She'd made her decision. Time to move on with her life.

Tomorrow she would tell Greg they were finished.

She could hardly wait.

Maggie made a cup of instant chai latte and waited for her laptop to power up. The second the distinctive Windows opening tune played, a sense of peace and satisfaction settled over her. Life wasn't always about making safe choices. Sometimes a person needed to step up and jump into the unknown, despite the haunting specters of the past.

She logged onto her blog and started to write.

Yesterday, the thing that worried me most about my new interest in spanking was telling my boyfriend. I worried he'd consider me weird. Kinky. Well, okay. I'll admit to the kinky, since this is a blog about spanking, but call me weird, and I'll deny it strenuously.

Today, I have a new problem. It's obvious Mr. X and I aren't suited. I don't know why I didn't see it before, or maybe I did and was too stubborn to admit the truth. He wants a quiet woman who will stay in the background and support his career. Dinners with the boss, look after the kids—that sort of thing. I guess my quiet manner fooled him into thinking I was the woman he could mold into the perfect wife.

We're going to dinner tomorrow night, and I've made my decision: I'm going to end our relationship. Hopefully, I won't hurt his pride. We work in the same firm, and it's gonna be hell if he starts taking our breakup out on me there. We'll see.

Meantime, I'm short one boyfriend. I'm going to have to go through the entire getting-to-know-you phase all over again with strangers before I can even casually mention my interest in spanking. I feel like I'm playing Monopoly and have gone straight to jail without collecting two hundred. I'm no beauty queen, but my friends say I look cute when I smile. Evidently, I've got the whole girl-next-door thing going on, complete with freckles. I have long, dark brown hair. It's straight because I didn't eat my crusts as a kid. That's my mother's story—her hair is beautiful with a distinct curl. Normally I wear it in a braid, because it keeps my hair out of the way.

I have plain brown eyes to match my freckles, a straight nose and good lips. I like my lips. They're kinda plump and pouty. All this set in a plump face. My breasts are on the large side. Let's just say it's not comfortable to exercise or attempt to jog without a restraining bra. I'm tall and solid looking. My mother used to say I take after my father's side of the family. Considering she's five-foot two, and I tower over her, I'd agree.

The point of all this description? It's not gonna be easy to find a replacement, so my spanking experiment will be delayed.

I'll have to find my kicks online. If any of you have suggestions about the best places to find a new boyfriend, please let me know. Oh, and I guess I should continue to collect tips about how to tell a boyfriend I'd like him to spank me. Keeping positive might bring me some good karma.

Maggie proofed her post and hit the publish button. Her post went live, and she felt better after writing down her feelings. She smirked. Cheap therapy. Who knew?

Next, she checked the comments on yesterday's post. Her hands flew over the keyboard, bringing up the right page. A chuckle escaped, her wide grin stretching from one side of her face to the other. As she'd suspected, her friends had checked out her blog. They must have hot-footed it home to check on her sanity.

They'd made it easy for Maggie to guess who had made each comment, using recognizable nicknames. Along with their smart-ass observations, they'd left some remarks about what they really thought. The crux of their advice was honesty worked best. They thought she should tell Greg exactly what she needed from their relationship.

Maggie didn't think she'd get that far with him. She wasn't about to make herself vulnerable with the truth when their differences were more basic—a simple divergence of philosophies.

What was this? she thought with a flicker of excitement, moving down the page with her side bar. Someone else had commented as well, telling her to find a new man. This commenter had seen the writing on the wall before Maggie had. They always said it was easier to see the solution to someone else's problems.

A yawn slipped free, telling her to leave the computer and climb into bed. Email first. She logged on and found a message from the same person who had commented on her blog. She was tempted to delete it, thinking it could be a pervert until curiosity made her click on the open link.

Dear Big Bad Ass,

Ditch the man. He's not good enough for you. He sounds conservative and not right for an adventuress like you. Stretch your wings and search for a new lover. Look for interests outside of the bedroom as well as inside, because despite what most men say, sex isn't everything. Momentary passion won't fill a life of loneliness. You need both passion and friendship.

Tell me what you like to do during your free time. I bet we have more in common than you think.

Kinky Lover

Maggie was shaking, quivering. She couldn't help but wonder what Kinky Lover looked like. Tall, handsome? She started to hit reply, then changed her mind. No. He was probably old and bald with a pot stomach and a desire to turn back the clock by fucking a nubile female.

Pursing her lips, her imagination working overtime, a giggle erupted at the thought. Kinky Lover had a point. Any man she hooked up with should share her interests. They needed compatibility both in and out of the bedroom. Something she and Greg lacked, which was why their relationship had run into problems.

Jeez, who was she kidding? The chances of finding a man were bad enough without adding to the equation. Add kink to the list of necessary traits and she'd end up alone for a long, long time.

Which brought her back to Kinky Lover. He hinted he shared her interests. Did that include spanking?

She started writing a reply and deleted it. No, what did she know about him? He could be a rapist or serial killer.

But what if he was the answer to her spanking dreams?

Before she could change her mind, she wrote him a short email, asking him what he meant about their common interest, added a few basic details, and pressed send before she could change her mind. With her pulse still racing, she powered down her computer and went to bed, but she couldn't sleep. She couldn't stop thinking about Kinky Lover.

Would he answer her email?

And if he did, what would she do? Meet him for a spanking session?

Just thinking about it made her wet. Very wet.

Chapter Two

Dear Kinky Lover,
What do you mean about common interests?
You're right. I need a man who engages my interest outside of the bedroom and enjoys the same things I do. I like walking on the beach, watching rugby (I'm a New Zealander, so a love of rugby goes with the territory, right?), cooking and reading.

For a lover, I want a man who will dominate me, show me his love and understanding by taking control and becoming responsible for my pleasure. Don't get me wrong. I don't want a bully. I don't want a man who will traumatize me, although I'm not averse to a little pain. You can't have spanking without some soreness. I want to feel the sweet tingle after my lover spanks me, and savor the sting when I take a seat and eat at my favorite restaurant. I want to see the rosy blush on my ass when I glance in the mirror. I want that as much as I desire a kiss and the soft stroke of my lover's fingers across my face.

I'm smiling now, since this is probably more than you wanted to know about me. Thanks for visiting my blog.
Big Bad Ass

Connor couldn't restrain his smile of victory. Despite his exhaustion, he felt the urge to jump to his feet and boogie. He controlled himself, not wanting to attract attention from his two flatmates.

So Maggie was spreading her wings. About time. Exhilaration pulsed through him, making him feel as if he could leap tall buildings without breaking stride.

He scanned her email again, his smile widening. He needed a plan. He'd have to move slowly, take things easy so he didn't frighten her away.

Spanking.

Damn, that was different. Reaction arced through his body, heading straight to his cock. He gripped the arms of the office chair, breathing carefully. Even so, each breath emerged in a harsh gasp, as if he'd indulged in strenuous exercise.

He couldn't say if the idea of spanking or thinking about having sex with Maggie spiked his arousal. After his childhood experiences and his parents' subsequent divorce, the idea of striking a woman seemed plain wrong. Maggie. It had to be Maggie.

Lucky for him, he'd given in to his impulse and dragged her to the gym. It was a starting point, a way to keep close contact with her outside of work. Rugby was another way of seeing her on a regular basis. The rest of his plan would come later. The last thing he wanted was to scare her into the arms of another man.

He'd always liked Maggie, enjoyed her shy sense of humor. He couldn't wait to run his hands through her long, dark brown hair and see it loose, spread across his pillow, her golden brown eyes twinkling up at him. Her curvy figure haunted his dreams. She looked hot and sexy in her exercise gear. He'd noticed other guys at the gym checking her out, which hadn't pleased him. Yeah, time to make his move, and for once the timing worked fine because he was between girlfriends.

The spanking part he'd deal with later.

Connor picked up his cell phone and called Julia. She lived closest to him.

"This had better be good, Connor Grey. It's only seven in the morning." Her words emerged as a tiger-like snarl, the sort that came from pain.

"Headache?"

"No thanks to you," she muttered. "Have another drink. One more won't make any difference. You lied!" The outraged mockery brought a grin to his face.

"I prescribe coffee," Connor said. "Strong and black."

"Why didn't you warn me about that hurricane shot?" Julia

moaned.

"I didn't force you to drink another cocktail at the pub," Connor said, "or the bottle of wine at Susan's." He heard her snicker.

"Fair enough," she said.

He changed the subject. "You guys coming to watch our game this afternoon?"

"With this headache?" The sharp note in her voice made him curse under his breath. The woman was no slouch in the brain department. He'd have to tread carefully. He wasn't ready for his feelings about Maggie to come out into the open.

"We need all the support we can get," Connor admitted. "Frankly, our team sucks. We need someone on our side."

"If there's coffee involved," Julia said. "I might be persuaded to round up a team of supporters."

Connor checked his watch. "Coffee will be there in fifteen minutes."

"Done," Julia said. "Oh, while I think of it—don't tell Maggie we told you about her blog. She threatened to smother us with her breasts if we told anyone." She paused then added, "Those breasts of hers could do the job. Promise?"

"Her breasts?" Connor chuckled. "Yeah. Okay." He hung up, smirking. Death by breast smothering. What a hell of a way to go.

"Can you tell me what I'm doing standing on the sideline of a rugby field freezing my ass off?" Maggie tugged her wooly hat over her ears and pulled her knee-length coat tight around her waist. "Greg's not playing today."

"Clearing the hangover cobwebs," Julia said, moaning.

Maggie lifted her chin. "I wasn't the one who stayed up late drinking a bottle of wine after leaving the pub." She winked at her friend. Her complaints were only half-hearted.

Play came down the rugby field toward them, and she concentrated on the players, searching for number eight. There he was. Tall. Dark. Broad shoulders. Connor played with both determination and skill, the tight-fitting uniform fueling her fantasies. His slim hips tapered to a tight butt.

Although not traditionally handsome, when he grinned, his entire face lit up and made her want to smile in return. His blue eyes twinkled. And he was a nice person. There weren't many guys who could hang out with four girls and hold their own in wide-ranging conversations covering the gambit from work to make-up, sex and sport.

And everything in between.

There weren't many taboos once they'd had a few drinks, including masculine topics, which made Maggie wonder if perhaps they should cut down on the drinking. Nah, they chatted the same way during lunch breaks at work. They were a team. So why couldn't she stop fantasizing about Connor? They'd all met Gwen, his girlfriend. A requisite blonde with long, slender legs and loaded with sex-appeal, she seemed pleasant and perfect for Connor.

Why did that fact make her so miserable?

The game passed in a blur. Maggie had difficulty concentrating, still nursing a sense of dread since climbing out of bed this morning. She waited with Julia, Susan and Christina while Connor chatted with his team mates and members of the opposition.

"I wonder where Gwen is," Maggie said in a matter-of-fact voice, looking for the leggy blonde.

"Didn't you hear?" Julia asked. "Connor and Gwen broke up last week."

Christina quit ogling the players and snapped to attention. "What?"

"He never said anything to me." Surprise skittered through Maggie first, followed by excitement. Then that meant—

Don't go there. A relationship between the two of you wouldn't work, so there was no point in letting her thoughts drift in that direction. Besides, you made a promise to the others. Remember?

"Did he say what happened?" Susan asked, curious.

"No, just that the parting was amicable. I asked nosey questions, and he refused to answer," Julia said. "Shush, he's heading this way."

Mud covered Connor's face when he stalked to them, his eyes sparkling through the grime. "Hey, did you see the way I left the opposition in my dust?"

"Yeah, we saw," Susan said, trying not to sound impressed.

"Don't you mean mud?" Maggie said with a grin, striving to keep her voice natural. She couldn't let her feelings for Connor screw up their friendship.

Connor's smile burst with sunshine, despite the overcast day. "You girls coming for drinks?"

"Are you kidding?" Christina asked. "I intend to scope out the eligible men."

"You'll have to count me out," Maggie said. "I have to go home and change for dinner. I have a date with Greg."

Susan's brows rose. "But didn't you—" She came to an abrupt halt, shot a swift glance at Connor before offering Maggie a weak smile. "We'll miss you," she finished lamely.

"You can tell me about it tomorrow." With a sigh, Maggie refrained from looking at Connor and turned away.

"Hey, wait—" Connor grabbed her hand and grasped it firmly, spinning her back toward him. Maggie stumbled and would have fallen if he hadn't seized her. The musky scent of male sweat, mud and wet clothing filled her nostrils while a shiver rocked her to the core.

"I'm such a klutz." She froze, tipping back her head to stare him in the face.

His thumb made a slow pass over her cheek. "Sorry about the mud," he explained in a husky voice. "But I wanted to remind you about our date at the gym tomorrow."

"I won't forget," Maggie promised.

"Don't drink too much tonight," he teased. "I'm warning you, I'll drag you out of bed tomorrow by your...toes."

"Um...okay." Maggie pulled away, aware of the hard muscles of his chest, the rush of blood to her cheeks and the lingering tingle from his touch. She contemplated sleeping in late on purpose. Connor had a free ticket into her bedroom any time. He just didn't know of his incredibly good fortune yet.

"You're gonna make her go to the gym on a Sunday?" Susan backed away, hands raised in front of her, an expression of horror contorting her face into a comical mask. "I hope this craziness isn't contagious. No way will you find me anywhere near a gym on the weekend."

"I'm trying to get fit, Susan," Maggie said, then turned to the sexy man standing beside her. "Don't worry. I'll be there. Have fun tonight, everyone."

Blowing them a kiss, she turned toward the parking area before temptation zapped from her brain to her limbs. It was all too easy to imagine the reaction if she grabbed Connor. The pact between her and her girlfriends was suddenly in dire danger of smashing wide open.

Temptation played a siren song inside her.

No. No way would she be the one to break the pact.

The second Greg slammed from her apartment, angry and upset, Maggie stomped straight to her laptop. She was still shaking when she put her fingers on the keyboard and logged onto her blog. Without taking a breath, she started typing furiously.

My dinner tonight with Mr. X went from bad to worse. I can still feel the embarrassed glow on my cheeks. He blames me for what happened. How was I meant to know he'd invited his friends to dinner with us?

When he came to pick me up, I tried to tell him then I didn't want to go out with him again—that it was over between us. The man wouldn't let me get a word in and hustled me from my apartment before I could tell him. I tried to talk about breaking up in the cab on the way to the restaurant. That's when he informed me we were dining with his business friend and his wife.

During the last six months I've met most of his friends. Some are okay. The particular couple we were dining with wasn't in the okay *group. The woman stands firmly in the* bitch camp, *while her husband had a different agenda. He belongs to the* wandering hands *club. He wandered his hands over my ass and breasts when his wife and Mr. X weren't watching.*

By the time we arrived at the Italian restaurant on Nelson Street, my temper simmered. This particular restaurant specializes in great food, and for entertainment, they have budding opera singers performing several live segments during the evening. Not only did I have to spend time with Mr. X, I had to put up with his friends and the opera. So shoot me. I like rock and pop. I can even listen to country when the mood takes me. Opera, not so much. It makes my head hurt.

I tried to escape into spanking fantasies. It worked until a hand on my upper thigh jerked me rudely from my steamy dreamscape.

All this, combined with several glasses of wine and my irritation, loosened my tongue and lowered my inhibitions. When I couldn't take the husband staring at my breasts any longer, I stated my opinion. Loud and clear.

"If I wanted you to look at my breasts, I'd take off my clothes. Give you a good look at them. I'd even supply a tape measure so you could see if they measure up," I added, my tone nasty.

"M!" Mr. X's aghast expression suggested I'd stepped out of line. "Apologize to R for that remark."

"Why should I? Are you saying it's okay for R to perv at my breasts and pinch my ass every chance he gets? You want me to sit here and take his abuse?"

"Eat your dinner," Mr. X said.

I reached for my wine, but Mr. X slid the glass toward him before I could grab it.

Do you believe it? He blamed the entire incident on me.

After that, the rest of the night was pretty uncomfortable. The wife glared at her husband. Mr. X glared at me. I can tell you I received more than my fair share of glares. The only reason the husband didn't glare at me was because he'd land in bigger trouble than he was already.

The minute we were alone in the taxi, Mr. X started telling me off, listing my infractions which, according to him, were many.

"You made a laughingstock out of me."

"I'm sorry," I said. "But you didn't give me a chance to talk to you. You see...I don't want to go out with you again."

"Don't be stupid," Mr. X said, not taking me seriously. "You drank too much. Everyone makes mistakes. I'm not going to hold a little overindulgence against you. I admit I wasn't happy with your outspoken comments. Next time just ignore the attention. He was only looking. Anyway, you shouldn't have worn such a low cut top. It encouraged him."

My fault? Pompous pig.

Fuming, I didn't answer Mr. X. I was afraid of what I'd say next. I could see the taxi driver watching in his rear view mirror. He was listening to everything we said. Instead, I bit my tongue and stared out the window at the lights of the city, the glowing red and green Sky Tower, lit for mid-year winter celebrations, and St. Matthews Church. I remained silent as the cab headed up Hobson Street to the motorway. I could have sliced the silence with a knife and served it on my grandmother's heirloom china.

When the cab pulled up outside my apartment, I thrust open the door and climbed out. Mr. X followed me.

"Wait for me," he told the driver then shouldered his way through the entrance door before I could stop him.

I stomped to my apartment and unlocked the door. Mr. X followed me inside and the instant the door closed behind him, I whirled around to confront him. I couldn't hold it in any longer.

"Will you spank me?"

"What sort of a question is that?" Shock vibrated in him, pulling him upright so he appeared taller than normal. "I've never hit a woman in my life."

"What if I wanted you to spank me? Would you?"

His mouth dropped open and confusion clouded his face. "You're joking, right?"

I shook her head. "I can't go out with you again. Your friends were disrespectful, and you blamed me. As if I asked for him to stare at my boobs and grab my ass."

"I—"

"Please go. I don't want to see you again."

"You're serious, aren't you?"

Jeesh, what part of that didn't he understand? "Yes."

"Don't you realize I'm doing you a favor by going out with you?" His dark brows drew together until they were a slash across the top of his eyes. Shock transformed into outrage.

"Get out," I said in a firm voice. "Now."

"You'll come to your senses," he snapped. "And when you do, don't bother crawling back to ask forgiveness. I don't do second chances." He slammed the door so hard my ears rang, ending our date with crashing finality. Not exactly a stellar *evening.*

But guess what? I'm footloose and fancy free.
All I need to do is find a man.

A grin formed on Connor's face when he read the blog entry. Most people would label it a smirk. Hell, he knew exactly where Maggie could find a man. *He* was that man. Damn, he couldn't take this. He had to talk to her today, come to an understanding.

Half an hour later, he leaned on the intercom button, and a curious neighbor let him inside—probably to stop the racket at such an ungodly hour on a Sunday morning.

Taking the stairs two at a time, he raced up to the second floor and thumped on Maggie's door. It took her a long time to answer. Finally, the door flew open. Maggie...her hair. It was the first time he'd ever seen it loose, and it rippled all the way down her back, stopping just above the curve of her ass.

"Hey." *Weak, Connor.* He cleared the lump from his throat and sought something witty to say. His gaze slipped to her breasts. Rounded and sexy. Tempting. A distraction.

"Connor!" A soft blush crept over her cheeks and down her neck. "Having a good look?"

Connor wanted to explore the pink glow with his lips. "You shouldn't answer the door dressed like that."

"You're early." Maggie scowled, crossing her arms over her chest.

Watching her butt, he followed her into the kitchenette, mesmerized by the dark locks glinting under the artificial light. It took him another four steps before he realized all she wore was an oversize T-shirt. He glanced down. Great legs. Normally she hid them beneath ankle length skirts or baggy sweats.

"Should I make coffee?"

"Yes. I need a shower." She padded down the passage and disappeared into a room at the end. Connor didn't move until he heard the rattle of pipes and the distant spray of water. A visual formed in his mind. Dark hair dripping wet, nipples playing peek-a-boo while Maggie lazily soaped her body... *Hell.* The last thing he needed right now was to imagine her naked.

Coffee. Yeah. He forced himself to walk into the kitchen, arousal shooting through his veins and pooling in his groin. He needed to stick to the plan he'd formulated in the early hours of this morning, after he'd seen her blog entry. *Talk to her today.* Part A of the plan. Part B was keeping her permanently, but that was on a need-to-know basis.

Spanking—that might cause a few problems too, but first things first.

Coffee...

Connor was familiar with the layout of Maggie's apartment since the Tight Five often hung out at her place. It didn't take him long to make coffee. By the time the shower stopped, water dripped through the coffee filter and the fragrant scent of ground beans filled the kitchen.

He waited. Where was she? Five minutes passed, then five more. He imagined her drying her body, smoothing on her body lotion smelling of old-fashioned lavender, brushing the knots from her long hair and restraining it into the braid she favored.

He grasped the edge of the table until his knuckles whitened. Damn, he had to get his lust under control. He couldn't touch her, except on a friendly basis. Not yet. *Patience, man.* Cursing softly, he grabbed two white china mugs from the cupboard and poured coffee into them. He steeled himself when he heard footsteps. Seconds later he smelled lavender, and Maggie breezed into the kitchen.

"Why are you so early?" she asked. "Didn't you see Gwen or whoever you're going out with last night?"

"I'm not dating Gwen anymore. I'm solo for the moment." As soon as he said the words, he regretted them. Damn, why did he sound like Romeo between Juliets? Despite public opinion, his bedroom didn't have a revolving door.

"Since when? Won't you walk lopsided now without a babe to balance you?" Maggie grinned and dropped into a stool beside him at the breakfast bar. She leaned over to switch on the stereo, her V-neck T-shirt gaping to display creamy white curves. His mind blanked, his fingers itching to touch her. Instead, he wrapped his hands around his mug and took a sip of coffee. *Baby steps and patience.*

"I thought you liked Gwen," she added.

"I *do* like her, but I felt like I was dating my sister."

Maggie's brown eyes widened. "Ouch. You didn't tell her that, did you?"

"No. Our parting was amicable." Her compassion made his heart melt. He wanted to hug her for caring about a woman she'd met only once.

"Do you have your eye on someone else?" She sipped her coffee and glanced at him over the rim of her mug.

"Not really," he said, seeing an opening. "Gwen was always complaining about rugby season during winter. With training and Saturday games, I don't have many free nights. I'm not desperate for a replacement. Why do you ask?"

"It's just that you always have a woman." White teeth nibbled her bottom lip. A cute furrow formed and vanished between her eyes, as if she didn't believe him.

"Maggie, contrary to public opinion I don't always have a woman around."

"Can I ask a personal question?"

"Sure." He wouldn't guarantee a reply, but her expression told him she knew that.

"What about sex? I mean, I like sex. The closeness and sleeping with a guy." She paused, looked him straight in the eye. "Do you miss sex when you're not going out with someone?"

Connor laughed. This conversation couldn't have gone better if he'd scripted it. "Sure, I miss sex." He hesitated, wondering how honest he should be with her. "This is just between us, right?"

"Of course. I would never share a private conversation with any of the others."

Connor knew it was true. While their other friends did gossip amongst themselves, he'd never heard Maggie repeat anything confidential. Not once. "Yeah, I miss sex," he said. "I love to explore a woman's body, her scent and taste, her soft curves. Masturbation doesn't bring the same pleasure. My hand never feels quite the same as tight, hot pussy."

Color shaded her cheeks, although she nodded. "I know what you mean. It's the empty feeling inside afterward that gets to me." Her smile was rueful. "I'm probably every man's nightmare because I like to cuddle. Sleeping alone and self-pleasuring isn't the same."

He was going to ask her. *Right now.* The timing couldn't be better.

A feeling he recognized as terror speared his gut. A lot rode on her reaction to his next question. Connor placed his coffee mug on the counter. "Will you kiss me?"

"A kiss?" A surprised laugh escaped her. "Why?"

"I have an idea, but I need a kiss first."

Smiling, Maggie leaned close and pressed her lips against his cheek. She moved back before he had a chance to react.

"That wasn't quite what I had in mind." Blood rushed through his veins, his heart thudding against his ribs in an erratic manner. Hell, sex between them would be good, if this innocent little kiss was any indication. "A real kiss."

Connor closed the distance between them and grasped her head firmly in his hands. She jumped at his touch, stared at him, a spark of indefinable emotion darkening the golden brown of her eyes to chocolate. His gaze dropped to her mouth. God, he'd always loved her mouth, fantasized about kissing it, seeing her lips wrapped around his cock. He snorted inwardly. Like that idea would score him points. Connor brushed his lips against hers. Soft. So soft. The rest of his body went on high alert, cock filling to press against his fly.

She sighed and he took advantage, slipping his tongue inside to taste her. Coffee and a faint minty flavor danced across his taste buds. At first he kept the kiss slow and gentle, then he lifted his head to study her. He liked the dreamy expression on her face, but he enjoyed kissing her more. He wanted her to respond to his kiss, needed to know she felt even a little like he did. Her eager lips and the hands threading through his hair, holding him in place as he wrapped his arms around her again, shot all his doubts to hell.

Slowly, he pulled back. They were both breathing fast. "Okay. That answered my question."

Maggie smoothed her tongue over her bottom lip and watched him with a touch of confusion. Judging by her expression, she thought she'd taken a wrong turn from the bathroom and stepped into an alternative reality. "What question?"

"Would you be interested in a *friends with benefits* deal with me?" He held his breath and waited for her answer, knowing he'd never wanted something so much in all his life.

Her mouth opened and closed three times. "Friends with benefits? You mean...we'd sleep together?"

"If we weren't seeing anyone else." *Damn, please don't say no.* His gut jumped with nerves. He'd pushed her too hard. Of course she'd reject his offer and wonder about his motives.

Maggie picked up her mug and took a sip of coffee, grimacing faintly. She stood and walked over to the coffeemaker, returning with the carafe. "Do you want a top up?"

"Sure." He held out his mug.

She took a long time, fiddling with the coffee, the mugs and the Granny Smith apples sitting in the fruit bowl.

"Are you going to say something?" he asked.

"Doesn't a deal like this have the potential to blow up in our faces?"

"Why should it?" he asked, trying to convince her. "We're not kids."

"I still don't understand why you'd choose me." She started pacing up and down, making him nervous.

"You're a friend. I like you. I trust you." Connor wasn't going to ignore the many pitfalls. That wouldn't be smart. "We'd set boundaries before we started anything between us. Stop pacing. Sit next to me. I'm not gonna bite." Not yet, but if things went his way he would in the future. He'd enjoy marking her, leaving her body wearing his badge of possession.

To his relief, she joined him at the breakfast bar, sliding onto one of the wooden stools.

"What brought this on? Why are you asking me instead of one of the others? Julia isn't seeing anyone at the moment."

"I've always felt comfortable talking to you about anything, including sex. You don't gossip and you have integrity. I like you." *Nothing less than the truth.*

"Oh." A cute crinkle marred the smoothness of her brow. "I like you too. You're one of my best friends." She paused a beat. "Are we still going to the gym?"

Damn. Her words didn't fill him with hope. He'd made her uncomfortable.

"Of course. I'm not letting you off that easy. You'd have to go through the sore muscle stage all over again." Had he scared her off? Or worse, she didn't find him sexy.

"Good. I'm flattered, but I need to think about your...proposition while I'm on the treadmill." She tried to smile. "Can we talk later?"

Thank you, God. She intended to give him a chance. "Sure, we can. I'll spring for lunch afterward."

"I'd like to go to the beach." Her eyes lit up at the thought. "I do my best thinking at the beach."

"You do? Why didn't I know?"

She shrugged. "I guess it's never come up before."

"Do you have plans for tomorrow?"

"No, apart from sleeping in and having a lazy day. The usual holiday stuff."

"My parents have a holiday home at Port Waikato. Would you like to drive out there with me this afternoon and stay the night?" Before she could say no, he added, "We can sleep in separate rooms." Connor had the absurd desire to grab her and stuff her inside his car. Kidnapping. Old-fashioned ravishment. Yeah. All that stuff. Something about Maggie brought out a dominant gene in him, the need to protect.

"Could I walk on the beach?"

"Anything you want."

When she wrinkled her nose, his heart sank. He knew what was coming next. She'd tell him to take a flying jump. There went a great friend. He knew he was taking a risk, but it had been worth it. There was no way he could have lived with himself if he'd done nothing and stood aside while another man scooped her up first, from under his nose.

Maggie picked up the empty mugs and stacked them in the dishwasher. "Okay, you've got a deal—"

"Then you'll sleep with me?" he asked.

She laughed. "Not so fast. I'll go with you to the beach. The other part needs more thinking." Her grin was a flash of white teeth. "I'll let you know. Promise."

Relieved, Connor nodded, brain working at speed. *Way to go!* He could be very charming, especially around Maggie. And persuasive, especially when he was going after something he wanted.

Looked like his charm gene was in for a major workout today.

Chapter Three

Friends with benefits.

What did that mean? Maggie wondered, breathing hard, her pulse racing as she stepped onto the treadmill. Wild, monkey sex whenever they felt the need? No-strings sex? Organized or spontaneous?

Connor's suggestion stunned her so much her mind had blanked. She had to admit it was difficult to pass *Go* when her brain commenced a continuous loop centered around a splendidly naked Connor.

She jogged in place on the treadmill, the pounding beat of a song with lyrics about someone who was crazy filling her head. The music wasn't loud enough to drown out her thoughts, although when the next song mentioned *fools in love* she thought about kismet and serendipity. Did she really want to do this? Have sex with Connor?

Hell, yes.

Was it a good idea?

Probably not.

So many things could go wrong. What if they found themselves incompatible in bed? The last thing she wanted was to lose Connor's friendship. She had to admit it wouldn't make her popular with the rest of the Tight Five. They all agreed he hadn't steered them wrong when it came to advice about the male sex. Susan, in particular, felt strongly about the friends-only rule because her ex-friend—the one she'd had since pre-school days—had waltzed off with Susan's fiancé one day before the wedding. Susan didn't like to talk about it much, but she put loyalty first in any argument. And Maggie had a feeling that Christina was more interested in Connor than she'd let on.

The thought gave Maggie pause. She hated the thought of hurting her friends and had tried to cast her growing feelings for Connor aside. It wasn't working. The wretched man taunted her in dreams, steamy naked dreams that had her waking in a real state. It made every other man pale in comparison.

Connor's track record was part of the reason she'd consider this friends with benefits deal, although she needed more details about how this arrangement would work.

And lastly, there was also the fact he changed girlfriends on a regular basis. If he did that with her, she didn't think she'd recover—she liked him that much. Something to ponder. Oh, and the fact she'd be breaking the pact she made with her friends. Could she live with a guilty conscience? That was a real biggie.

Then there was her father and stepmother. The treadmill program went into warm-down mode, slowing before coming to a stop. Grabbing her towel, Maggie wiped the sweat off her forehead and throat while the next song started on her iPod—the New Zealand band OpShop singing about one day. She didn't hear the lyrics. All she could think about was that there might never be another chance with Connor. Despite her father's lectures about scandal and keeping a low profile, she'd kick herself if she said no and had to watch Connor with yet another woman. She didn't think she could handle that—not again. Only a fool would let this opportunity slip through her fingers. Benefits. Yeah, she could see them, but the pitfalls, the potential for pain and loss...was it too much to risk?

She couldn't forget her promise to her friends. If she messed up with them, no doubt there would be huge consequences. She'd have to lie to them, and that didn't sit well with her. She let out her breath slowly.

The rest of her workout passed in a daze, and by the time she exited the changing rooms to join Connor, her head whirled with mental arguments, but she'd decided to take a chance on love. Surely wanting love wasn't such a bad thing? If Connor still wanted to change the dynamics of their relationship, she'd risk it and go along with the idea, keeping her fingers crossed for the future.

She hoped she wouldn't regret it.

"Hey, how was the workout?" Connor asked, giving her an admiring glance.

She clutched the bag containing her workout gear closer to her chest. She had to admit she was nervous about this whole arrangement.

"Good." A laugh escaped and her features contorted when she pulled a face. "Nah, that's a lie. Exercise hurts like hell."

What Maggie didn't tell him was that she realized for the first time she'd managed to get through the entire workout without worrying about collapsing in the middle of the gym and drawing attention to herself. Thinking about Connor and his proposition had let her zip through the workout without too much stress. *Amazing.*

"How about we go back to my place so I can pack a few clothes?" Connor said. "Then we'll stop at your apartment and grab a few groceries at the supermarket on the way?"

"I've never visited your apartment before. Do I get the tour?" Their gazes met. A flutter started in her belly. *Oh, boy.* Maggie took half a step toward him, intent on touching, brushing her fingers across his jaw to test the roughness of his stubble. She inhaled sharply. Yes, this would be so easy between them. So easy to let go and let the emotions rule her. Lust. Sex. Togetherness.

"You want to see my bedroom?" he asked, a husky note entering his voice.

"If you want to include your bedroom on the tour," she tossed back with a casual shrug. Inside nerves quaked while anticipation banked, arousal taking off like a sprinter to race the length of her body. A distinct dampness pooled between her thighs. "Will your flatmates be there?"

"Probably not. They're away for the weekend." He offered her a sexy smile. "We're gonna talk. That's all." He brushed a strand of hair off her face, tucking it behind her ear. "Hash everything out between us so there's no misunderstanding later when we hit the bedroom."

"All right," Maggie said, surprised not a single qualm

41

remained in her. She trusted him to keep his word.

During the drive to Connor's central Auckland apartment, they talked about rugby, exercise and the upcoming work function neither of them wanted to attend. Unfortunately, the partners frowned upon employees who dodged their gatherings.

Maggie was surprised to see that Connor's apartment was small with two bedrooms—not much space for three men. If she stood on tiptoes and looked out the window of the compact lounge, she could see a sliver of Rangitoto, the dormant volcano island that dominated the harbor. The distinctive cone was visible from most parts of inner Auckland.

Turning back to Connor, she said with a smile, "Great view."

"Yeah, I like it." Connor reached for her hand and tugged her down a short carpeted passage to a bedroom. "Sit on the bed while I grab some clothes."

Maggie noted with interest the king-size bed and modern streamlined furniture constructed of white pine and chrome. A shelving unit, bulging with books of all sizes, covered part of one wall. So the man had an intellectual side as well. Interesting. She took two steps and plunked onto the corner of the bed. The cotton duvet cover made a crinkling sound when she settled on it, the bold tribal design and spice, ochre and black shades making her think of ethnic art and exotic lands. A large window filled most of another wall with views over the harbor. The water sparkled, despite the sluggish winter sun, and two yachts flew across the white-tipped waves, their white sails billowing in the breeze. Yes, she could learn to like it here. No doubt.

Connor opened a wardrobe and grabbed a green bag. He tossed in sweats, a pair of jeans and a couple of T-shirts, along with a sweater. Maggie turned to watch him, her heart rate accelerating as she studied his taut backside, his ease of movement. Soon, very soon, touch between them would be acceptable. Excitement flared deep inside her, a shiver of anticipation working free to give away her state of mind and rapid arousal.

A cough cleared the thickening in her throat. "What sort of things do we need to discuss?" She had a fair idea but wanted him to tell her. Of course, whatever he said would have a final bearing on her decision. Although she lusted after him, she wasn't foolhardy. An agreement of sex between friends had explosive potential, and not necessarily all confined between the sheets. Heck, who was she kidding? She'd already made her decision.

The thought brought her parents to mind. Immediately, she shoved their stern faces away, locking the door on mental lectures. Geographical distance and her adult status meant their opinions didn't count. Despite what her furious and distraught father said, she was nothing like her mother. One bad experience hardly compared to several torrid affairs and three marriages to public figures with the resulting messy divorces.

"First, it's essential we have complete honesty between us," he said with a serious tone. "If you have any doubts, tell me. This won't work if we're not honest with each other. We need to communicate."

His intent gaze told her he was sincere when it came down to nothing but truth between them. She thought back to previous boyfriends, the lies—both big and small—and nodded without hesitation and scarcely a flinch. Honesty remained important to her in a relationship.

Tingles sprang to life, tickling across her skin like champagne bubbles. An image formed in her mind, one of her draped across the arm of a chair. Connor standing behind her, a hairbrush in his hand. Heat stained her cheeks until they were as hot as her bottom would feel after several loving blows.

Her pulse quickened, imagining the scene. "What else?"

"Safe sex."

Oops, something she hadn't considered and should have. "That goes without saying. Are there more rules?"

"We don't date."

"No dates? I'm not sure I understand. Do you mean with each other or with other people?"

"What I mean is no courtship rituals are necessary. If you agree, we have sex whenever the mood strikes both of us." He paused, his eyes looking her up and down, making her shiver, then continued. "If either of us starts seeing anyone else, we tell the other. If we meet someone else and decide to sleep with them, we talk about it. It might mean we continue sleeping with each other and it might not."

He opened a drawer and pulled out socks. Out of another, he grabbed underwear. Connor stuffed both items in his bag and zipped it closed. "We don't tell the others. This remains strictly between the two of us because I don't want to answer their nosy questions." His gaze drilled into hers, as if he wanted to impart the importance of the rules. "Also, respect for each other. And most important of all, we need to keep our emotions out of this. If your feelings change about our deal, you need to tell me. I'll do the same. Any questions?"

A tight band formed around Maggie's chest, growing tighter as she listened to Connor spell out the rules in his husky voice. What was she getting into? Lovemaking should be spontaneous. It shouldn't come with rules.

"Have you done this before?"

"Once, when I was at university in Dunedin."

"Oh." A flash of envy struck her. Heck, why not call it jealousy, because that's what it was. The idea of Connor with a lover fanned the flames of resentment. Another woman in the same bed made her feel even worse, so how would she cope if he decided to call off the agreement between them to date someone else? "How long did you—?" She broke off to gesture with her hands when the words wouldn't come.

"We were together for a year. We stopped seeing each other when I finished my computer course and came to Auckland. Karen stayed in Dunedin."

"I see." Words deserted her entirely. The woman had a name. Karen.

Connor picked up the bag. "Think about it. We don't have to do anything straightaway." He picked up his bag. "You ready to go?"

Maggie stood and followed Connor out the door, aware of him in a way she hadn't been before, ultra conscious of her clothes and the way they fit her body. No thinking required. She wanted Connor so much, but tangled emotions filled her. They were there in her mind, hovering on the fringes like scared children riding a rollercoaster.

Could she have sex with Connor and keep her emotions at bay? And more important, could she keep out of trouble and juggle all the lies without dropping a ball?

Two hours later they drove down a narrow gravel road, and Connor pulled his SUV into the driveway of the last house on the dead end road. Maggie breathed in the tang of the sea filling the air. To her right, the distinctive black sand rose in rolling hills as far as she could see.

With her stomach doing somersaults, Maggie followed Connor inside, feeling a little like Alice stumbling into the unknown. She hoped Connor would head straight to the bedroom. Temptation thrummed inside her, urging her to act on her instincts. *Jump him.* She curled her hand around the handle of her overnight bag, digging her fingernails into her palm, determined to keep it together and act with decorum instead of desperation. It didn't help when her parents' voices kept jumping into her mind, urging her to consider the consequences of her actions. They didn't want another public scandal of the Penisgate variety in the family.

Connor led her into a large open room that looked like a combined lounge and kitchen. She scanned the room with interest. The furniture was old and mismatched, a little on the scruffy side, but everything appeared spotlessly clean, not musty. A breakfast bar divided the kitchen from the rest of the room.

Connor dropped his bag on the floor, and taking his cue, she did the same. "We have time for a walk before it gets too cold," he said. "That will give you time to do your thinking in the fresh air."

"Sounds good."

Perhaps if she compiled a list of pros and cons, her decision would be easier. The question of spanking would definitely make the list. Dare she mention it to him? Maggie shot him a swift glance and saw the intensity seething in his face when he returned her scrutiny.

"If you don't mind walking in the dark, we could go for a walk after dinner as well." His eyes narrowed, and suddenly he morphed into predator, unnerving her. Tall. Dark. Deadly.

Her mouth dried. Her heart flip-flopped. She took a step backward. "Yeah, sure."

"Do I make you nervous?" His soft purr curled her toes, made her body bloom with eagerness.

"A little." Everything was happening too fast for her to process and agonize over in her normal manner. For once she'd reverted to gut instinct...

"I'd never hurt you. You know that, right?"

She nodded. "I know." Her attention centered on Connor, watching him shrug out of his denim shirt. He dropped it, his clothing fluttering to the ground. Her throat worked in a swallow, her eyes on his bare chest, the hard expanse of muscles. She'd never let herself look and linger to appreciate this magnificent male specimen before because she hadn't wanted to spoil things with her girlfriends. She'd never wondered what the Celtic knot tattoo on his biceps would taste like.

Friends only.

Maggie gulped. And now they were going to have sex. The mutual scratching of an itch. She had it bad. But could she really do this? The warmth in his eyes not only made her heart beat faster, but turned her limbs to jelly.

This time she advanced instead of retreating, reaching out to touch him. His skin burned her fingertips, and Maggie jerked her hand away, her head lifting to study the sensual sweep of his lower lip. She'd felt his mouth on hers, knew how soft it was, and wanted more.

"Touch me." This time his purr tempted her like rich, bitter chocolate. She had no defenses.

"How do you want me to touch you?" *Let me count the ways.*

"Run your fingers over my chest. Use your mouth. Anything you want, babe. I need you to touch me."

A dream. Christmas and birthday gifts combined in one. *What was she waiting for?*

"So we're not going for a walk after all?"

"Not unless you want to." His laser-sharp gaze contained questions.

"No," she whispered. "Maybe later." With a trembling hand, she reached out and pressed her palm against his chest, basking in his warmth, the soft grin curving his mouth. His heart beat with a solid thud. A faint sprinkling of dark hair covered his pectoral muscles, soft to her touch. He smelled of soap and the aftershave she'd given him for Christmas. She loved his scent. Clean and masculine. Sexy and tempting, and he was all hers.

Grasping his shoulders, Maggie leaned into him, heard his sharp intake of breath. A small sign he wasn't as calm as he pretended. Her lips touched his skin, and his solid muscle bunched in a visible reaction. Maggie dragged her tongue along his collarbone and nipped him. Connor groaned and moved so fast she blinked. One moment she stood, the next she lay on her back, staring up at Connor's intense face. He wasn't even breathing hard after his rapid trip down the passage and into his bedroom.

"You okay?" he asked.

"Yes." He'd acted like a caveman, tossing her onto the bed as if she were a lightweight. When Greg had tried the same thing, he'd dropped her and she'd borne bruises on her backside and hip for days. And he'd had the cheek to tell her she needed to lose weight.

This time it wasn't anger coursing through her veins. This time excitement pounded in time with every beat of her heart. Invisible energy crackled in the air between them. She stared up at him with wary fascination, wondering what he'd do next.

"That's good." He removed her shoes, dropping them with a clunk onto the hardwood floor. Her socks joined the heap. After unlacing his boots and peeling off his socks, he joined her on the bed, pinning her to the mattress with his chest. He kissed her, taking instead of cajoling, his mouth covering hers hungrily. Sensations skittered through her mind and body one after the other, heat licking across her skin. He tasted her, yet didn't probe for her tonsils as Greg did when he was excited.

What was she doing? It wasn't right to compare the two men. She wasn't with Greg and this thing with Connor was all about fun and mutual pleasure. That's all.

She pushed Greg from her mind and drifted as in a dream,

wallowing in the skillful mastery of Connor's mouth, the easy thrust of his tongue that made her think of penetration in another area. Jolts of pleasure rocked her with little explosions, moistening her body, preparing her for his possession. Had he packed condoms? They'd need a lot because once or twice wouldn't douse the flames searing her body.

"Connor." She clutched his shoulders, sighing softly when his mouth left hers to graze kisses down her jaw, her neck. His teeth scraped over her pulse and her hips bucked sharply upward, pressing against his hard body, loving the firm weight of him.

"I like that," she whispered, deciding to state her likes and dislikes up front. Otherwise, how would he know? Besides, they were friends and friends didn't judge each other. She admitted that didn't stop her nerves from going into overdrive, the whisper of her conscience. He repeated the move, his lips sucking lightly. When he lifted his head, a moan of complaint nearly escaped her lips. Almost. She trapped it inside by biting her lower lip.

"Do you mind if I mark your skin?" His probing gaze sought a reaction.

"A love bite?"

"Yeah."

She drew in a sharp breath. Hot intent and desire darkened his face, passion simmering between them. Her tongue darted out to moisten her lips, and he followed the move with avid attention, making her pulse race faster. "I suppose that would be okay," she said, "as long as I can hide them beneath my clothes."

A love bite. *Wow.*

"Good. I'm hungry."

Satisfaction rang in his words. He levered his body away from hers, and immediately she missed the solid weight of him. A protest built inside her, only to fade away with understanding when he tugged her woolen sweater over her head and started on the pearl buttons fastening her pale blue shirt. One tiny pop at a time, the expanse of bare skin growing larger. Tension replaced the sexual excitement when the realities of baring her body to him came closer. *Plump.* She knew this was coming, but that didn't mean it was easy for her. Her body stiffened. No point sugarcoating the truth.

"Don't tense up, babe." Grasping her shoulders, he shook her lightly, an edge to his words. "I like the way you look." He stopped undoing the buttons and pressed a kiss to her mouth, nibbled at her bottom lip before soothing the sting with the lave of his tongue. Her breath came in short gasps when he finally lifted his head. "I like your curves and I can't wait to see you without your clothes. Don't try to hide from me. Please."

His fingers strummed across a throbbing pulse point at her jaw, making it beat impossibly fast—she could feel the rapid tic—and embarrassment flooded her cheeks. Heat. Arousal. She clamped her thighs together, intensifying the hot fire between her legs.

"Connor, I..." What could she say? Her body was one big throb.

"If you want me to stop, I will."

Her gaze flew to his, consternation replacing or at least shoving aside her anticipation. He wouldn't. *He couldn't.*

"If you stop now," she said in a hard, no-nonsense voice, "I'll grab you by the ears and manhandle you."

"In that case..." he teased, daring her to go through with her threat.

Given the way he'd tossed her on the bed, grabbing his ears might take some doing. She grinned. She'd give it her best shot. He wasn't getting away that easily, not when her body pulsed from head to foot, her breasts heavy and tight, nipples aching for his touch. Without a doubt, using her own fingers to get off this time would leave her feeling empty, hollow inside.

"I'm a bit nervous," she said. "I don't want you to stop. Do you hear me?"

Connor chuckled. "I'd like to see you try to manhandle me. Sounds interesting."

His eyes sparkled with amusement and echoed in his curved lips. He stood and stripped off his jeans, returning to her side dressed in tight black boxer-briefs that left nothing to her imagination. Taking her hand, he pressed it to his groin, silently encouraging her to touch him. Her pussy clenched as she measured the length and girth of his cock with her fingers, judged his size and savored the heat of him. He made a soft sound and, when checking his reaction, she noticed his tight jaw, his stillness. The tension in his body.

"See how much I want you?" Raw desire blazed in his face, twisting his lips and darkening his eyes. "I suffered from a hard-on for the entire drive out here. Never doubt I want you."

His words slid over her like a soothing balm, calming her ruffled nerves. Along with relief, a grin surfaced. "Then what are you waiting for?" she whispered.

"I'm all about mutual pleasure..." He paused, as if weighing his words. "...but I like to do things my way. Is that okay with you?"

Maggie cocked her head to the side, amusement bubbling inside her. If only he knew how much she wanted to give over control to her lover and enjoy the loving, the pleasure between them, without having to perform, without having to worry about a report card being thrust at her during a future disagreement. "I'll let you know if it's not."

"Good."

She noticed an air of approval stamped his demeanor. The man was brimming with confidence. She liked that. It boded well for the future. Spanking...

He continued unfastening the buttons on her blouse, and this time she tried to relax, to enjoy every brush of his fingers against her bare skin. When he parted the fabric to reveal her lace-encased breasts, her bravery faltered a fraction, even though his steady gaze glowed with masculine appreciation. While she was busy sucking in her stomach, he unzipped her jeans.

"Lift your hips for me."

Bemused by his assured manner, she obeyed and let him tug her jeans down her legs. He lifted her upper body and removed her shirt, leaving her dressed only in matching pale blue bra and panties. Thank goodness she'd shaved her legs earlier after her workout at the gym.

"Damn, you're sexy." He traced a forefinger along the lacey top of one bra cup, the drag of his finger making a prickle of yearning spring to life. He retraced the same path with his tongue and dipped into her cleavage. A shiver worked free. To think she'd almost missed this. Her hands cupped his head, fingers twining in his hair. A small croak of dismay escaped from her when he lifted his head. He grinned. "Don't panic. I'm not going anywhere."

"Condoms," she said with a trace of impatience.

"I have some in my bag. It's out in the other room."

"You should go and get them." She gave him a nudge. "Immediately."

"Great minds think alike." He paused to kiss her again, a sensual sliding of lips that grew into more. A rough growl vibrated in his chest as he feasted on her mouth. When he finally lifted his head, they were both breathing hard. "Don't move a muscle," he said. "I'll be right back."

As if she *could* move. Her limbs felt like strands of cooked spaghetti after his kiss. Sighing, she parted her legs and ran her hand down her torso. Her fingers skimmed over her panties, and she wondered if he'd spank her for misbehaving. When she strummed her fingers over her clit, hot pleasure radiated from her core. Her eyes fluttered closed to better concentrate on the sinful sensation. The crotch of her panties grew damper, her folds swollen with arousal.

"I thought I told you not to move."

Maggie gasped, her eyes flying open. She stared at him with guilt. "I...um..."

"Are you wet for me?" He prowled from the doorway to join her on the bed. Dragging her close, he gave her a playful swat on the butt.

She gasped, the jolt on her ass electrifying her entire body, zapping through her nerve endings like a fork of lightning. *Ohhh, that was amazing.* Could she get him to do it again? She chewed on her bottom lip, indecision paralyzing her voice.

"Answer me, babe." Connor stroked her ass firmly, intensifying the sensations rippling through her body.

"Yes," she murmured. *And how!*

"Show me."

The softly voiced order reverberated between them as they stared at each other. Panic kicked Maggie in the stomach. *What did he want her to do?*

Connor said, "Show me how you like to touch yourself."

She swallowed hard. "You want me to masturbate in front of you?" she asked, her voice barely a whisper. All her bad girl exhibitionist behavior seeped into the mattress.

He grinned. Wide. "I didn't expect to do all the work myself."

She pulled back, her emotions shooting through her like a bee in a tizzy. Although she had to admit, along with his command came a dark thrill.

"Get started," he ordered. "No secrets, remember?"

He brushed the back of his hand over her cheek, making her slow her breathing. When she was certain no amusement or anything sinister lurked in his face, she relaxed. *Showtime.* Lifting her hips, she whisked her panties off and spread her legs to flash her glistening folds.

His breath hissed out, approval glinting in his eyes. "Pretty. I like knowing you want me."

His appreciation and praise sent her confidence soaring. She brushed her fingers down her slit, coating them with her honey before returning to tease and circle her clit. A gentle pleasure filled her and she closed her eyes to savor the blissful hum. So good. Knowing he watched her every move pushed the sensations even higher.

"Let me taste you."

Her eyes flew open. She removed her hand, expecting him to move between her legs. He didn't. Instead, Connor lifted her hand to his lips and took her finger inside his mouth. Warm heat seared her digit, a dart of sensation spearing down to her pussy. When he sucked her finger, she couldn't contain the hungry groan of pleasure emitting from her throat, her sheath clenching with need.

"Connor," she moaned. Even her voice contained hunger. Yearning. She needed him so badly she couldn't hold back, knew she'd suffer if he didn't take her and yet they'd barely started. Their gazes met, desire rippling between them in silent code.

With a final swipe of his tongue, he released her finger and smiled. "I want to see your breasts."

Maggie thought of his mouth on her nipples and gulped.

Hard. "Yes."

His brows rose at her taut whisper, his mouth curling into a knowing grin. With a competent flick of his wrist that gave her pause, he removed her bra and, after licking a finger, gently circled one areola. Together they watched it pucker, pulling to a tight crest. His blunt-tipped fingers traced across the plump curve. Maggie sighed, enjoying his explorations, feeling the moment rife with possibilities.

"Tell me what you like." He pinched one nipple, rolling it between finger and thumb, watching her reactions closely until her cheeks glowed with heat because of his scrutiny.

"Everything," she whispered. *She liked everything*, which reminded her of the slippery slope she teetered on with Connor. She had to remember to keep a firm grip on her emotions. Any relationship between them was sex for mutual pleasure. That's all. No long-term partnership. No expectations. Just sex.

He repeated the move, dragging her attention back to the present, the jolt of pain smoothing out until she drifted in a heavy fog of desire, each lingering caress ratcheting up her sexual appetite. Her pussy throbbed, clenching with fresh hunger at each pinch, every sensual kiss.

Connor watched the play of emotions over her face, the desire and growing hunger. It echoed in him, burning like an inferno. He'd imagined how it might be with Maggie. Wondered. Nothing he'd come up with did justice to the reality. She was beautiful. Responsive. Captivating with her honest reactions. They'd barely started, and he wanted to keep her forever.

Yeah, like she'd want to hear that. If he told her the truth, she'd run a mile. He was pushing things now, proposing a *friends with benefits* arrangement. His bloody reputation didn't help the situation. Forcing aside his doubts, he leaned over and cupped her breast, taking a nipple into his mouth. Her soft groan sped straight to his balls. They pulled tight, pre-come dampening his boxers.

"Connor." Her harsh whisper told him she felt the magic between them. A start. He had to believe there would be more.

Connor lifted his head to stare at her. "I wanted to go slow, babe. Explore you, but if I don't get inside you right now, I'm going to explode."

"Yes." The grip of her hands on his shoulders signaled urgency on her part, which suited him fine. "Me too."

Connor yanked off his underwear. Seconds later, condom in place, he settled between her legs. Fire and chills warred within his body, the need to hurry pounding him. Instead, he pushed only the head of his cock into her, resisting anything more, wanting their first time to be memorable for her. Their lips met, the kiss seductive and without haste, a mating of mouths that promised so much more.

Maggie wriggled beneath him, pushing him deeper into the tight heat of her pussy. Damn, he couldn't go slowly. He thrust, filling her completely with one seamless stroke. Fully embedded, he paused to savor her heat, kissing her again without haste. Tenderly. She undulated against his body, pressing sexy curves to his chest and tempting him to move.

"I'm a weak man," he admitted. "I honestly wanted to go slow, but—"

"Fast is good," she murmured before nibbling the cords of his neck.

Taking her at her word, he started to thrust, watching her face and monitoring her reactions. Her pussy rippled around his cock, squeezing it tight. They fell into an instinctive rhythm, the slap of flesh and sounds of fucking loud and unrestrained. Frissons of excitement whipped him. She felt so *damn* good. The tiny noises she made at the back of her throat, a sound between a whimper and a cry, pushed at his restraint. He thrust harder. *Faster.* Her fingernails dug into his shoulders until he felt the edge of pain. It rippled straight to his cock. Damn, if she kept touching him that way he'd lose *all* semblance of control.

He manacled her wrists above her head, curbing her wandering hands. A low groan emerged when he started to move faster again, pounding into her pussy with controlled passion. Hot. Tight. *Perfect.* Her slick heat caressed him, a surge of wetness making his cock buck.

"I love the way you feel," he murmured, needing to let her know how much he was enjoying making love with her. "Tight and wet."

"More, please." Her needy whimper whispered past the rim

of his ear, while her pussy gripped him sweetly.

"I don't want to come first."

She ground against his erection, panting slightly when the walls of her sex pulsated. "It doesn't matter. We can do it again."

Connor plundered her mouth. *Anytime.* Hell, yeah. He'd take any excuse to touch and explore her body.

He thrust again. Once. *Twice.* Clawing tension rose until he couldn't control it any longer. His cock jerked in explosive contractions, heart pumping while he froze, deeply embedded in her. He gasped at the pleasure roaring through his body. His own private fantasy turned into flesh. He didn't think he'd ever felt this good before. In the past sex had been all about getting off. With Maggie it was different because he *cared* for her. Cared about what happened to her, her feelings, her needs. He came back to reality and realized he was probably squashing her.

"Damn, I'm sorry." He pulled free and dealt with the condom, wondering if his early climax would cause a problem between them. Women were funny about that sort of thing, even though she'd encouraged him to take his pleasure. "That hasn't happened before. I'm usually more disciplined."

Maggie laughed, setting his fears at rest. "Don't apologize. I've enjoyed it." She cocked her head to one side, teasing him. "So far."

"Only enjoyed? I'll have to see if I can do better."

Grinning, Connor moved between her legs, lifting her to his mouth. Her sweet flavor exploded across his taste buds. He parted her folds, rasping his tongue over her clit. Her groan was music to his ears. He'd do almost anything to hear more of the ragged sound, the whimpers she couldn't contain.

He pushed two fingers inside her and settled in to give her pleasure. A puff of air against her engorged clit. A stroke of his tongue. He pumped his fingers, curling them to hit her sweet spot. She shook and moaned, hips jerking beneath his touch. When he covered her clit with his mouth and gently sucked on it, the tiny bundle of nerves pulsed. He felt the rhythmic clenching of her pussy around his fingers. Groaning, she jerked beneath his touch, shaking uncontrollably before slowly relaxing. After a final swipe of his tongue, he lifted his head and moved up the bed to draw her into his arms.

Maggie curled into him, her soft sigh filling him with contentment.

His.

She mightn't know it yet, might fight the idea, but he had enough patience for both of them.

Boy, did he.

Chapter Four

I dreamed about spanking. Not surprising considering the subject loomed large in my mind. I found myself in a meeting with one woman and two men.

"Why do you want to be spanked?" the woman asked. She wore a prim black suit with a crisp white shirt. Her blue eyes glinted with intelligence from behind horn-rimmed glasses.

I stiffened, my spine hitting the back of the chair. It was her attitude, her intense scrutiny. She made me feel like a freak.

The men sitting with us laughed, whispered asides to one another.

"Spanking is considered kinky," the woman said. Her tone implied not normal.

"It's hard to explain," I said. "I read an erotic romance where the hero spanked his heroine. Just reading about their romance made me hot all over. It made me consider the possibilities. The couple really bonded. They seemed so intimate. They communicated. The couple was close and attuned to each other's needs. I wanted that."

"A book?" the woman scoffed. "You got all this from a book?"

"She's confusing fiction with reality," a dark-haired man said.

"Bottom line, she's weird," the second man said.

"Haw. Haw! Bottom line." The dark-haired man smirked. "She wants a few thwacks on her ass, and you call it the bottom line. It's her ass all right, her bottom." He leaned over and poked my hip with his forefinger.

Suddenly I was naked.

Applause rang through the room. I whirled around and found myself face-to-face with hundreds of men. They varied in age, but had one thing in common.

A leer.

I let out a horrified shriek.

"Maggie. Maggie!"

Her eyes flew open, heart pounding.

"Are you okay? You were screaming."

"Connor?" Maggie suddenly realized she was naked, the cotton sheet pooled at her waist. With a gasp, she grabbed the sheet and tucked it around her breasts. She inched away from Connor. The events of the previous night came back to her. They'd made love...had sex. The *friends with benefits* thing.

"Don't you think it's a little late for that? I've seen you, touched you." Connor's voice grew husky. "Kissed you." The amusement twinkling in his eyes intensified. "I've explored your body, babe. I know what you like, the little sounds you make when you come."

Maggie closed her eyes briefly, heart pumping far too fast. She'd done it now, slept with him.

All night.

He hadn't run off to sleep in another room.

Greg had never liked sleeping all night in the same bed with her.

"You're shaking." Connor drew her into his arms and pressed her against his chest. "Are you going to tell me why you woke up screaming?"

Maggie swallowed, recalling the vulnerable feeling of being naked in front of a fully dressed crowd. She imagined how coming out about her interest in spanking would make her feel the same way. Exposed.

What would Connor think if she asked him to spank her?

Greg hadn't thought much of the idea. But now it was all she could think about. A rush of heat exploded in her lower belly. She opened her mouth to speak and shut it again, hiding her face to mask her topsy-turvy emotions. The need to continue with her experiments in spanking ate at her. Giving up wasn't an option.

"Aren't you talking to me today?"

Maggie lifted her head to meet his gaze. "I had a really weird dream. I was a bit disorientated when I woke."

"Do you want to talk about it?"

"No," she said, then realized she'd lost another opportunity to state her wants.

Connor nodded, his face strangely serious for a change. "In that case, how about if I distract you?"

"I'm listening." If he suggested coffee or breakfast she'd be crushed. This *friends with benefits* thing wasn't as easy as he'd made it sound. She felt as if she were navigating a mine field. "What did you have in mind?"

His eyes twinkled with definite mischief. "This," he said seconds before he moved.

Without warning Maggie found herself on her back with Connor leaning over her. His strong arms caged her in position as he stared down at her. "Now I have you exactly where I want you."

"What are you going to do to me?"

His grin never wavered. "Why don't you wait and see?" He leaned closer and kissed her, a gentle kiss that pierced her objections.

He could do anything. Anything at all, if he continued the pleasure he'd started last night. The wet rasp of his tongue over the pulse point at her throat made her breath stall. This close she could see the dark stubble on his jaw and feel the faint rasp against her more tender skin. He looked up and caught her staring. He had flecks of gold in his eyes and eyelashes long enough for most females to envy.

"What? Don't you like that?"

"I like it," she admitted, although she was sure he knew that. Her body wasn't exactly holding back on visual clues. Her breath caught each time he touched her.

"I'm going to explore every inch of you," he said between kisses. Slowly he worked down toward her breasts, nibbling her collarbone, nipping then laving the sting away.

"And do I get a chance to explore?"

"Not yet." He grinned at her before lowering his head and licking around one nipple. They both watched when it pulled tight.

Sighing her enjoyment, she plunged her hands into his hair, silently encouraging him to continue.

"No touching. Hands above your head."

Maggie frowned. "But that's not fair. You're touching."

"My game. My rules."

Is that all this was to him? *A game?* She stared at him, trying to read his mind. And they said women were bad. He had an impassive thing going and she didn't have an inkling of his thoughts. Clearing her throat, she said, "Is this a game to you?"

"What we're doing right now. Yes. But our *friends with benefits* deal is serious. I'm not playing games or stringing you along. I promise." Not a hint of humor showed on his face or in his blue eyes.

She needed to trust him. It was that simple. Letting her breath ease out, she relaxed. A tremulous smile communicated her acceptance of his conditions.

"Hands above your head," he ordered. "Grasp the headboard and don't let go."

Maggie hesitated a fraction before following his instructions.

"Good girl," he said with a grin.

"Should I wag my tail?"

Connor chuckled. "Maybe later." He ran his fingers down her torso, bypassing her breasts to skim across her ribs and trace around her belly button.

"That's ticklish."

"Ah," he said, his mouth moving against her skin as he spoke. Gradually, he moved down her body. A kiss here. A touch there.

She thought he'd hurry things along and get to the good stuff. Instead he explored her body, learning what she liked. A nip on the tender skin of her inner thigh. The firm stroke of his hands down her calves. Her breasts grew heavier while clawing tension swelled inside her.

"Connor, no more."

"You want me to stop?"

"No more teasing. I can't take any more."

"What do you want me to do?"

"Fuck me," Maggie said bluntly. "That's what I want."

The air crackled with sudden tension as he stared at her. A grin crept across his face and glittered in his eyes. "I like your plain speaking, Ms. Drummond." Without taking his gaze off her, he reached for a condom. He ripped open the foil packet and rolled the condom onto his erection. Instead of pushing into her pussy, he rolled onto his back and grinned at her. "Ride me. Put me through my paces."

A splutter was the only sound to pierce the silence that fell in the bedroom.

"Well?" he prompted, placing his hands beneath his head, his grin never wavering.

A dare. He thought she'd refuse. Little did he know. Maggie clambered over him, parting her legs so she straddled his hips.

"Take what you want, babe."

She sucked in her stomach, self-consciousness hitting her. With the morning sun streaming through the net curtains, he could see her clearly. It made her uneasy, and brought back bitter memories of Greg explaining to her why she should lose weight. Her hesitation made her clumsy.

"I want you. Never forget that."

His soothing voice lent her courage, and she guided his cock to her entrance. "How do you know exactly the right thing to say?" she asked with a hint of chagrin.

"Natural talent," he said with a boyish smile.

"Is that right?" Maggie inched downward, impaling her body on his cock, parting sensitive tissues and filling the empty spaces inside her. "Does that feel okay?" But not ridding her of all the doubt.

Connor reached for one of her hands and interwove their fingers. His smile warmed her, boosted her confidence and she found herself returning it. She started to ride him with steady strokes, shifting her body, experimenting to find the perfect angle. Her breasts bounced, the hot intent in his eyes pushing her to the edge of control much quicker than normal.

"You're doing a good job." Connor's hands rose to grip her hips. His fingers branded her flesh, the bite of pain bringing relief.

She quickened her strokes, reaching for pleasure. Her womb fluttered, tension creeping through her limbs. The pleasure swelled, soared, pressure climbing with each rapid slide of his cock then fading. It was like a wave had splashed over her on its run to the shore, and she desperately wanted a return of the blissful sensation.

"Help me, please," she pleaded.

"My pleasure." He slipped a finger between her legs and wiggled it across her clit. "Like that?"

"Yeah." Her eyes closed to focus on the sweet agony of his touch. Inside and out, he knew how to touch her with delicate precision. They fell into a rhythm. She rose and fell on his cock and on each downward sweep, he delved between her legs, fingered her clit. It was a slow buildup this time. She soared each time he stroked her clit. Her head fell back and the tension ramped up, her teeth sinking into her bottom lip.

"Come for me, babe. I want to hear you, feel you clasp my dick tight." His erotic whispers pushed her off the plateau, and she shattered, the ferocious heat of the pleasure pulsating the walls of her sex.

When she came back to herself, she fell forward, wrapping her arms around him, still breathing hard.

"Damn, I wish you could see yourself when you come," he whispered, stroking his hand over her hair in a rhythmic manner. "You're so pretty with your pink cheeks and your tits bouncing, your loose hair. Let me kiss you, babe."

She offered her lips and he took. He ate at her mouth, consumed her until the passion roared between them again. His fingers tangled in her hair, holding her in place, slanting her mouth to fit. He nipped and licked and took possession, stroking their tongues together in a sensual dance that could only lead to one place. Greed and hunger burst to life, heat and lightning flaring between them.

He lifted her off him and seconds later, he had her on all fours in front of him. He stroked her ass, cupping and squeezing the globes of her bottom. Then he took possession, sliding his cock into her wet, sensitive pussy, his warm breath teasing the whorl of her ear. She grew wet with want, loving his unrestrained passion, his need for her. Short, sharp strokes massaged her inner tissues, then he started in on the long, slow slides that drove her crazy. She trembled with each smooth erotic glide, overwhelmed by his demand, his masculinity. He was hard, thick, just what she needed.

"Come again," he ordered.

The sensations gathered at his words, growing like a whirly wind. An abrupt explosion and she milked him with recurring squeezes. Connor plunged his cock into her and stilled, his release starting even before she finished. Together they toppled into ecstasy, and all Maggie could think was there was no way she could give up this kind of magic.

"I tried to ring you in the weekend," Julia said. "Where were you?"

"I needed to...um..." Cripes, she had to take care. She couldn't blurt out the details about her time spent with Connor. A wash of color heated her face. Think. "Um...I needed some time alone...to think."

"What were you doing?" Susan asked.

Christina scrutinized her. "Your nose is sun burnt."

Maggie squirmed, trying not to act guilty. She failed. She felt her blush spread down her neck.

"Did you do something with spanking?" Julia asked, wriggling her eyebrows up and down until she looked as if she belonged in standup comedy.

"Don't tell the world," Maggie snapped.

As one, her three friends stared at her, varying degrees of interest showing in their faces.

"It's just us," Christina said in a mild voice. "We're your friends. We're not going to judge you."

"I find it hard to talk about. Susan, you don't like talking about your ex-fiancé, and Christina, you never talk about that married man you dated. It's the same thing." And wasn't that the truth. Maggie hadn't found either the words or the time to tell Connor what she wanted. Part of it was fear and the other part was Greg's astounded reaction still ringing in her ears.

Ever since Connor had dropped her at her flat, doubts had set in like a plague. She offered her friends a weak smile. "I'm sorry. Give me time, okay?"

Julia patted her hand. "Of course we will."

"Take all the time you need," Susan added.

"Not too long," Julia said. "I'm dying here."

Connor appeared, grabbing the seat they'd saved for him in the lunch room. He tweaked Julia's nose. "Curiosity killed the cat, you know." He grinned at them all. "What did I miss?"

Maggie didn't know how he did it. Not a flicker of guilt crossed his face.

"Maggie won't tell us what she did in the weekend," Susan said. "She says she needed time alone to think."

Connor smirked. "Looks like our girl saw some sun. Her nose is sun burnt. Did you burn anywhere interesting?"

"Only the sheets." Aghast, Maggie clapped her hand over her mouth, eyes widening in shock. Her heart beat out three distinct thumps before stalling. It only started racing again when she dragged in a harsh breath.

Connor's eyes glinted with real amusement and his mouth curled into an evil grin. "Our girl got some. Good for you. Don't say Greg—"

"Where were you this weekend?" an irate voice demanded.

Maggie's stomach swooped to her toes. She closed her eyes. Perhaps if she couldn't see him he'd go away.

"Maggie, I'm talking to you." Greg grasped her shoulder and shook her. Her head jerked back and forward with the force of his shake before she jerked from his touch.

"I went to the beach," Maggie said.

"There's no need to rough her up," Connor snapped.

"Leave her alone," Julia hissed. "Can't you see you're hurting her?"

"Sorry," Greg said in a stiff voice. "I wasn't thinking. I wouldn't hurt you for the world. I was worried. You didn't answer your phone and you weren't at your flat when I went around."

Maggie clasped her sweaty palms in her lap, struggling for inner calm. Could this day get any worse? "We can't talk now.

People are staring."

"You're right," Greg said. "I have a client appointment in five minutes. I'll come around to your flat after work." With that, he strode away, leaving the lunch room.

Mortified by his outburst, Maggie glanced at her friends to check their reactions.

"He can't go around treating you like that," Christina said.

"I agree. You need to break things off with him," Julia said.

"I have," Maggie said. "After our date on Saturday night. That's why I went to the beach for some alone time. I need to tell him again."

"Why didn't you ring one of us?" Susan demanded.

"I want to know about the sheets," Connor said, his evil grin back in evidence. "Whose sheets did you burn?"

Maggie's mouth dropped open. She snapped it shut.

"I'm with Connor. I want to know about the sheets. If you weren't with Greg, who were you with?"

Now she'd done it. Her mouth flapped open and closed again. She picked up her coffee for something to do with her hands. They shook and she hurriedly set the mug back on the table.

"I don't want to talk about it. What did you do for the weekend?"

"I washed my hair," Julia said. "But we're talking about you."

"What beach did you go to?" Susan said.

"Yeah, I spent most of the weekend at the beach," Connor said.

"I thought you and Gwen were finished," Susan said. "Who did you take and how did you find a replacement so quickly?"

"There are more fish in the sea," Connor said smoothly. His eyes glinted, and Maggie stiffened waiting to see what he'd say next. She thought she might quite possibly kill him the next time they were alone together.

"What beach did you go to, Maggie?" he asked.

Killing was too good for him. She'd put itching powder in his sexy black boxer-briefs.

"I went to Maraetai beach," she lied through gritted teeth.

"That would be why I didn't see you," Connor said. "I went to Port Waikato."

"Do you surf?" Susan asked. "I'd love to learn."

"I can surf, but I haven't done it for a while."

"Good. You can teach me," Susan ordered.

Connor saluted. "Yes, ma'am."

"I want to know about Maggie," Julia said, neatly turning everyone's attention back to her.

"I'm not telling," Maggie said primly. "Look at the time. I need to get back to work." She stood, her chair scraping across the hardwood floor. With a wave, she started for the door.

"You can run but you can't hide." Susan's singsong voice stopped Maggie in her tracks. Slowly, she turned to face her friends.

"I'm not hiding anything."

Connor winked at her and Maggie groaned inwardly. He, more than anyone, knew she had secrets. The wretch. As she strode down the hall to her cubicle, her mind grappled with a way to get her revenge on Connor. Payback was a bitch, as he'd soon learn.

Connor found it difficult to concentrate on work. It had been bad enough during the morning but after seeing Maggie in her blushing confusion his mind rejected any work-connected thoughts in order to playback their weekend together. Hot. The woman had his heart. She just didn't know it.

A tap on his door heralded Julia's arrival. When Connor looked closely, he noticed circles of fatigue under her eyes. Somehow he didn't think she'd had a weekend full of sex. She didn't glow like Maggie. She looked…sad.

"You okay, sweetheart?"

Julia sat on one of the two chairs facing his desk. "I'm fine. Just a bit tired." She tossed her head. "I'm worried about Maggie. Did you see the hickey on her neck? If she's not sleeping with Greg, then who did she spend the weekend with? I'd hate someone to take advantage of her."

The satisfaction Connor had felt on seeing his mark on Maggie died with Julia's words. He wasn't taking advantage of her. They'd had a bloody good time together. It was a mutual thing between them. He hadn't pressured her. She'd agreed to go with him.

"She's a big girl. I'm sure she knows what she's doing."

Julia frowned. "You don't think she'd pick up someone so she could get into spanking, do you?"

Not if he had anything to do with it. "We'll have to make sure she doesn't."

"How? How are we going to do that? She's an adult. We can't make her do anything."

"We all make mistakes," Connor said slowly. Julia had made him aware of a few problems he hadn't considered. Spanking. He hadn't known how to approach the subject with her, and since, she hadn't said anything, he'd remained silent too. "Maybe we should research this spanking thing," he said. "Let Maggie know we support her."

"You can't let her know that we told you," Julia said. "She'll never tell us anything if she knows we broke our word."

"Damn." An open approach was out for him. He'd have to research on his own.

"I like your idea, though," Julia said. "The more we know, the better we can help her. Help keep her safe."

"We'll have to compare notes when she's not with us," Connor said.

"All right."

"And next time you girls go to the pub for margaritas make sure I'm there too."

"You ready to hear about blue pubic hair?" Julia asked with a smart-ass grin.

Connor's attention jerked from his computer screen to Julia. "Blue?" he said in a faint voice.

"That's what I thought." Julia stood to leave.

"Wait, you can't leave without giving me details. Who has blue pubic hair?"

Julia laughed and tapped her nose. "For me to know and you to find out."

"Hell, I'm going to have to make Friday night drinks," he said. "I'm missing out on all the good stuff."

Maggie hadn't intended to blog about Connor until he'd teased her. She was still considering the itching powder in his boxers, but this would do until then.

How do you tell someone you're into kinky sex, that you want them to spank you?

Today I'm feeling a bit like the columnist from Sex and the City. I hooked up with a guy in the weekend. I know him a little bit, but not well. And yes, our relationship is casual. The sex was great. Hot. Blazing hot. The best I've had for some time. But all the time we were together, I kept thinking about spanking. I wanted to ask him to spank me. At one stage he swatted me lightly on the butt. Just a teasing sort of thing. It made me so hot I almost came immediately. I wanted more but didn't know how to ask.

So my question is how do you communicate your spanking needs? And what do you do if the idea of spanking horrifies your partner? What do you do if your partner thinks you're a deviant?

The buzz of Maggie's doorbell dragged her away from her blogging. It was two minutes after six and she remembered Greg saying he was going to drop by. The sound of a key in her front door made her hurriedly sign off her blog. She logged off the Internet as she heard footsteps.

"Maggie, are you here?"

A flash of irritation made her scowl. What didn't Greg understand about over? Sighing, she rose and went to meet him. She had to get her key back from Greg.

"There you are," he said. "Why didn't you answer me?"

"I finished sending an email." The lie slipped out without a qualm. Maybe if she practiced a bit she wouldn't have such a bad time lying to her friends. Practice made perfect. "Would you like a drink? I'm about to have a glass of wine."

"You shouldn't drink alone," Greg said.

"If you have a glass of wine with me I won't be alone." His pompous attitude made her more determined to finish the relationship.

"What is wrong with you? You never used to be so snappy and sarcastic."

"Because you didn't used to treat me like a belonging." She had to get her key back before Greg left so he couldn't enter her apartment again without her permission.

Greg raked his hand through his hair, leaving the blond curls messy and making him appear more approachable. "Hell, I'm sorry. It's just you're acting a bit strangely and it threw me. I didn't mean to hurt you this morning."

Maggie didn't reply. She padded into the kitchen and opened the fridge to grab the bottle of Sauvignon Blanc she'd opened the previous night after Connor dropped her off. She poured two glasses and handed one to Greg.

"I wanted to ask if you'd attend the partner dinner with me," Greg said, taking a seat opposite her on the two-seater.

Maggie stared at him in shock. "But we're not going out together." She stood. "I think you'd better leave."

"But we haven't talked," Greg said. "And what do you mean we're not going out together. I didn't agree. I left to give you time to think."

"I don't want to go out with you again. We're finished. Give me your key and leave."

"I don't—you're making a big mistake." He set his glass down hard on the wooden coffee table and stalked to the doorway.

"My key?"

With a glare, he retrieved it from his pocket and threw it at her. The slam of her apartment door told her he'd finally left.

Reaction set in and her legs trembled so much she had to sit on the nearest chair. He hadn't mentioned the spanking part of their previous conversation, which worried her. What would happen if he told everyone at work? She'd hoped he'd keep quiet because the subject had been so distasteful to him. Damn, when had her life become so complicated with lies and half-truths?

Taking her wine with her, she returned to her computer. She waited while the computer started and loaded the Internet. There were no comments so she decided to do some research. Surely she couldn't be the only novice interested in spanking?

69

The doorbell went again. Maggie huffed out an impatient breath. The melodious sound repeated, and she realized she'd have to answer. She peered through the peep hole, suspecting it would be Greg again.

"Connor."

Maggie opened the door and stood aside for him to enter. "I shouldn't talk to you."

He grinned. "Maybe I don't want to talk."

"What if Julia or one of the others decide to pop in for a visit?" A shudder of horror sent an icy chill speeding down her spine. This was a dangerous game they were playing. She shut the door and retreated to the kitchen, automatically pulling out a beer for him.

"Don't worry." Connor closed the distance between, took the beer and put it on the bench. Then he grasped her hands. "I wouldn't do anything to upset you." He tugged her closer and wrapped his arms around her.

With a soft sigh of surrender, she leaned into him, shuddering when his hands slipped down her back to rest on her butt. Her mind slid into a quick, dirty daydream. A bared bottom. A wooden hairbrush.

A hand cupped her butt cheek, squeezing, building the anticipation simmering through her. Heat suffused her entire body and her folds moistened, the thoughts of spanking an erotic assault on her mind. The tension inside her amplified and a soft, needy sound emerged from deep in her throat.

The hand caressing her bottom stilled.

"Are you okay? Am I hurting you?"

Oh, heck. How embarrassing. How did she fix this? Admit her desires? Even as she opened her mouth she knew she was going to take the coward's way and say nothing. "I was thinking about the weekend," she whispered, words tumbling over each other she spoke so quickly. Anything to fill the pause. If the silence lasted any longer it would become uncomfortable. It would sound as if she was hiding something. She was but that was beside the point. "It was…amazing." An understatement. Amazing didn't come close to describing how great it had been between them, not only the lovemaking but the way she and Connor talked. They'd missed the awkward getting-to-know each other phase because they'd already done that.

"It was great," Connor said, his blue eyes sparkling.

She liked to think it was with remembered pleasure, but it could have been the angle of the light.

"That's part of the reason I came around. I wanted to be with you again." He lifted one hand off her ass and caressed her cheek. Their gazes met and looking at him made her knees wobble. He was with her. The weekend hadn't been a once off as part of her feared. He wanted to repeat their lovemaking and really meant the friends with benefits thing. The thought hit her with the strength of a sucker punch.

"It can't be here," Maggie said. "The girls drop in all the time, usually unannounced."

"We can meet at my apartment. You're the only one who has ever visited me there. I can't see that changing. What do you say?" He interspersed each word with a kiss to a different part of her face.

Her lips parted in silent invitation. They were alone. There was no reason they couldn't kiss and touch. They were adults. Things wouldn't get out of hand.

Connor tugged her blouse from the plain black skirt she still wore—her work clothes. Simple. No-nonsense. Conservative. His hand wandered over her warm skin, his fingers callused slightly, although the sensation wasn't unpleasant. The faint drag stirred desire and awakened her hunger even further.

"Are you ticklish?" His words were muffled against her throat.

"No, not really."

"So I can't tease or torture you that way."

"No." He could drive her crazy with lust though. "Are you? Ticklish, I mean."

"Afraid not." His hand traced across her rib cage, constructing a sensual bubble around them.

Connor took such care with her, made her feel treasured and desired. The contrasts with her previous lovers brought the realization she'd allowed them to shortchange her, allowed them to take what they wanted from her without demanding equal time for herself.

"Touch my breasts," she suggested.

"My thoughts exactly. That was next on my to-do list."

Maggie spluttered in half laughter and half disbelief. "You don't have a to-do list."

"Don't I? How do you know?" His mouth closed over her earlobe, the faint play of teeth sending messages of pure delight skittering through her. Then he peeled back one bra cup and stroked her puckered nipple with the back of his hand. One finger ran around her nipple and around again. His finger diverted to stroke the small bruise he'd left on the upper curve of her breast during the weekend.

"I like seeing my mark on you," he said.

Maggie shuddered, her head falling back, eyes squeezing shut while she greedily gathered sensations to recall later when she was alone. His fingers rolled her nipple before tugging lightly. The sensation grew until it was almost painful, but it was a good pain. It echoed in her pussy, a short jolt of desire.

"Connor."

"Do you like that? A little bit of pain in your loving?"

"I don't know." Her eyes flicked open. "I like that, so I must. Does that make me weird?" Her heart beat rapidly while she waited for his reply. She scanned his face and didn't see any disgust. She didn't see anything except intense interest. Desire.

"You're not weird." He laughed. "What would you say if I said I'd like to shave your pubic hair so you're nice and soft? So you'd feel every flicker of my tongue, every stroke of my fingers. Would that make me weird?"

Maggie thought about that for two seconds. "Yes," she breathed, unbearably turned on by the request.

His stroking finger stilled. "Yes, I'm weird?"

"Yes, you can shave me. I like the idea."

Connor laughed again, a strange expression on his face.

"You're teasing me." Maggie pulled away, hurt and embarrassed. "You didn't mean it." She wrapped her arms around herself, a form of armor, and backed away until the countertop halted further retreat.

"Don't, Maggie." Connor moved swiftly, blocking her from moving. He hugged her so hard she felt the ridge of his cock prodding her stomach. "I was joking, but your reaction has convinced me."

"I don't think so." Maggie's voice emerged stiff with a touch of anger. "Let me go."

"Dammit, I'm an ass," he muttered. He stopped teasing and kissed her, really kissed her, exploring and savoring her mouth like a fine glass of wine.

The fight seeped out of her and she clung to him, desire grabbing her with an urgent tempo, the hunger between them razor-sharp. When Connor pulled away, they were both breathing hard and color highlighted his cheekbones.

"I want you."

"Yes," Maggie agreed. "The bedroom."

"Not yet," he said. "Let's stoke the fire a little hotter first." With competent hands he unfastened the pearl buttons on her white blouse. Her bra, already askew, held one breast while the other pebbled in the cool air. "I want to taste you, explore some more before we end up in the bedroom. Some things shouldn't be hurried."

He dipped his head and licked her bared nipple. Wetness pooled between her thighs with each of his kisses and touches until an achy sensation filled her pelvic region. She wanted him bad.

His mouth closed over her nipple and sucked. Maggie fought a whimper and clenched her thighs together. Her hands crept up to his head, and she leaned back on the counter, Connor following without letting up on his ministrations.

"Connor, that feels good."

He lifted his head and stared at her wet nipple. "God, I love the way you respond to me."

"Can we move this to the bedroom?"

"Maybe you're right. My jeans are strangling my cock."

Maggie's gaze went to his groin, licking her lips when she saw the large bulge. "I can fix that."

He laughed with real amusement. "I'm counting on it, babe. Do you have condoms? I didn't bring any with me."

He really had come to talk. The knowledge brought a warm glow. He cared enough to drop by without expecting sex, despite their agreement. "I have condoms. You remember the sex party Julia had last month?"

"Yeah. Julia wouldn't let me go. She said I'd spoil all the fun."

"It was fun. I bought a few things, including condoms."

Connor dragged her toward her bedroom. "What else did you buy? Can I see?"

"Later," she said. "I'm not in the mood for playing with toys. I need hard, sweaty sex right now. I need your cock inside me."

Stopping, he gave her a passionate kiss. When he finally lifted his head, he said, "I had no idea how talking about sex with you would make me so hot. I like it when you tell me what you want. Don't stop, okay?"

She nodded, but secretly wasn't so sure. The misguided joke about shaving had made her cautious. She wouldn't tell him about her desire for spanking until she was sure of him. Meanwhile she'd explore on her own, look at spanking toys, read research and visit blogs and spanking forums. Admitting her need for spanking was one thing, but spelling out her desires to a man was another thing.

Connor pulled her into the bedroom and ripped off his shirt. "Where are the condoms?"

Maggie kicked off her shoes and opened her bedside drawer to grab the packet of condoms. She hadn't opened it yet since Greg had turned up his nose at them.

"Strip," he ordered. "I'll take care of the condoms."

The doorbell rang as Maggie finished peeling off her panty hose. They both froze.

"Hell," Connor swore. "I bet that's one of the girls."

"We can't let them find us like this." Panic roared through her at the thought of discovery. She'd promised Julia, Susan and Christina that she wouldn't make a move on Connor. They'd all agreed he was out of bounds. And as Christina said, the man had enough women in his life without adding them to the mix. Guilt hit Maggie hard. What was she going to say?

"Calm down. We haven't done anything wrong. I've popped into visit you before. We're friends, for God's sake. Friends visit each other. Besides, it might be a salesman. Go and answer the door."

The doorbell rang again and, biting her bottom lip, she turned to go to answer it.

"Maggie." Connor's chuckle halted her. "You'd better sort out your bra and blouse first before you answer the door."

Maggie glanced down at her bare breast and blushed. "Don't want to shock a salesman." With trembling fingers, she pulled her bra cup back into place and fastened her buttons.

"Good girl. Go an answer the door. Everything will be all right."

On autopilot Maggie went to the door, jerking it open without checking to see who it was on the other side.

"Maggie!" Julia said. "I'm glad you're home. I just about gave up. What took you so long to answer?"

Chapter Five

"I was looking for a beer and glass for Connor," Maggie blurted, sure her face was on fire, her guilt clear for Julia to see.

"Why are you so flushed?" Julia's eyes narrowed. "Is that a hickey on your breast?"

Bother, she'd missed a button. Two buttons. "Great. Why didn't Connor tell me my buttons were undone?"

"Why is Connor here?" Julia sounded distinctly suspicious.

"He's probably at a loose end," Maggie snapped. "I was glad he came because Greg was here."

"I thought you and Greg were finished."

Thankfully, mention of Greg distracted Julia. "I thought so too. Greg wasn't clear. I'm sure he's clear now. Come and have a glass of wine." She'd prefer to continue in the bedroom with Connor but could hardly tell Julia to go away without making her suspicious.

"Where is Connor?"

"He must have gone to the bathroom," Maggie said, biting her lip again. She turned away to grab a glass from the cupboard. He'd have to wait for his erection to subside since he could hardly walk out here sporting a hard-on. Julia would notice that straight away. The distant flush of the toilet sounded. She handed Julia a glass of white wine and hunted through the cupboard for a packet of crackers. They might as well have cheese and crackers with their drinks.

"Hey, Julia." Connor grabbed his can of beer and took a sip. "What's up?"

"I needed to get out of the apartment so I decided to walk over to see Maggie."

"Did you want to talk about girl stuff? Do you want me to leave?"

Maggie was torn, unable to decide what was worse. The idea of facing Julia alone or suffering through the self-consciousness after their interruption.

Julia decided for them. "Don't be silly. Maybe we can gang up on Maggie and find out who gave her the hickey on her breast."

"Do you have a love bite on your breast, Maggie?" Connor's smirk was wicked and sent desire zapping through her. "Are you going to give us details?"

"No," Maggie said. "I'm not talking. You can't make me."

"How much wine have you got? We should put some more in the fridge," Julia said with a sly grin at Connor.

Maggie reached for the phone and hit speed dial. "Indian Hut? Good. I'd like to order banquet number four. You can deliver that to Apartment Five B, Eleven Mason Street in Newmarket. Half an hour? That sounds perfect." Hanging up, she said to Connor and Julia, "If we're going to drink more wine, we'd better eat as well. It's the responsible thing for a host to do. Haven't you seen the drink-drive ads on television?"

"Which would be fine if I'd driven here," Julia pointed out. "I walked."

"I'm saving you from walking into a lamp post. Your nose is very attractive as it is. If you broke it, you'd end up with a kink."

Connor snorted. "Julia has enough kink in her life already. Blue pubic hair..."

Maggie sniggered. "You know about her blue pubic hair?"

"I do now," Connor said, laughing.

"Oops." Maggie slapped her hand over her mouth.

"It's all right," Julia said. "He tricked you. I was here and heard him. The man is sly. You should watch yourself. He'll have the name of your secret man out of you before long. He's slick."

Connor and Maggie exchanged a look. Luckily Julia

misinterpreted the guilt for something else. "Your days are numbered, Maggie Drummond. We'll get the truth out of you. Don't doubt it."

Maggie picked up her wine and took a sip to moisten her dry mouth. This scheme with Connor was madness. She had to stop before someone got hurt. Aw heck, who was she kidding? She couldn't stop. The sex with him was the best she'd ever had, and she actually liked him when they weren't in bed. No, she'd have to watch herself. They'd both have to be careful.

In the erotic romance I read, the hero smacked the heroine with his hand. I still imagine the sound of his palm hitting her bare bottom. The sudden crack. Her cry of both pleasure and pain. Her elevated breathing. The soft sigh when a second and third smack heats her bottom and radiates all the way to her clit. The arousal.

Yes, I get hot just thinking about this couple, and they're fictional. I start to think how it could feel if it were my bottom and arousal swamps me. Should it worry me or is this natural? I don't know. All I know is that I have to try spanking. Somehow, I have to find a man who is willing to experiment with me, a man who is open and supportive. A man who likes me exactly how I am and doesn't want to change me. I'm not putting up with a man who expects me to diet and lose weight to fit his ideals. That's not me.

Not anymore.

Since I read the book, I've done a lot of research on the Internet. There's so much to think about. Of course, the biggie is finding a partner or communicating with an existing partner and talking about incorporating spanking into a relationship. Then there're positions and tools. I hadn't thought beyond a man dragging me over his knee and using his hand, but I've learned about people using hairbrushes, paddles, floggers. Canes. I'll admit the idea of a cane frightens me. Too many memories of school. The principal used to cane in extreme circumstances until the Parent-Teachers' Association outlawed it.

A hairbrush doesn't seem so harsh and a paddle actually intrigues me. It will be interesting to learn how my body copes with a spanking. Will I bruise easily? How long will it be uncomfortable to sit? Will other people realize or will it remain my guilty secret? Will spanking change me?

At first I worried I was a freak. My research has shown there are lots of other people out there who enjoy spanking. I'm not alone.

I'm ending this post with a question—how did you know you wanted to explore spanking? What made you take the leap into the world of spanking?

"Jesus," Connor muttered, scrolling through the comments on Maggie's blog. Her posts were attracting regular visitors, and each person had honest opinions for her. Some had fallen into spanking by accident, while partners and lovers had introduced others. Maggie was really serious about spanking. That fact came through in her posts and the way she interacted with her visitors.

What did he do now?

He'd always thought he was a skilled lover, giving his partners pleasure. With giving came receiving. His stepfather had told him that during an embarrassing but enlightening talk on sex. Connor grimaced. No one liked to think about their parents having sex, and even less the fact that they did it often and enjoyed the act.

His stepfather had changed his life in so many ways. Positive ways. His mother had bloomed under his stepfather's attention. His life, which had been like open warfare while living with his real father, had evened out. He'd gone back to being a kid again, while his mother had lost her scared, pinched look and the bruises had faded.

How the hell could he hit Maggie when he'd sworn he'd never lift a hand to any woman, no matter what the provocation?

Maybe he could talk to his stepfather? He toyed with the idea and reached for the phone before deciding he'd wait.

Spanking is only beneficial if it enhance the lives of both partners.

A visitor left the comment and it had stuck with him. He was crazy about Maggie. He loved spending time with her, even if they didn't end up having sex. But spanking? How would it enrich his life when he hated the idea of violence and had taken a vow never to hit a woman?

The peel of his cell phone broke into his introspection. Probably just as well since his thoughts were chasing in circles. "Yeah?"

"It's Julia. Do you fancy coming around for a drink? I'm sick of my own company."

Connor frowned at the downbeat note in her voice. "You must be scraping the bottom of the barrel to ring me," he teased, hoping to coax a smile from her.

"I'm not...seeing anyone at the moment," she said. "I thought—" She broke off abruptly, but Connor heard the tears in her voice. "How about if I drop around after rugby training? In two hours. I'm about to leave now."

"Thanks. I need to buy some groceries anyway. I'll make dinner for us both."

"Don't forget to buy some beer," Connor said.

Rugby training went a bit over two hours, but Connor arrived at Julia's flat just after eight. When she opened the door, he checked for evidence of tears and found none, to his great relief.

"Hey, sorry I'm late. The coach kept us longer than normal."

"Dinner won't spoil. All I need to do is put on the steaks."

Connor followed Julia through to her kitchen. "I checked Maggie's blog before training. She's serious about spanking."

Julia turned on the gas and placed a heavy griddle on the heat. She grabbed a hair scrunchie from the fruit bowl and pulled her hair into a ponytail to keep it out of her way. His friends were all beautiful in their own way, but Julia was stunning. She'd even placed in the Miss Auckland contest a few years ago before throwing in the beauty contest circuit for the party one. Lately she'd seemed quieter, more restrained, although she still wore her confidence and sexiness like a badge.

"Maggie surprised me with her blog," she said. "It was unexpected but she seems more confident. I was glad she told Greg to take a hike. The man's an ass."

"Why don't you tell it like it is," Connor said, his tone wry. "Do you want a beer or a glass of wine?"

"I'll take a glass of the Chardonnay please. And you know Greg isn't good enough for Maggie. She's a sweetie and needs someone who will take care of her."

"You won't get an argument from me." *Someone like him.* Connor grabbed a beer for himself and opened the wine. He handed her a glass, put the wine back in the fridge and settled on one of the barstools at the breakfast bar.

Julia placed two steaks on the hot griddle, glanced at her watch and joined him at the breakfast bar. "Greg doesn't want to let go. He's started annoying her at work."

"Annoying her how?" Connor's voice was sharp. Maggie hadn't mentioned it to him.

"He requests her to help him with his clients' accounts, sends her flowers and rings her most days. It's nothing over the top, nothing that she can complain about to management."

"Maybe I should say something to him."

"We've already offered to help her, but Maggie says she needs to deal with him herself. She really has changed."

"But he's not listening to her."

"If he pushes her any harder, she'll lose her temper. I hope I'm around to see the fireworks. Maggie is slow to lose her temper, but when she does, she's a real dynamo."

"I've never seen her lose her temper before," he said, intrigued.

Julia checked her watch again and stood to turn the steaks. The scent of cooking meat filled the kitchen with a delectable aroma, reminding him he hadn't eaten for hours.

"Our Maggie is like an iceberg. She has hidden depths," Julia said as she removed two baked potatoes from the oven.

"Can I do anything?"

"Nah, sit there and look cute," Julia said with a hint of her usual impish humor. "What do you think about Maggie and her spanking?"

She retrieved two salads from the fridge: one green and the other one looked like the pumpkin salad his mother often made containing feta cheese, black olives and chickpeas. She placed a tub of sour cream, butter and some oil and vinegar on the counter. A few minutes later they were eating.

"I'm not sure what to make of it," he said. "I guess as long as she's happy and doesn't get hurt." No way was he going to say what he really thought.

Julia's cell phone rang. She answered it, listened for a second and said, "Christina, can I ring you back. Connor's here and we've just started our dinner." She laughed and said, "Twenty minutes. No, you guys can't come around. It's the middle of the week and if you come around, I'll drink too much. I'm getting too old to go to work with a hangover." Grinning, she disconnected the call and put her phone on the countertop.

"It's not like you to turn down the chance of a party."

Julia shrugged. "People change. I haven't felt in a party mood recently."

Connor waited for her to say more, but she didn't, cutting off a corner of her steak instead and popping it into her mouth.

"Most of the people posting on Maggie's blog live overseas. She's not going to find a prospective lover online," Connor said.

"People do these days. It's not unknown."

"Would you?"

Julia swallowed a mouthful of wine. "I don't know. It depends on the circumstances, the people involved. It's not always easy to meet a compatible partner these days. People have busy lives. Where do you meet prospective lovers if you're too busy with work?"

"I don't know. I hadn't really thought about it." Connor finished his meal and pushed his plate away with an appreciative sigh. "Great meal. Thanks." Julia had made him think. He didn't know if Maggie was actively looking for another man or not. He wasn't looking but that didn't mean she couldn't. The idea of her with another man made him...uneasy.

He wanted Maggie and didn't want to lose her to another man.

Dear Kinky Lover,
How will I know I've found the right man? I don't know. I guess finding a lover who is into spanking will be much like

finding a life partner. Some men will suit me and others will suck. I know it's not gonna be easy. You don't have to warn me about safety and security. I know and believe me, I've taken it into consideration.

The thing that will probably get me is my impatience. I want this so much that I know I'll have a tendency to rush into a relationship wearing blinkers.

Maybe, as you say, I'll be disappointed because I've built things up in my mind and the reality won't compare to my daydreams. I hope not. I'm a glass half-full kinda girl. I like to think positively, and hopefully, that's all I'll need.

Individuals are different and complex. We all go into relationships with our own set of baggage. I've already found that incorporating spanking into an existing relationship is difficult. My ex-boyfriend laughed at me and called me a freak. That's part of the reason he's now my ex.

We're all fragile in our own way. It's easy to misinterpret, which is why communication is so important. Everyone I've spoken to online stresses honest and open communication. Stating my needs isn't easy though. I have a casual relationship and really like the guy. The sex is so good, but he made just one comment while we were making love that made me reconsider talking to him about spanking.

Patience is a thing I need to work on. I've had a long time to think about spanking and consider the implications. My prospective partners haven't, unless they're already into spanking. Another thing I've learned is that spanking isn't a one-size-fits-all kind of thing. What is right for one couple won't work for another.

See how much there is to consider. Don't worry about me, Kinky Lover. I am considering all angles of this subject. I'm not going into spanking wearing rose-colored glasses. I appreciate your advice.

But one thing, you didn't tell me how you discussed your spanking needs with your partner. How did you get your partner to see the advantages spanking can bring to a relationship?

Best wishes,
Big Bad Ass

Connor spluttered on reading the last line, swallowing his mouthful of coffee quickly before his computer screen wore it instead. *How did he get his partner to see the advantages of spanking?* He snorted a laugh, keeping far away from his coffee. He was the lucky son-of-a-bitch who had a partner who already wanted a spanking. The confusion was all on his side, along with hang-ups about hurting his partner or turning into a monster. Maybe it was time to visit his parents. Perhaps he could take Maggie with him. Introduce her as a friend. He'd mentioned her and the other girls to his parents before. They wouldn't think much of it, not until he asked Frank about spanking.

The more he thought about it, the better he liked the idea. His mother had a birthday coming up soon. Perhaps he could wrangle invitations for all the girls. It would throw the heat off him a bit because his parents wouldn't know which girl he was talking about.

Feeling happier about his decision, he composed an email to Maggie.

Dear Big Bad Ass,
I didn't have to bring up the spanking discussion. My girlfriend brought it up for me and we went from there. My advice to you is to be honest with your partner, tell him what you want. Communicate. Sometimes you just have to put your heart out on the line. Take a big breath and jump...
Let me know how it goes.
Kinky Lover

Chapter Six

"That's a try for the Hawks. Connor Grey is having a good game today," the announcer said.

"Go, Connor," Julia screamed.

Maggie jumped up and down, cheering with the others. Something was up between Greg and Connor though. She'd seen them exchange words.

"They might actually win a game for a change," Susan said.

Christina rubbed her hands together and tugged her bright red and white hat lower over her ears. "How much longer to go? I don't know about you girls, but I could do with a cup of hot chocolate."

"The weather is always horrid when the Hawks play," Maggie said. "The sun will probably peek out the instant the final whistle blows."

"Why don't you all come to my place for hot chocolate and we can start our Maggie makeover?" Christina suggested.

"Good idea," Julia said.

"I'm there," Susan said. "I can't wait to get my hands on Maggie."

"Should we book a room?" Maggie asked, her mouth quivering with silent laughter.

Susan punched her on the arm. "You know I didn't mean it like that. But seriously. You're very sexy, and by the time we're finished with you everyone else will know it."

"So you'd turn gay for me?" Maggie smirked at the shocked silence. Teasing her friends was fun.

"Would that mean I'd need to spank you?" Susan asked.

Maggie pretended to frown. "I hadn't thought that far ahead, but yes. Probably. Spanking is now part of my psyche and non-negotiable."

"Oh, hark at her. *Spanking is part of my psyche.*" Christina mimicked her with perfect nuance.

The four women burst into laughter and started discussing who they'd turn gay for.

"Not the Prime Minister of New Zealand," Julia said firmly. "Oops, we've missed another try. What is wrong with the Hawks today? They're actually going to win a game."

"Better not let Connor hear you say that," Maggie said. "He'd probably spread rumors about blue pubic hair."

Susan and Christina giggled along with Maggie, but Julia didn't.

"Are you ever going to let me forget that? The color is growing out, okay?" The testy note in her voice stripped their laughter away.

"I'm sorry, hon," Maggie said, giving Julia a swift hug. "I didn't mean to hurt your feelings."

Julia sighed. "Put it down to the time of the month. I'm sorry I snapped."

The final whistle blew and the spectators and teams started to disperse.

"Are we going to tell Connor we're leaving?" Maggie asked.

"I guess we'd better. I really don't feel like fending off flirting males today in the clubrooms," Susan said. "It would be nice to have a girls' afternoon."

"Maggie, you look sensational," Susan said, her tone one of awe.

Maggie turned slowly, trying to take in the transformation in the mirror. "So you really would turn gay for me?"

"In a New York minute," Julia said, leaning over to kiss her on the cheek. "Spanking and everything."

Maggie turned her attention to the mirror again. She couldn't believe the difference Christina's makeover had made. The girls had talked her into having her hair cut. The hairdresser had fit her in at late notice and had worked wonders with her straight hair, taking six inches off the end, giving it a better shape and lighter highlights that shimmered under the artificial light.

"Your highlights will look beautiful in the sunlight," Susan said. "But wait until we finish. Make-up and clothes come next."

"Maybe I should try one thing at a time. The hair is change enough for now."

"Don't be such a coward." Christina propelled her from the hairdresser salon with a firm hand in the small of her back.

"But I need to pay," Maggie said, digging in her heels.

"I've got it," Julia said in a decisive manner. "This is my treat."

Maggie found herself hustled down the busy street, full of Saturday shoppers. Cars crammed the hectic intersection, fumes heavy in the air when they paused at the lights for the pedestrian signal to turn green.

Susan sneezed when a bus sped past. "Tell me why this is a good idea again."

"That's what I want to know," Maggie inserted before the others could answer.

"Forget it," Christina said. "I've wanted to get my hooks into you for a long time and you're not wriggling out of this makeover."

"Light's green. Let's go," Julia said, linking her arm through Maggie's. "I've got her. She won't get away from me."

"If I'm naughty, will you spank me?" Maggie said in a loud voice.

"Really," an elderly lady said with a sniff. With a withering stare in their direction, she led her young grandchildren across the road.

"Oops," Maggie said. "I didn't mean to offend anyone."

"Too late," Julia said, tugging on her arm. "Let's go before the wee man starts blinking red."

They crossed the road and headed for Smith and Caughey, a well-known Newmarket institution. A wave of perfume greeted them when they entered the make-up department.

"Where to?" Maggie asked, finally accepting that her friends wouldn't let her change her mind. She hoped Connor liked the result. *Connor*. Holy Hannah. What was she thinking? It didn't matter if he liked the end result or not. They were friends and casual lovers. That was all. She was taking part in the makeover because she wanted it. She wasn't going through this for a man.

"Over here," Christina said. "I have a deal I've worked out with this company. I really like their products and they do both skincare and cosmetics. They don't do animal testing on their products either. What?" she said. "I care for animals and the environment and want to do my bit."

"Of course you do," Susan said.

"We're impressed you're incorporating that sort of thing into your new business," Julia added. "Some businesses go for the easiest and quickest way to make money."

"Not me," Christina said. "I made a list before I started. I've always used natural cosmetics and I wanted to continue. It was important to me."

"You've never said anything before," Maggie said.

"You never said anything about spanking before," Christina countered.

Julia licked a finger and pretended to mark an invisible scoreboard. "Touché. We all have our secrets and little hot buttons we don't discuss in case people laugh or tease us."

Christina stopped in front of a make-up counter and pushed Maggie onto a high stool. "We have to pick up this conversation again. Next time we have drinks at the pub. I don't care if it's a Friday night or not."

Julia chuckled, but Maggie thought her response held uneasiness. It made her wonder what was going on in Julia's life. She thought about Friday night drinks and shuddered. She knew there was one secret she'd never spill, no matter how many margaritas she drank.

An assistant arrived, a bright smile on her face. Christina explained what she wanted, and Maggie found herself under the spotlight again.

An hour later, she stared in the mirror in shock. Although she wore make-up, she hadn't done much with it or purchased new products in ages. "I didn't realize it would make such a big difference."

"You look gorgeous," Julia said. "And I know just the outfit to top off your new look. Susan and I have scouted the clothes department for you."

A whirlwind shopping trip later, they went back to Maggie's apartment and collapsed with a bottle of wine and some Thai takeout.

Julia waved her glass of wine in the air. "Maggie, I didn't know you were so curvy. You've got a great figure."

"No wonder Greg doesn't want to let go," Susan said.

"I guess I fell into bad habits," Maggie said. "Thanks so much to all of you. I wouldn't have done this without your prompting and I think I really needed it. I'd like to propose a toast. To Christina for making the initial suggestion, and to friends for helping me to carry it through."

"You don't need to toast me," Christina protested. "You're going to be my walking advertisement." She raised her glass, making her golden bracelets jingle musically. "To friends."

"To friends!" they chorused. Their wine glasses tinkled as they clicked together.

The ring of a cell phone broke in on their chatter and laughter. Susan, Christina and Julia all dived for their handbags and Maggie chuckled. She knew it wasn't her phone because it sat on the kitchen countertop and wasn't making a sound.

"It's mine," Julia said. "Hi, I'm not in at the moment. Leave a message after the—" She broke off and listened, her smile reaching her eyes. She looked beautiful in that moment. Happy. Maggie realized Julia hadn't smiled much lately. Standing abruptly, she walked from the kitchen, leaving them staring after her.

"What was that?" Susan whispered.

"Shush, I can't hear," Christina muttered.

"You can't eavesdrop on a private conversation," Maggie said. "It's not nice. How would you feel if it were you? Let Julia have her privacy."

Christina frowned. "But I want to know what's going on. She isn't usually secretive like this."

A loud sigh sounded from Susan. "Maggie is right. Julia will tell us when she's ready."

"I tell you, we need a margarita session very soon. All this suspense is killing me. How is your spanking blog going, Maggie?"

Maggie laughed. "Oh, no you don't. You can't turn this on me. Besides, you all read my blog and don't try to deny it. You know I'm heavy into research at the moment, and that's as close as I'm getting to my spanking."

Julia returned to the lounge, her eyes bright and cheeks glowing. "I have to go."

"Where?" Susan asked.

"I'm meeting up with a...a friend," Julia said. "I'll see you at work on Monday." Quickly, she gathered her handbag and gave a wave. The rapid tap of her high heel sandals signaled her retreat.

No one spoke until the click of the door closing told them she'd gone.

"What was that about?" Susan demanded.

"No idea," Maggie said. "No doubt we'll find out eventually."

"She looked so different," Christina said. "It's made me realize how quiet she's been lately. Do you think it's a man?"

"Of course it's a man," Susan said. "Do you think Connor will know anything?"

"If he does, the man won't tell," Maggie said. "He's as tight as a clam with secrets."

"I've noticed a real swagger in his step recently," Susan said. "They're very close. You don't think..."

"Julia and Connor?" Christina laughed and then looked thoughtful. "I don't think so. Surely we'd pick up on it if there were something romantic between them."

Guilt roared through Maggie, and she bit down on her bottom lip to stop herself from saying something. Anything. Good grief, if the girls found out about her and Connor...

"Besides," Christina added. "We made a pact about Connor. I like having a male friend and talking to him. I don't want that to change."

"None of us do," Susan said. "I like the way he's honest

when we ask him tricky questions."

And he was that way with her, Maggie thought, the guilt almost overwhelming her. He was honest and truthful, yet she couldn't give him the same honesty when it came to her need for spanking. Everything she read said honest communication was the most important thing between partners. She would have said the same even if spanking wasn't in the equation. The couples who stayed together were the ones who had great communication.

"I don't think Julia and Connor are together," Maggie said, knowing she was floundering in dangerous territory. "I think it's someone else."

"Do you know something?" Susan asked.

Maggie sucked in a breath and let it ease out. It did nothing to slow the rapid beat of her heart. When she glanced down, she noticed the tremor of her hand and hurriedly placed her glass on the coffee table. "No. All I know is that Julia looked really happy. I'm pleased for her and I hope whoever was on the other end of that cell phone realizes how great she is." A quick glance at both of her friends told her they'd bought her comment and didn't suspect anything about her and Connor.

Her cell phone rang and she rose, retrieving it from the kitchen. A swift glance at the screen told her it was Connor. She stabbed the answer button, trepidation causing butterflies to stomp around the pit of her stomach.

"Hello."

"What are you wearing, babe?"

She closed her eyes on hearing his husky voice, thankful that she had her back to Christina and Susan. Searing heat emblazoned her cheeks, signaling her guilt clearly to anyone who took a close look.

"I'm sorry, Greg," she muttered. "I can't go out with you. I have friends with me."

"Who?" Connor asked, his voice sharp and miles away from the lover of seconds before.

"Susan and Christina."

"I'm at home and would really like to see you. Come over when they leave."

"I don't know." Clear doubt shaded her words, propelled by

a heavy dose of remorse.

"Please. I really want to see you." He hung up without saying another word.

Maggie closed her cell phone with a snap and returned it to the bench. She walked back into the lounge to join Susan and Christina, praying they didn't ask too many questions because she hated lying to them. In that moment she hated Connor and the position he'd put her in with his *friends with benefits* deal.

"Is Greg still bothering you?" Susan asked.

"Yes," Maggie said, answering with relief. Greg couldn't get it into his fat head. She didn't want him. It was all about Connor. Anxiety replaced her momentary relief when Connor filled her mind again.

Susan flicked her long hair over her shoulder and scowled. "Maybe you should complain at work. Place a formal charge."

Maggie picked up her glass and played with it. Her hand trembled but she hoped they put it down to the phone call. "A charge for what?"

"Sexual harassment," Christina said. "He's bothering you at work and during your personal time. He shouldn't be allowed to get away with it."

Maggie stared at her friends, her hand gripping her glass so tight it was a wonder the stem didn't snap. "But that would ruin his career. He'd have to leave and find another job."

"But he's using the job to get to you," Susan said. "He's not going to stop until you make him. Christina is right. You need to file a complaint."

Maggie didn't think she could do that. She's talk to him first. Hopefully their last chat had put an end to his hopes for a future with her. "I'll think about it."

"You should." Christina put down her glass. "I don't know about you two, but I'm exhausted. I have a client to take care of tomorrow and need my beauty sleep. I think I'll head home."

"I might go too," Susan said. "Will you be okay if we leave you alone?"

A whoosh of relief almost floored Maggie. She'd wondered how she'd manage to get rid of her friends, even though shame filled her with every thought. Her need for Connor, for his touch and companionship, raged hotter than her self-reproach.

"Maggie? Will you be okay?"

With a start she returned to the conversation, castigating herself yet again for letting Connor sidetrack her thoughts. "Why shouldn't I?"

"Wasn't Greg coming over?"

"I told him you were here and were spending the night. I don't think he'll turn up because I was pretty sharp with him." *Lies. All lies.* Could she dig herself a deeper trench?

Susan cocked her head. "Are you sure?"

She reminded Maggie of an inquisitive bird. "I'm sure. Besides, I want to handle Greg if necessary. I don't want group participation."

Christina pushed her glasses up her nose and grinned. "But group participation is so much fun."

Maggie's brows rose in surprise. She hadn't misinterpreted Christina's comment, had she? A faint tinge of color appeared on her friend's cheeks. No, she hadn't. *Interesting.* It seemed she wasn't the only one harboring secrets.

Susan snorted. "You'd run a mile if a man suggested he bring along another party—either male or female—for a sexual fling."

The color in Christina's cheeks deepened, and Maggie thought she looked pissed now rather than amused.

"Not everyone follows a traditional path," Christina snapped. "We all want different things, like Maggie with her spanking. It doesn't make us weird, and don't get me started on kinky. I hate the label *kinky*. Wanting personal fulfillment, no matter what form it takes, makes us human. And before you say it, I don't mean non-consensual sex in any shape or form. That *is* sick. I'm talking about relationships in the normal sense. Dreams, hopes, aspirations—a person shouldn't push them away, and that includes sexual things." Her chest rose and fell with each rapid breath, her eyes sharp like a sergeant-major conducting drills and looking for mistakes.

The three women were silent for a long moment. Maggie wasn't sure where to look until sympathy filled her in a crashing wave. If Christina wanted to move into untraditional sexual practices, that was fine with her. It wasn't as if she was thinking along traditional lines. The Tight Five had supported her when she said she was into spanking. The least she could do was support Christina in turn.

"Good for you, Christina," Maggie said, breaking the yawning silence. "Do you want to talk about it? Are we allowed to ask questions?"

Christina gave an uneasy laugh, picked up her glass and realized it was empty. Maggie noticed her hand shook when she replaced the stemware on the coffee table. "I think I've had too much wine. I didn't intend to mention a thing."

"You can't leave us hanging like this," Susan protested, her eyes glittering with curiosity.

"Yes," Maggie said before Christina had a chance to answer. "She can. Christina knows we're here if she wants to talk."

"Thanks." Christina stood and hugged Maggie, the pressure of her hands on Maggie's shoulders telling of her gratitude. "I really need to go because I do have to work tomorrow." She glanced at Susan. "Do you want to share a cab?"

"I need to do laundry and sort out a few other things before I visit my parents tomorrow." A grimace slid across her face. "I promised I'd make a bacon and egg pie to take for lunch." She wrapped Maggie in a hug. "It was fun watching your makeover. You look stunning. Our Christina does a great job."

"She does," Maggie agreed, infusing her voice with warmth. "I feel like a new woman. It's like looking at stranger in the mirror."

Maggie walked her friends to the door and, with final hugs and kisses, they departed. After closing the door, she glanced at her watch. Just before nine. Connor had said to come over no matter how late her visitors left. A sliver of guilt slipped into her mind again, but she quashed it. Christina was right. She wanted to spend time with Connor. She wanted to explore spanking. Tonight, she'd tell him exactly what she wanted from their relationship. The worst thing that could happen was he'd say no.

Connor answered the door with a smile on his face. *Maggie.* He yanked open the door and gaped.

"Maggie?"

She smiled, a wide, bright grin that did nothing to hide her apprehension. "Who else were you expecting?"

"I don't know—the Easter bunny?" *Holy hell, what had she done to herself?* She looked incredible. Amazing. Not that she hadn't looked great before.

"Wrong time of year. Try again."

"You look beautiful." An understatement.

"Thanks. Christina and the others did a makeover today. My bank account is looking a bit sick, but other than that, I enjoyed myself." She sashayed into his apartment, balancing on heels that put a dent in their seven-inch height difference. His gaze dropped to the gentle rock of her hips, the faint bounce of her ass, and lust roared through him. *Was she wearing a new outfit?* He couldn't wait to see what she looked like under the coat.

"Would you like a drink?" he asked, not wanting to be rude and jump her straight away. His mother had brought him up right.

"No thanks. I've had enough wine tonight. If I have any more I'll fall asleep." She loosened the belt on her black and red coat until it dropped free and unfastened the buttons. "I wouldn't want to waste *this* on sleep."

Connor froze. His mouth dried of every trace of spit.

"Do you like?" she asked in a saucy tone, cocking one hip with sexy attitude.

"Hell, yeah," he croaked, staring at the wee bit of nothing she wore "I think red is my new favorite color." He prowled across the distance separating them and pushed the black and red coat off her shoulders. It fell down her arms and dropped to the floor with a whisper of crisp fabric.

She might as well have been naked because the lacey bra and panties she wore didn't cover much. They were all enticement rather than functionality. He tucked a lock of her dark hair behind one ear, still trying to take in the transformation from Maggie to siren. He ran his hand over her collarbone and across her shoulder, his attention on her beautiful breasts. The red lace was translucent and he could see her nipples. As he touched and skimmed his hands across silky skin, her nipples hardened, pulling to tight crests that just begged him to kiss.

"Come to bed," he said, his voice husky and full of desire.

She smiled. "I thought you'd never ask."

He grabbed her hand, wanting to go slow despite the urgency thrumming through his veins. Even so, he couldn't prevent a surge of impatience when he grabbed her, swinging her into his arms and striding for his bedroom. He tossed her on his bed, part of his mind thinking how right she looked there. *His.* He couldn't muck this up between them. Not when it felt so damned right.

Connor followed her down to the bed and plundered her mouth, nipping. Tasting. Seducing.

"I want you so bad," he muttered.

"So, what's stopping you? Take me. I'm all yours."

If only she really meant that.

He licked the sweetness of her mouth, pushed his tongue in at the corner of her lips until a choked, breathless sound came from her. His hands mapped her body, committing her to memory while he continued to make love to her mouth.

When he finally lifted his head, they were both breathing hard.

"This lingerie is more thought than covering," he said, tugging on one of the shoulder straps.

"Yeah, great, isn't it? It makes me feel sexy and feminine."

"Newsflash, you are sexy and feminine, babe."

"Prove it." Her tone was a lazy invitation and it lit a match under his libido. The urgency took over and he removed the bra in seconds flat, latching onto a nipple and sucking hard. His cock started to throb and he ground his erection against her leg, groaning softly around her nipple at the resulting surge of pleasure. *So damned good.*

Maggie whimpered, and he would have stopped, but she grasped his head in her hands and arched into him. With his control at breaking point, he tried to go slow, but her silent encouragement urged him on.

He dragged down her panties, the sound of ripping of lace making him freeze. "Hell! I'm sorry. I'll buy you some new ones."

Maggie groaned. "I don't care. I want you inside me. *Now.*"

She struggled to kick the torn panties off her legs and puffed out an exasperated breath when she failed.

"Let me." Connor grasped the flimsy material and ripped them right off. Maggie parted her legs and he moved over her, surging inside her with one quick thrust of his hips. Her snug walls gripped him.

Hot. Tight. So perfect.

Fire exploded in his groin, forcing him to move. Clenching his butt muscles, he plunged into her sex, sheer need driving him. He surged, retreated, stoking the pleasure that fired his body, his famous control history.

Maggie bucked and moaned beneath him, arching and taking every one of his hard thrusts. The slap of flesh against flesh filled the air along with the tart, spicy aroma of arousal.

Primitive hunger gripped him, and he couldn't stop the plunge into pleasure. His balls lifted and suddenly his climax took him. He thrust hard then stilled, his heart hammering against hers as he gave into the firestorm in his body.

Connor came back to himself and realized he'd placed all his weight on Maggie. Cursing under his breath, he lifted onto his elbows. Then he realized a couple of other things. One, he'd just taken her like a Neanderthal without care for her pleasure and two, they hadn't used a condom.

Chapter Seven

"I didn't use a condom," Connor blurted.

"You also came before I did," Maggie said, her heart still thudding from the experience. She didn't even care she hadn't come. A small problem. Connor would take care of that soon.

"Did you hear me?"

"Of course I heard you," Maggie said. "Don't worry. I'm not at the right time in my cycle, but to set your mind at rest I'll go to the doctor tomorrow and get the morning after pill." Maggie felt a pang saying the words, but she knew it was the right thing to do. While she wanted children in the future, it wasn't right to have a child to hook a man. And besides, she couldn't exactly explore spanking while pregnant. That sounded plain wrong.

"I'm sorry." Connor's voice was hoarse. His eyes held remorse, and Maggie knew he was being too hard on himself. She shared the blame.

"Hey, there are two of us in this bed. I didn't notice the lack of condom until you said something. It will be all right, and to make sure I'll ask the doctor for a prescription for birth control. Okay?"

Connor dipped his head and kissed her hard, pouring apology and passion into the kiss. She felt it clearly.

"I really am sorry. I didn't mean to manhandle you like that. I've never treated a woman like that before. I don't know what came over me."

Maggie frowned. Manhandled? He'd ripped her panties and taken rather than coaxed. So what? She hadn't felt in danger or scared at any time. In fact, she'd enjoyed every moment of their lovemaking.

"What are you talking about?" She pushed at his shoulders so she could see his face. "Explain."

"I was rough with you."

"You didn't hurt me. I like that you felt you could let go with me. I won't break, you know. Besides, I have a mouth. If you ever do something I don't like, I'll tell you."

Connor blinked, a wealth of emotions passing through his blue eyes. Too quickly for her to decipher them. "You enjoyed it? Me being rough?"

Maggie's mouth twitched. "Apart from not coming. That bit sucked."

He seemed to hesitate before the tension seeped from his shoulders. "I can fix that."

"You should get right on it then," Maggie said, allowing her teasing to rush free in a sassy grin. "I'm all agog to see how you're going to do it."

"Agog?"

"Yeah, it means eager and impatient."

Connor groaned. "I know what it means."

Her brows rose. "So?"

He snorted, shook his head once and pressed a swift kiss to her lips. "Don't talk. I need to concentrate."

"It's true then. Men really can't multitask?"

"That's a myth put out by women."

"Prove it."

"I can't talk and use my mouth on you at the same time."

Maggie suppressed a giggle and shook her head in a mournful manner. "All talk and no action."

A snort escaped him. "Someone should have spanked you when you were younger."

"Ah, but they didn't, which is why I need it now." She waited, taut with excitement, for his reply. It was the closest they'd come to a discussion about her sexual needs. Would he take the hint?

His brow furrowed then he moved down the bed. "We'll see if you're singing a different tune after I'm finished."

"Promises, promises," she taunted even though frustration roared through her. Why couldn't she articulate exactly what she wanted? Where the heck were her big girl panties?

The touch of his mouth sent every thought flying from her head, the slow laps of tongue firing lust to life. Damn, he was good at that. He found all her sensitive spots until heat and pleasure curled through her. A whimper escaped, one she couldn't contain. A flush of heat crept up her body, and she sucked in a hoarse breath.

"That feels good, Connor. Don't stop. Please don't stop."

He laughed, the sound a puff of heat against her sensitive flesh. His lick across her clit pushed her over the edge. She convulsed against his lips, her pussy fluttering in orgasm.

"Connor," she cried, almost sobbing because he made her feel so good.

When he lifted his head, his stubble rasped against the delicate skin of her inner thighs. He moved up the bed and kissed her. She sank into the kiss, tasting her juices on his lips. Murmuring softly, she wrapped her arms around his neck and held tight.

Connor rolled away, settling her comfortably at his side when she protested.

"Where did you grow up?" he asked.

"In Wellington. Why?"

"I realized I didn't know much about you."

"It's not as if it's a secret." Her voice held a note of caution, the same caution she always experienced when discussing her family. It wasn't as if she could come out and say, *Oh, you know Elle Walker, the aging socialite who's always in the gossip columns? That's my mother. Oh, yeah and after one dumb mistake in my late teens my father is still convinced I'm exactly like her and will screw up again.*

When she thought about it, she didn't know much about Connor either. He was right. Whenever they were with the others, they talked about work, about the present, about rugby. They didn't get into personal things.

"How did you end up in Auckland?"

"My parents divorced when I was five. My mother took me for a while but having a child didn't work with her schedule and

I went to live with my father. My mother had family in Auckland and moved up here. My father has three other children with his second wife."

"And you get on okay with your stepsiblings?"

Maggie laughed. It was easy to laugh now, but her childhood hadn't been easy. "Mostly. My stepmother is good for my father. They have a lot in common."

"What about your mother?"

"She remarried as well. I don't see her very much." Maggie bit her lip, knowing she'd left huge gaps in her potted history. "Actually, to tell the truth my teenage years were difficult and it wasn't an easy time for me or my father and his new family. We didn't get on and I left as soon as I could. We get on better now with time and distance between us." But he still managed to slip in a lecture each time they spoke or visited.

Connor stroked her upper arm before grasping her hip and pulling her into the cradle of his body. "My parents separated when I was four. My father used to hit my mother. He beat her so bad he put her in hospital a couple of times. When he started hitting me as well, she decided to get out of the marriage."

"Oh, Connor. I'm so sorry."

"It was a long time ago now. My mother remarried and my stepfather is a wonderful man. Frank's been more of a father to me than my real father ever was."

"That's good." Maggie didn't say anything else. She couldn't. No wonder he'd worried about being rough with her.

"Sometimes I worry I might take after my father."

"No! Connor, no. You mustn't think that." Maggie pulled away enough to search his face. "I've known you for a couple of years now, and you've never shown a sign of violence. You are not your father."

"Blood will out, according to my grandmother."

"Your grandmother is a silly old woman," Maggie said in a fierce tone, thinking at the same time the woman bore a resemblance to her father when it came to outspokenness. "You mustn't believe her. You're a good man, Connor Grey. I wouldn't be here with you if I didn't believe that." Unsure if she had convinced him, she kissed him. Hard. It was a bruising kiss designed to make him pay attention. Once she was sure she had him, she softened the kiss, taking it into loving and seductive. When he groaned and his cock started to prod her thigh, she knew she had his full attention.

This time their lovemaking was slow. They dragged out every last sensation in no hurry to finish. Their breaths mingled and each soft, tormenting stroke created an empty ache in her womb. She ran her hands down his back and dug her fingers into the taut globes of his ass, silently encouraging him to move. They only parted for the length of time it took for Connor to don a condom before coming together again. Strained breathing and sighs gave way to pleasure, the coil of energy in her pussy exploding into a shattering climax only seconds before Connor came. They stayed clasped together for a long time while their breathing returned to normal.

Sleepy and content, Maggie let her mind drift. As usual her mind went straight to her blog and spanking. She thought about Connor and her promise to herself to strive for honesty. She even opened her mouth, ready to speak until another thought occurred. If Connor worried about turning violent like his father, how would he react when she asked him to spank her?

Sunday passed quickly. Maggie had expected Connor would leave her to visit the doctor on her own, but he insisted on going with her. After a quick stop at her place so she could grab clothes, they went to a walk-in clinic in a part of town they knew no one would see them and saw the doctor together. The doctor suggested they both take blood tests, so they did. They left armed with prescriptions and advice to use condoms until the birth control protection was viable.

That evening, alone in her flat, Maggie thought over the hours she'd spent with Connor. He made her feel cherished, and she knew without a doubt, he would never hit her. He'd never tread the same path as his natural father. Now all she had to do was convince Connor of something she knew was fact.

How do I approach my partner and ask him to spank me?

The Bottom Line

I've met a man I really like. The sex is great. More than great. And even better, we have a good relationship out of bed. I want to take our relationship to the next stage. How do I ask him to spank me when I know something in his background makes him abhor the whole idea of this sort of kink?

I really don't know what to do now. It's true I've had more time to think about spanking and the repercussions of adding it to my sex life. When I approach him, I know he'll be both shocked and reluctant. But I also know myself. I won't be happy until I try this. The more I read both online in blogs and forums and also in erotic romances featuring spanking, the more I want to explore this for myself.

I was ready to ask last night. I've decided honesty is something to strive for—a good thing, I think. Anyway, I opened my mouth to state my desires and he started talking, asking questions about my childhood. I didn't mind answering. Like many New Zealand children, I come from a broken home where both my parents remarried and I was plunged into a blended family. Some of you are probably nodding because you're in the same situation. But what do you do where your partner comes from a violent background? What do you do if he's worried about turning into the same violent monster his father was? How do I get him to come to terms with the fact that if I give him permission to spank me, he's not dropping into the same dark pit that haunted his father?

I've tried patience. I really have. Some of you might say I should forget this and grasp the happiness I've found already. I can't do that because that would be allowing myself to settle.

I don't know what to do, how to approach this problem. My mind is going in circles, and I'm starting to get frustrated. I don't want a stranger to spank me. I know I could do that—pay to have someone spank me—but I know in my heart that it wouldn't work. I want love and laughter along with my spanking. I want rich fantasies and silly role-playing. I don't want to settle for second best.

If you have any advice for me, I'd love to hear it. How did you introduce spanking to your relationship? Did it happen by accident or was it a planned thing introduced to bring spiciness to your relationship?

Connor read the post with growing alarm. His heart thumped so fast it felt as if he'd run a hundred meter sprint. He wanted Maggie, not just for now, but for the future. They were good together. A curse slipped free.

Why the hell had she picked up that bloody book?

With a glance at his watch, he grabbed his car keys and slammed from his apartment to do what he'd been putting off. He'd hoped Maggie would let go of this spanking idea. But no, she continued to blog on a regular basis and had attracted quite a following. A sensation he identified as jealousy clutched his chest, squeezing so tight it felt as if someone had applied a vice, clamping it shut around his ribs.

He didn't know a lot about his mother's first marriage, mainly because he'd been a child when it happened and she'd protected him from the worst of the violence. But right now, he needed answers. He needed to reconcile his love for Maggie with her desire for spanking. And he needed to do it quickly, before he lost her to another man.

Half an hour later, he knocked on his mother's door before opening it and shouting a greeting. Two cars sat in the driveway, so he knew they were at home. He'd been so wound up he hadn't thought to call ahead.

His mother appeared from the lounge. "Connor, what are you doing here?"

Frank appeared beside her and wrapped an arm around her waist. "What your mother means is that we're pleased to see you."

He exchanged a grin with Frank. "Aren't I allowed to pop in to see you whenever I feel like it?"

"Of course you are," his mother said. "We were about to have a barbeque. Can you stay? You are still coming for my birthday?"

"I'd love to have dinner, and I wouldn't dare miss your birthday," Connor said. "Although isn't it a bit cold for a barbeque? It looked like rain when I was driving up here." The crash of thunder punctuated his words and rain rattled the windows with enough force to make them all look outside.

"You brought that rain with you." The twinkle in his

mother's eyes belied the stern words.

Connor grinned again, pleased he'd come, despite the circumstances that brought him. "Don't you ever listen to the weather forecasts?" Although he'd thought about inviting Maggie and maybe the others for his mother's birthday, he'd changed his mind. It would be like making a statement of intent, and he didn't want to do that, not publically at least.

"I look out the window," his mother retorted. "I make the right forecast most of the time."

"What can I get you to drink?" Frank asked. "Gabby and I are drinking wine, but we have beer if you'd prefer."

"You two go and catch up," his mother said. "I'll get Connor a beer and start cooking the steaks."

Connor accepted a beer and followed Frank to the lounge. He sat then bound to his feet. He found himself pacing, unable to settle. Belatedly, he became aware of Frank studying him in a quizzical manner.

"Problem?"

With his round glasses frames, Frank reminded him of an owl. A wise old owl.

"Yeah. I'm not sure how to say this so I'm going to lay it out fast before I die of embarrassment." Connor paced another lap of the lounge, the movement helping him to concentrate. "I've met a woman, someone I really like and want a future with. She wants me to spank her as part of our lovemaking, and I'm worried I'll hurt her. I...I...what if I take after my father?"

"Connor," his mother said from the doorway. "Son, you're not like Larry. You have the most even temper I've known. I've never seen a hint of Larry's violence in you. *Never.*"

Frank smiled a gentle smile, the one that told Connor how much he loved both his mother and him. The same smile he'd always showered them with. "At least you stopped his pacing. I thought I'd have to spring for new carpet for the lounge because he was wearing a track."

"Mum, I'm sorry you had to hear. I know you don't like talking about him."

"Connor." His mother looked as if she might cry.

Hell. Connor glanced at Frank and wished he hadn't come to visit his parents. He took a couple of steps toward the door.

"Don't you dare leave."

Connor froze.

Frank chuckled. "Take a seat, son. You're not going anywhere until we talk about this."

"I want to hear about this woman who has you tied in knots," his mother said. "Besides, it's nasty out there. Do you want me to worry about you driving home in the middle of a storm?"

He caved, sinking into the nearest chair. What had he expected? That he could drop his bombshell and escape without taking return fire?

"Dinner won't be long," his mother said.

"Do you need any help?" Frank asked.

"I can cope with cooking a few steaks," she said. "You stay with Connor. Give him the talk." She winked and the adoring look that passed between them made Connor feel like a voyeur.

"Have you talked to her about what you're feeling?" Frank asked, getting straight to business.

Connor grunted, the sound containing severe irritation. "I've started to talk a million times but it's...I keep wimping out."

"I know it's not easy, son, but the main thing is communication." His eyes sharpened. "How do you know she wants you to spank her if you haven't discussed the matter?"

Connor felt his cheeks heat, aware his reply wouldn't show him in a good light. "She has a blog where she discusses spanking. One of our friends told me, so I've been reading it."

"And she doesn't know." Frank picked up his wine glass and took a sip, his manner slow and purposeful. Thinking-mode, Connor realized, remembering Frank looking the same way on numerous other occasions while he was growing up.

"She doesn't know I read her blog."

"Connor Grey," his mother said, barging into the room. "I can't believe you've been spying on this poor girl."

"It must run in the family," Frank said in a mild voice. "Gabby, I thought you were cooking the steaks."

His mother ignored Frank's quiet reprimand to focus on him. "Sweetheart, there's a big difference between abuse and consensual loving."

A vision swept his mind—one he'd rather not have. "Mum, I don't want to talk about sex. Frank, what do you think about those All Blacks? Man, they choked in their last game against the Wallabies."

His mother wrinkled her nose. "I do know about sex."

"Nah, you found me in a cabbage patch," Connor said. "How do you think the All Blacks will go against the Springboks?"

"I should have told the stork to take you right back and bring me a little girl. I'm sure she wouldn't resort to underhand behavior. Sweetheart, you need to talk to her, tell her what's on your mind and why you're having a problem with the idea. If everything is in the open, you'll find your relationship much easier. When can we meet her?"

"It's early days," Frank said, coming to his rescue. "Give Connor a chance. I'm sure he'll bring his friend to visit when he's ready."

His mother nodded. "Personally, I think the All Blacks will give the Springboks a whopping and send them back to South Africa with their tails between their legs. We'll win the rugby match by at least twenty points. I'd place good money on it."

Connor grinned. "How much do you want to bet?"

"Twenty," his mother shot back. "And a promise you'll bring your young lady to visit."

Connor's grin faded as he acknowledged the problems lying between him and a future with Maggie. Lies. Lots of lies. A good man would have left well alone, but Connor admitted the truth to himself. He wouldn't have done a thing differently. He and Maggie were good together. They could have a future. All he had to do was prove it to her.

Chapter Eight

"A speed dating event," Connor said with a distinct lack of enthusiasm.

Susan tossed her head. "You don't have to go. Guys have an easier time meeting women to date," she added. "But quite frankly, I need all the help I can get. I want to find a man and settle down. I want to have children, and I'm running out of time."

They all stared at her, and she met their looks with one of quiet determination.

Maggie hadn't realized Susan wanted children so bad. She risked a quick glance at Connor and found him studying her.

"I hope this maternal cluckiness isn't catchy," Julia said into the distinct uneasiness that had overtaken them after Susan's outburst.

"I'm not going to apologize," Susan said, tossing her head. "Besides, my mother is driving me nuts. All my sisters are married. She's convinced my ovaries will wither, and I'll die an old spinster."

"I hope you told her to butt out," Julia said.

Susan let out a loud sigh. "She means well. And I do want to get married."

"That doesn't mean you should settle for second best," Christina said. "Mr. Right doesn't always come along straight away."

"Look, I'm sorry. Forget I said anything." Susan forced a smile.

"We don't expect you to apologize," Maggie said. "You can't

help how you feel."

"The speed dating was a suggestion. I'm going and thought it might be fun if we all went."

Maggie felt bad for Susan. Wanting security and a child wasn't so different from wanting to find a man who would spank her. Deep down she wanted the same things Susan did: security with a man who loved her.

"I'll go with you," she said. "It sounds like fun."

Connor looked as if he might argue, and Maggie glared at him.

"I'm in," Julia said, breaking the uncomfortable silence. "It will make a change from drinks at the pub."

"Sign me up too," Connor said.

"Really?" Maggie asked.

"Yeah, really. Susan is my friend and I want to support her." Connor's voice held a trace of defensiveness. "When is it?"

"Are you trying to weasel out of it?" Maggie asked in suspicion.

"No, it's my mother's birthday coming up. If it clashes with the speed dating, I'll have to pass."

It was the first Maggie had heard of his mother's birthday. She blinked against a sudden surge of moisture to her eyes. Her throat tightened, and she swallowed rapidly to dispel the sensation. Despite constantly reminding herself she and Connor were casual lovers, she couldn't stop the possessive thoughts filling her mind. She wasn't even looking for another lover. Connor had spoiled her, and every other man came up lacking in comparison.

She wanted to do normal couple things. All the sneaking around had started to get old.

"It's next week. Thursday night at eight," Susan said.

Christina checked her PDA. "Works for me."

"My mother's birthday is on Saturday," Connor said.

"What about rugby practice?" Maggie asked.

"We have a bye this weekend." Connor picked up his beer and took a sip. "There's no training this week."

Maggie crossed her legs. "I'm free." She noticed Connor watched the move, his gaze lingering on the expanse of thigh displayed by her new skirt. Connor hadn't been the only one paying attention. She received requests for dates from two of the lawyers at the firm next to them. Greg also continued to ask her out, despite her firm negative answers.

Maggie stood. "I'm going to head home. I'm tired. Someone decided I needed to change my workout. If anyone tells you to take up running to vary an exercise routine, run far and fast in the opposite direction. My thighs are killing me."

Connor smirked. "Poor baby."

The other women grinned.

"You wouldn't catch me running," Julia said.

"You don't have to battle weight like I do. I just need to think about a dark, moist and decadent chocolate brownie and weight sticks to my thighs and butt." Maggie sniffed at their derisive laughter. "I'm going home to soak in the bath."

"I'm going too," Connor said, standing. "I'll walk you out."

"Night," Julia said, lifting her right hand in a casual wave. "Anyone for another drink? We could split a bottle of wine."

"Sounds good to me," Christina said. "I'll buy. I've taken on two makeover clients this week. Retirement from Barker & Johnson is looking better every day."

"Congratulations, Christina. I'll see you at rugby tomorrow." With a quick wave Maggie followed Connor from the crowded bar.

Outside, he took her arm, holding her protectively against his side to help combat the swirl of icy wind.

"Come home with me," he said.

"I don't know," Maggie said, fighting temptation. "We have work tomorrow and I really am sore after running." She also wanted to check her blog for comments. So far, most of her visitors had said the same thing. She needed to talk to her partner. Easier said than done. The last thing she wanted to do was scare Connor away. Besides, what happened if he met someone else and their *friends with benefits* deal ended? What would happen to her then?

"Doctor Connor to the rescue. I know just the thing to fix sore muscles."

He wrapped his arm around her waist and led her to his

SUV. Maggie fought her conscience for about two seconds before meekly allowing him to seat her in the passenger seat. She watched his face when he jogged around the front of the vehicle. As usual, he was smiling, his dark looks making her heart clench with longing. She wished Susan hadn't brought up babies. She'd love to have children. One day. A sigh escaped and she leaned her head back against the headrest, letting her eyes close. She hadn't lied when she'd said her body throbbed in one big ache. This running lark was killing her. She needed her head read. How had she ever thought running was a good idea?

Connor started the SUV and Maggie let herself drift.

"Wake up, babe. We're at my apartment."

"Sorry. I must have fallen asleep." Self-consciously, she stretched and fumbled for the seatbelt. "I didn't snore, did I?"

"Yeah, you did. The cutest little sound."

"You're making that up."

"You'll never know, will you?" Connor brushed the tip of her nose with his finger. "Come on. We'll get you in the shower before you fall asleep again."

Maggie climbed out the vehicle, grimacing and mumbling under her breath about running and people who should know better. "I wanted a bath. Don't you have a bath?"

"I never said I had a bath," Connor corrected. "I said I have something better. Come on, limpy-gimpy. Let's get you inside."

"If you think you're gonna get lucky tonight, you'd better rethink your plans," Maggie snapped. *Damn, it hurt to walk.* She was never going to run again. Only stupid people ran. Fools and idiots.

"I'm not a complete moron." Connor's face darkened, and she hurriedly looked away, biting her bottom lip in consternation. Even her conscience was working against her, trying to do the right thing and push him away.

Without another word he led her into his apartment. His roommates weren't home, although Maggie smelled curry spices and noticed a basketball and a sweatshirt tossed over the back of a chair. At least one of his roommates had been here recently.

Connor chucked his keys on the countertop and shunted

her down the passage to the small bathroom. Reaching in, he flipped on the tap and waited until the water ran hot.

"Get in and warm up," he said, leaving her alone.

Maggie shrugged out of her clothes, wincing and groaning when she lifted her legs to remove her pantyhose. Horrid things. Maybe she'd try stockings—some of those thigh-high ones that didn't require a garter belt. Leaving her clothes on a heap in the floor, she pulled back the shower curtain and stepped inside. For long moments, she stood there, soaking in the heat.

With a sigh, she reached for the soap and cleansed her body, driving out the last of the chill caused by the winter winds that had swirled across the city of Auckland today.

"All done?" Connor asked.

Maggie turned off the shower and stepped out, shivering when the cold air hit her wet skin.

"Feel better?"

"Not really." Maggie wished she'd followed her instincts and gone home.

Connor approached her with a large blue towel and started to dry her briskly.

"I can do it," she protested, trying to grab the towel.

"Of course you can," he said, resisting. "But I want to do it for you."

Once he'd dried her, he led her to his bedroom. While she'd been in the shower, he'd closed the curtains and drawn back the blankets on the bed. Only one bedside lamp lit the room, shadows playing across walls when they entered.

"Lie face down on the bed," he said, pulling the towel away from her body.

"Why?" A sharp note entered her voice as she grabbed for the towel. Fatigue weighed her down, and once again, she kicked herself for letting him bring her here.

"I'm not going to hurt you. I have some massage oil to help with your sore muscles. I'm going to rub it on for you. That's all."

"Oh. Okay," she said, slivers of guilt nipping at her. She'd sounded distinctly bitchy. *Way to go, Maggie. Drive him away. That will make you happy and appease your guilty conscience at the same time.*

She stretched out on her back in the middle of the bed. "The fronts of my legs are really bad. Could you do them first?" Thank goodness for the scanty light. Although he'd seen her naked, she felt vulnerable in an unclothed state. She snorted quietly. And wasn't that great? Imagine a woman who wanted her ass smacked and yet she didn't want to show her boyfriend her naked butt. A few contradictions there, that was for sure.

To her relief, Connor smiled, unperturbed by her grumpiness.

He reached for a small glass bottle. "Your wish is my command." Unscrewing the cap of the bottle, he poured some of the contents into his palm before setting it aside. He rubbed his palms together before joining her on the bed.

Lavender, sandalwood and an herby scent she couldn't indentify filled the room.

"It might be a little cold at first," he warned, straddling her legs.

She winced at his first touch, but the oil quickly warmed as he rubbed it on her right thigh. His fingers glided smoothly over tense muscles, rubbing with gradually increasing pressure, a combination of kneading and feathering strokes that felt good after the initial pain. He moved up and down her legs and gradually, Maggie relaxed, letting her eyes close to savor his magic touch.

"I'm going to stop to get some more oil," he said, his voice husky.

"Okay." He could do anything he liked if only he continued touching her with those magic fingers.

The mattress shifted when he moved, depressing again when he returned. He massaged her calves and feet before moving up her legs again. She expected him to tell her to turn over but he started to massage the rest of her body, moving slightly and parting her legs. His fingers stroked across her inner thighs and slipped closer to her labia, skimming near enough for the massage to take a distinct turning into sexual territory.

Then he moved, his hands gliding across her hips, her waist. Taking his time he worked up her body. Although disappointed in the direction of his massage, she wasn't about to tell him to stop when it felt so good. Already her sore muscles were a dim memory. Maggie breathed slowly, enjoying the rich tang of the massage oil and the soft sound of Connor's steady breathing.

He stopped to get more oil and worked it into her breasts. He circled them, gradually working closer and closer to her nipples. With a finger and thumb, he stroked them, tugging slightly in a manner that sent a bungee cord of pleasure to her pussy.

"Does that feel good?"

"Really good," she purred.

Gradually, he released the pleasure and worked upward, stroking her shoulders and rubbing in the oil until she felt like a puddle and pleasure skimmed her body along with his touch.

"Turn over for me, Maggie."

Her eyes flew open.

"May as well do the job properly, babe."

She turned over, grinning into the pillows, despite a sliver of unease. Maybe Connor would get lucky tonight. Need pulsed through her. Although her muscles felt loose and limber, other parts of her were decidedly tense. When he straddled her body again, she felt the heavy weight of his erection. Her grin widened. Looked like they would both enjoy themselves tonight.

Connor started with her shoulders, nimble fingers rubbing, stroking and feathering her flesh until her mind wandered in blissful relaxation. Gradually he moved down her body, his talented hands working closer to her butt in all its naked glory. What would he do if she asked him to give her a swat or two?

Her breath caught, arousal unfurling inside as her imagination took flight. She chewed her bottom lip, trying not to tense up and undo his good work.

Connor stroked her shoulders, letting his thumbs press into her muscles, his fingers glided over her smooth flesh. He liked touching her like this. Having the freedom to touch without restraint or worrying about anyone else noticing.

His hands drifted downward, lightening his touch when he skimmed over her lower back working her upper glutes. Her backside was curvy. Rounded. Uncharitable people might call it plump, but he liked the way Maggie looked. He pressed his fingers into the muscles, his mind drifting to spanking. Maybe he could give her an experimental swat or two at the end of the massage.

The last time he'd given her a swat had made for great sex. Hot sex. But no matter how much he rationalized spanking in his mind, told himself it was something she wanted, he hesitated. He couldn't reconcile the idea of pain and sex—good sex—together.

Yeah, he'd read Maggie's blog posts, he'd done a little research on the Internet. Hell, he'd even swallowed his embarrassment and talked to his mother and Frank. It might have been easier if he could have talked to Maggie about spanking, but he couldn't tell her he knew about the blog and her inner desires when Julia had sworn him to secrecy.

And, as far as he knew, Maggie hadn't actually experienced spanking in person. Thinking about doing and actually doing it were two different things. What would happen if he spanked her and she hated it? What would happen if their relationship changed because of the spanking?

Mind in turmoil, he carried on massaging her on automatic pilot. He skipped down to her thighs and calves, paying close attention to the muscles used most in running.

"You're very good at that," she mumbled.

"I'm good at a lot of things."

"Like what?"

"Is that doubt I hear in your voice?" he asked. "Because I'm telling the truth. I have lots of hidden talents."

"Tell me."

Connor laughed. "Where's the fun in that?" He ran his fingers up the back of one thigh, his hand coming to rest on her butt. "You need to find them on your own."

"I think you're blowing smoke."

"But I'm good at massage. I have you purring like a kitten."

"That's true," she murmured. "You have magic fingers."

"And I make you hot." She made him hot. Connor tried to ignore his rising need for her, but the tight jeans were crowding his cock.

"Also true."

Satisfaction filled him at her admission. He wanted her to need him, as much as he needed her. For the first time in years, he hadn't even looked at another woman or started to get uneasy in a relationship. He didn't want out. "I told you this would work between us."

"It does, but I don't like keeping secrets."

"We could tell the others—"

"No," Maggie said immediately, her raised voice echoing with finality. "I don't want them to look at us differently or speculate about when we'll breakup. I don't want to explain our arrangement."

Connor frowned. "Are you ashamed of being with me?"

"No, of course not." Maggie turned to look him in the face. "I like being with you."

Connor gave a swift nod, although her reply didn't reassure him. "Turn back on your stomach. I'll finish your other leg."

She followed his instructions, placing her face in her arms and relaxing. Being with Maggie was what he wanted, but it was a minefield trying to keep everything straight. He hated the dishonesty. Tangled bloody webs and juggling balls. Connor snorted and feathered strokes across her hamstrings, working his way back up to her glutes.

"Finished," he said, staring at her backside. *Do it. Give her a quick swat.* It's what she wants. Before he could think a second longer, he lifted his hand and gave her a half-hearted slap across her buttocks. "All done." He stared, trying to measure her reaction. Pity he couldn't see her face. "How do you feel?"

"Good."

"My massage skills must be lacking if it was only good."

She turned over, a broad grin on her face. "One problem. Your massage skills are clearly superior, but I don't feel relaxed." Her lids lowered and she ran her tongue across the sweep of her bottom lip. "I feel..." She paused again, teasing lighting her eyes. "...incredibly horny."

Horny? Hell, worked for him. Connor climbed off the bed and shrugged out of his shirt. He unfastened the button on his jeans and slid down the zipper. The low whine sounded loud in the quiet room. He pushed his jeans and boxer-briefs down over his hips and grabbed a condom.

"Let me put it on for you."

Connor shrugged and handed it over. He watched her while she ripped open the foil packet.

"Come here." She patted the bed beside her. "Lie down."

"Are you seducing me, Ms. Drummond?"

Maggie let out an unfeminine snort. "Look at the state of you. You're easy."

"I wasn't the one who admitted they were horny."

"True." She fumbled slightly when she rolled the condom onto his erection. The tiny flash of uncertainty and nerves charmed him. Made him relax. "It's all your fault."

He placed his hands under his head and watched her, enjoying the sway of her breasts.

"You know you've turned me into a breast-man," he said. "I used to think I was a leg-man. I was wrong. Your breasts do it for me."

"Ah, thanks, I think." With the condom rolled onto his cock, she seemed to hesitate. "Stop staring at me."

"Why? It was a compliment. I find you very attractive. Sexy."

"Here's the thing. Most women don't like their bodies or there are things they'd like to change about them. I try to like my body. I really do. It's just that it's not always easy. Some men take pleasure in tearing a woman down, telling her she's too fat or needs to exercise more."

"I'm not one of those men."

"I know you're not. Even when you dragged me off to the gym or when you told me I should try running, you never made me feel as if I should exercise. It was a suggestion. You were being my friend."

Friend. Wow, that stung. "I always feel better after a workout. I thought you would too." Connor studied her expression and jumped to a conclusion. "Did Greg tell you to lose weight?" His voice emerged in a low growl.

"Once or twice."

"You did a good thing when you told him to take a hike."

Maggie nodded. "I think so, but I don't want to talk about him when we're both naked."

"And alone," he added.

"Exactly."

"Babe, I'm all yours. Do whatever you want."

"I..." Confusion flooded her face and she started to chew on her bottom lip again. That must hurt after a while. He grinned inside, guessing her problem. Yes, she touched him when they made love but normally he gave her orders or took charge. His offer had surprised her.

"Go on. It's your chance to discover what I like."

Her gaze darted to his cock and he laughed.

"Good start, babe."

A cheeky grin bloomed and he stared, smitten by attraction. Lust. Need. *Damn, he wanted her.*

"Where should I touch you first?" Maggie leaned over him and kissed his neck, his chest. Her mouth was hot and wet on his skin, her eyes heavy-lidded when she paused to stare at him. She clambered over his body, lifted up and pushed down again, taking his shaft inside her. Heat. Hot pressure. Slowly, she worked him into her pussy, looking like a siren with her hair swinging around her shoulders, her cheeks faintly pink and the sway of her breasts.

"Damn it, woman. Are you trying to kill me? Move faster."

"This was your idea," she countered, continuing at the same slow pace.

"Two can play at that game," he said.

Rising up again, she tossed her head. "I don't play games."

She didn't either. A fact he both liked and appreciated.

Maggie paused. "I've never been able to come like this. What am I doing wrong?"

"I can touch you or you could touch yourself." Why the hell couldn't she ask him about spanking like that? Straight out. He'd never laugh at anything she said or treat her like an idiot. "We'll experiment until we get it right."

Intense concentration marred the smoothness of her brow. She rose and fell getting into a rhythm.

"Try changing the angle," he suggested, hoping like hell he

could hold off long enough for her to experiment.

She twisted and squirmed and slipped the fingers of one hand between her legs. Her head fell back and soft, needy sounds emerged. Connor didn't think she'd ever looked more beautiful.

He reached up and stroked one breast, using a bit more pressure when his fingers trailed over the tip. "Feel good?"

"Yes," she said, moving quicker, her eyes fluttering shut.

Connor watched the play of emotions over her face. If she thought he intended to let her go easily, she could think again. Now that he'd made love to her, spent time with her, he was more convinced than ever that they had a future. He started to move with her, knowing she was close now. Releasing control, he allowed the heat and pressure to rampage through him as they slid together with exquisite friction. He pinched one distended nipple, flexed his hips.

Without warning she cried out, convulsing around his cock. She stilled and the clawing tension burst inside him. His cock jerked with explosive contractions, blistering waves of pleasure and satisfaction taking him. He tugged her into his arms and held her, luxuriating in the aftershocks and the feel of a soft curvy woman in his arms. His curvy woman.

Somehow he had to show Maggie her heart was safe with him. He'd hold all her secrets close and nurture her dreams. All she needed to do was trust him.

Chapter Nine

Greg studied the group of friends as he passed the lunch room. It looked like they were studying the gossip pages probably discussing the latest scandal to hit parliament. A politician found in bed with a married woman. At least Maggie had the sense to feel embarrassment because her cheeks glowed and she fidgeted with discomfort. Greg made a scoffing sound. He had no idea why Maggie spent so much time with the bunch of losers. None of them had any ambition. Granted Connor Grey had brains. The head of the IT department held him in high regard, but the man was a womanizer. He had a different woman on his arm every time Greg saw him.

Greg continued along the passage to his office, ignoring the traces of envy curling through him. The leggy blondes who spent time with Connor never gave him a second glance.

And as for the three women. Julia acted like a slut—the female version of Connor. Greg didn't know the other two very well, since he tended to steer clear of them in the work environment. They were both secretaries and his accounting assistants dealt with that side of his work.

What was he going to do about Maggie?

She refused to talk to him at work, wouldn't take his calls at home. The answer phone was getting a workout, and he'd given up leaving messages.

Greg dropped into his chair. He picked up a pen, tapping it on his pristine blotter pad while he tried to think of a way to speak with Maggie. He needed to get an accounting team together to work on the Silverstone project. Of course, she wasn't qualified, but it might not matter. At least she'd have to spend time with him. Work late if necessary to meet deadlines.

Perfect, he thought, mentally flitting over names to fill the rest of his team for the project. At worst, she could always make coffee and run messages, liaise with the office and IT departments.

"Maggie, dear. You're not getting away from me, not after all the time I've invested in you."

He gave a fleeting thought to one of their last conversations. *Spanking.* Now that had been weird. Way out of character. Surely, she couldn't have been serious?

Connor scanned the room and shuddered at the speculative stares he intercepted from some of the women. He felt like a duck in the sights of a shooter's rifle. No wonder sensible ducks headed for ponds situated in the middle of reserves come shooting season. A dark corner of the pub next door would work for him.

"How long does this last?" he mumbled to Julia.

Julia caught a woman staring at him and snickered. "Don't be a baby. They won't hurt you."

He glanced at Maggie. All he wanted to do was grab her and run. She didn't belong here anymore than he did. Not that he could tell her that. He cursed himself for allowing this situation to develop. What he should have done was tell Julia and the others he wanted Maggie and gone from there. Nah, that wouldn't have worked. They would have pressured Maggie to turn down his request for a date. The four women thought he was incapable of settling with one woman. A touch of frustration brought a deep frown. Once, that would have been true.

Even six months ago the accusation would have contained the ring of truth.

Things changed. *People changed.*

A strident bell rang and a woman approached the waiting mike on the small stage at the front of the room. The din of excited chatter faded to quiet expectancy.

"Welcome to the very first Auckland Speed Dating event. Thank you for coming tonight. Your attendance fee is going to a good cause—to aid research for the Multiple Sclerosis Society of

New Zealand."

Thunderous applause erupted, and the apprehension in Connor abated. Each time he started to feel like a duck in the sights of a hunter, he'd remind himself this was for charity. And he'd be able to keep an eye on Maggie. He didn't want anyone else to get ideas about her.

Maggie belonged to him.

She just didn't know it yet.

"When you registered for this event, you each completed a form with your details. When you checked in tonight, you received a number. That is your number for tonight. You should also have a second sheet with other numbers. Those numbers will be your dates for tonight."

Connor shot Maggie a swift glance but failed to grab her attention. Irritation burst in him when he realized she was scoping out the competition. Scowling, he checked them out too, trying to decide what she might see in them. Call him big-headed, but they were a geeky-looking bunch. The closest guy looked as if he might run at the sight of a rugby ball. A dazed expression froze on his face when a woman approached him. Connor felt sneaking sympathy. *Don't make eye contact!* Too late, the guy gave the woman a tentative smile. She pounced.

"Hey, Connor. Seen anyone you like the look of?" Julia asked.

"Don't you dare move away from me," he muttered.

Grinning, she backed up, and he grabbed her arm. "Don't even think about it. They can't see through my clothes. Can they?"

Julia blinked. "They're trying to will them away. Now you know what women feel like when we pass a building site."

"Huh, Susan told me you girls make a special detour to pass the building site at the bottom of Queen Street."

"Busted." Julia's eyes glowed with silent laughter. It made Connor realize her behavior bordered on reserved recently.

"How are things with you, Jules? I haven't seen you much lately." Although they'd never slept together, they were close, and he often stopped by her apartment to visit. Since hooking up with Maggie, he hadn't done that as much.

"I'm fine. Nothing a holiday in the sun wouldn't fix."

Connor knew the feeling. He'd love a week on a Pacific Island with Maggie. Time in a place without interruptions and where they didn't need to hide they were a couple sounded like heaven. Rarotonga or maybe Samoa. Even Fiji.

"See anyone interesting?" Julia interrupted his daydreams of sand and sun, Maggie in a bikini. Maggie naked.

"I'm too scared to look at any of the women."

"Good men are hard to find," Julia said. "That's why a function like this has more women than men."

"So why did you agree to come?"

"Bored with my own company," Julia said.

"But—"

"Despite popular opinion, I'm not a slut. I don't have a constant parade of men through my bed."

Connor blinked. "Of course you don't. I never said you were. Are you sure nothing is wrong?"

Julia sniffed. "Positive." The sheen of tears in her eyes said otherwise. Momentary panic hit him, his relief when the woman in charge of the event approached the mike on the stage again almost palpable. Crying women always got to him because he never knew how to comfort them. Sometimes it didn't matter what a man did. They cried regardless.

"Gentlemen, please find the desk with your number on it and take a seat. They're clearly labeled behind the screens. Ladies, the numbers of your dates are all in the same area. We'll get started in a few minutes, just as soon as the gentlemen are seated and ready to proceed. Remember you have five minutes with each date. The bell will go when your time is up and you move onto the next one. At the end of the dating, everyone will complete a form, detailing the numbers they're interested in meeting again. We'll take things from there and contact you with your list of prospective dates. Good luck, and have fun!"

Applause filled the hotel ballroom, some clapping with more enthusiasm than others. Connor fell in the lukewarm category.

"That's your cue," Julia said, sending him a wink.

"Right." With a last glance at Maggie, he strode away to find his desk behind the screened off area of the ballroom.

"I've been looking forward to this all week, but now that I've seen the men I'm not so keen," Susan said in a glum voice.

Privately Maggie agreed with her, although it wasn't right to judge by appearance. "There are a couple of guys who look okay." And one of them was Connor. She'd noticed the way some of the women had looked at him, like a dieter studied a chocolate bar.

She tried to tamp down the jealousy blooming inside her. No reason for it, she told herself. They'd both agreed they were free to date others.

A bell interrupted her jumbled thoughts. "Ladies, the gentlemen are ready for you. If you're a bit lost and not sure where to go, look for the ladies wearing the bright yellow T-shirts. They're stewards and will help with directions."

"I'm starting to feel like I'm at school," Christina said. "And look how the women outnumber the men. I feel like I'm in a competition and that makes me nervous."

"You and me both," Susan agreed.

"I'm going to need drinks after this," Julia said. "Anyone else want to hit a bar with me?"

Maggie nodded. "I'm in. We can discuss our dates. Good luck. Something tells me we're going to need it." There were some beautiful women present tonight. Old insecurities surged back to haunt her. If they couldn't find dates, what hope did she have?

She slipped into the seat opposite her first date and forced a smile. "Hi, I'm Maggie."

"Stewart," he said. "I like stamp collecting and reading Superman comics."

"That's nice."

"Can you cook?"

"Yes, I like cooking," Maggie said.

"Good, I need a woman who can cook. My mother said that's important."

Maggie stared, shocked. In her worst nightmares she hadn't thought the men would be this bad. She glanced at her watch. Another hour. A drink was looking good, and she'd barely started. "What else are you looking for in a woman?"

"I want a woman who is a good cook, does a good job of housework and won't mind looking after my mother."

"I'm not very good with sick people." Maggie had no experience with ill people and didn't want to learn unless it was for someone she cared about. "Maybe you should hire a maid?"

His mouth dropped open.

Just then the bell went.

Saved by the bell. Surely the dates couldn't be all as bad as Stewart?

She slipped into the next seat and smiled a welcome. To her relief he wasn't as bad. He just wasn't very interesting either. Her mind drifted to spanking and her blog.

"Is there anything you'd like to know about me?" he asked. "Maggie?"

"Yes, what do you think of the idea of spanking in a consenting adult relationship?"

The man's mouth opened and closed before he replied. "Spanking? During sex, you mean?"

"That's right," Maggie said in a crisp voice. She almost felt sorry for him. *Almost.*

"I haven't thought about it," he said. "Er...I suppose I could try it. What would you spank me with? Would it hurt?"

"That wasn't quite what I had in mind," Maggie said, the need to laugh out loud taking her by surprise. Maybe the night wouldn't be so bad after all.

The bell went and she moved on to her next date. She grinned and took her seat. "Hi, I'm Maggie. How do you feel about spanking?"

The man stared at her, his mouth curling into a delighted grin. "I haven't been naughty."

"But you're thinking about spanking. Surely that's worth a swat or two."

"And I came tonight under protest," he said. "Where have you been all my life?"

"So you could be interested in spanking?"

He winked at her. Maggie grinned back. Not bad. The man edged into cute when he smiled.

"Stranger things have happened," he said.

"Have you spanked anyone before?"

"I'd be willing to learn."

The bell went and with a quick wave, Maggie sashayed to her next date. Maybe this speed dating wouldn't be as bad as she thought.

"Spanking?" her fourth date asked. "Isn't that a bit kinky?"

"And your point is...?"

"None of the other girls have asked me that question. Is spanking a new fad I haven't heard about yet?"

"Just ordinary run of the mill kink, I think," Maggie said, managing to keep her smile at bay. "Do you have any interests?"

"Nothing to beat spanking. You really like getting spanked? It turns you on?"

Maggie allowed herself a secret smile. "That's for me to know and you to find out." Good grief. This flirty siren wasn't her. She didn't want to attract the wrong sort of man. It was fun, though.

The bell rang. Maggie stood. "Nice to meet you.

Three dates later, she came across Connor. "Hi." She grinned at him. "Are you having fun?"

"Fun is not the word I'd use to describe this speed dating thing."

"So you haven't met anyone interesting?"

"I didn't expect to. Did you?"

Maggie thought about her dates so far. "I've met a few interesting men." And she'd shocked some of them speechless. A couple had seemed intrigued.

Connor leaned closer, lowered his voice. "What are you doing afterward? You want to come around to my place? Spend the night?"

"I don't know. The others were talking about the pub. I'd already said I'd go for drinks. They'll think it's strange if we both change our minds."

The bell sounded, loud and strident.

"That's my cue to meet my next date." Maggie blew him a kiss. "Only four more dates to go and we're out of here."

Connor groaned. "Don't remind me. I'm gonna start making

things up soon. I'm tired of the same old questions."

"Poor baby. It sounds like you need a drink."

"I need more than a drink. I need a shower. I feel dirty after being stared at so hard."

With a laugh Maggie went to her next date, a spring in her step.

Connor wished he'd never agreed to come along. All he could think about was Maggie. He wasn't interested in other woman. Once, maybe. But not anymore. Hiding and skulking around wasn't working for him. He wanted to tell everyone that he and Maggie were together. The *friends with benefits* deal meant he couldn't do a thing.

Hamstrung by his own cleverness.

The final bell rang.

Thank God. Connor stood and joined the rest of the men. "I'm pleased that's over with. I came under protest."

"I don't know," one of the men said. "There were a few interesting dates. One girl asked me about spanking."

"You too?" another man asked. "She was fun—she didn't look like the kind of girl who would be into kinky stuff."

"No one asked me about spanking." Suspicion rioted through Connor. "What did she look like?"

"A bit on the plump side. Long dark hair." The man held his hands up in front of his chest, a leer forming on his face. "Big tits."

Maggie. Hell, why hadn't she asked him about spanking? Why would she ask complete strangers and not ask him?

"She's on my list of dates," another man said. "I like adventurous women."

Connor's mouth tightened. Maggie wasn't going anywhere with these men. *Not if he had anything to do with it.*

He left the men talking about the woman who was into spanking. When he exited the screened area, a crush of chattering women met his gaze. *Hell.* He stilled like a possum in headlights. Where were the girls? He'd had enough of feeling like prey. Julia. Good. Without making eye contact, he navigated the room.

127

"Drink," he said in greeting.

Julia gave a clipped nod. "Let's go."

"Where are the others?"

"Somewhere around the place. I saw Susan briefly. They're meeting us at the pub around the corner. God, if I ever agree to do speed dating again, shoot me. It was excruciating." She hooked her arm in his and dragged him toward the door.

Connor went unwillingly. He didn't like leaving Maggie here with all those men. What the hell had she been thinking, asking about spanking?

Chapter Ten

What would you do if a stranger started asking you questions about spanking? Run for the hills or feel intrigued enough to ask questions?

I don't know what came over me. I was in a social situation recently, bored out of my brain. I started thinking about spanking out of self-defense. Hey! Can I help it if spanking preys on my mind these days?

Anyhow, instead of the same boring getting-to-know-you conversation, I asked about spanking. It made the interaction interesting, livened things up a little. The reactions fell into two camps. The men were either for or totally against spanking. One guy was disappointed because he thought I wanted to spank him. Call me an innocent, but it never occurred to me a man would want to be on the end of a spanking. You learn something every day.

I learned something else too. Most of the men who were open to spanking immediately let their minds jump into the gutter. I could see it in their faces. They wondered what else I would do. One of them actually asked me if he could meet me later for a quickie in the car park. Another asked if I was open to anything. When I asked for clarification, he mentioned BDSM. His eyes glittered with a scary light when he mentioned whips and chains. He might have mentioned anal sex as well, but I was too busy trying to change the subject to take in everything. He was seriously creepy.

All of this made me realize I need to stop talking about my desires. I'm with a man who makes me feel good. The sex is pure dynamite between us, and I live for the times when we're together.

We've learned a lot about each other and something in his background makes it difficult for me to tell him what I'd like, what I need. I guess what I'm trying to say is I've come to care for him and I don't want to drive him away. On the other hand, I know I'm not going to be happy until I try spanking.

LOL, I've had a thought. What happens if the reality doesn't match my fantasies? What happens if, after all this time, I hate spanking and it does nothing for me except give me a sore bottom? Yeah, wouldn't that be a real kick? A spanking aficionado who hates receiving a spanking.

Maggie yawned and slapped at the alarm clock, wishing she could stay in bed for longer. Wasn't gonna happen.

She dragged herself out of the bed and stood. The twisted sheets told the story. She'd tossed and turned for half the night, worried about her most recent blog entry. The post got right to the point. What if she was all talk and no action? A pretender?

She padded to bathroom and flipped on shower. A decision. She needed one. Today.

Either she had to man up and tell Connor what she wanted—exactly what she wanted—or she needed to move on. Use the terms of their *friends with benefits* deal to find a man who would spank her without a qualm.

A man without baggage.

An hour later, she ran through the front doors of Barker & Johnson. No puffing. This fitness kick was good for something. Maggie hit the elevator button and tapped her foot while waiting for the car to arrive. Long minutes later the elevator let out a cheeky beep. The doors opened. Maggie stepped inside and waited for them to close.

They'd almost shut when a male voice called, "Hold the lift." A hand shot between the doors at the same time Maggie hit the hold button.

"Thanks. You know those days when nothing seems to go right?" He glanced at Maggie and continued talking without waiting for her reply. "I'm having one of those days. I'm late for an appointment."

He grinned, and Maggie couldn't help smiling back. Taller

than Greg but not quite as tall as Connor, the man had brown eyes that were full of humor and masculine appreciation. His glance darted to her left hand and back to her face. "I'm Kevin Grainger." His blond hair was cut short and he had a designer stubble thing going on. The casual look contrasted sharply with the charcoal gray designer suit and pale pink tie.

"Maggie Drummond," she said, taking his extended hand. His hand bore calluses and a few cuts. A distinct warmth emanated up her arm and she held her breath. Interesting. The elevator reached her floor and came to a halt. "I hope the rest of your day improves. Um, did you choose your tie?"

"I'm getting off here too," Kevin said with a chuckle. "My seven-year-old niece chose the tie. My sister thought I'd never wear a pink tie but my niece insisted on this one. I wanted to prove my sister wrong." He fluttered his eyelashes. "What do you think? Does it make me look gay?"

"Your designer stubble is a perfect foil."

"My thoughts exactly."

They walked out of the elevator together, both laughing.

"I know this is very forward of me, but could I take you out to dinner tonight? I'm not a weirdo. My accountant Greg Somerville will vouch for me."

"Anyone who cares about making his seven-year-old niece happy must be okay," Maggie said. "I'd love to have dinner with you."

"Great." Kevin pulled out his wallet and handed her a business card. "I'm staying at the Hilton on the waterfront. I can book a table at Whites for around seven. Would that work for you?"

"Seven is perfect," Maggie said. Out of the corner of her eye, she saw Greg approaching. "I'll meet you at the restaurant." With a wave and a quick smile, she turned away to head to her cubicle before she came face-to-face with Greg.

"Wait. I don't have your number," Kevin said.

"I'll be there. I promise," Maggie said. "I won't stand you up."

"Maggie, you're late. Is there a problem?" Greg asked, his stern gaze going from her to Kevin and back.

"No, no problem," she said quickly.

"Good," Greg said, his gaze dropping to the hem of her skirt. "I'll see you later."

Not if she saw him first. She hadn't missed the disapproval on his face when he'd seen her new look. Too bad. She liked it, and judging by the reactions of the rest of the males around the place, they liked the new-look Maggie. Besides, she'd scored a date. She couldn't wait to tell the girls. She wasn't looking forward to telling Connor quite as much.

Maggie practically skipped down the passage to her cubicle. As usual several of her fellow employees were playing solitaire and surfing the net. She wouldn't have time to check her email since she'd promised Tanya, one of the partners, she'd complete the Weston accounts this morning.

After switching on her computer, she immersed herself in work. She worked right through morning tea, printing off the final set of accounts before midday.

She delivered the accounts to Tanya and waited while she glanced through them.

"Great job," Tanya said. "Thanks for getting them done so quickly. Word is out about you."

"No problem," she said. "Pardon?" Tanya's final words registered. Fear clutched at her heart. What did she mean?

"Word is out about the great work you do. Greg has requested you for a special project he's working on next month. I understand you've done a few jobs for him recently."

"Oh," Maggie said. "That's...uh...great." What the hell sort of game was Greg playing? Yes, he'd requested her services for a couple of projects recently. Normally that wouldn't bother her, but when she reported for duty, he treated her like a glorified junior, getting her to make coffee and complete the filing. It was true she wasn't a qualified accountant, but she wasn't chopped liver, either. She was good at her job. "Was there anything else you wanted me to work on?"

Tanya ran through a quick list of assignments. "The Dobson accounts are next on the list. The Dobsons are coming in on Monday."

"All under control," Maggie said. "I should have them completed for you to check tomorrow."

Five minutes later, Maggie left her cubicle, desperate for a cup of coffee and something to eat. She spotted the other members of the Tight Five at their usual table, but made a beeline to the coffee machine. She purchased a salad sandwich and went to join them.

"What did you think of the speed dating last night?" Susan asked.

"I had a bunch of really strange men, apart from Connor. He wasn't weird," Maggie said.

"But you can't date Connor," Christina said.

"Why not?" Connor said in a mild voice. "What's wrong with me?"

"There's nothing wrong with you, Connor. Christina didn't mean it like that," Susan said.

"What did Christina mean then, 'cause I'm offended." Connor puffed out his chest. "I'm a perfect date. Ask anyone."

"But you don't keep the fish," Julia said. "You throw them back. Maggie wants a fisherman who keeps his fish."

Susan chuckled. "Isn't fish plural? Maggie doesn't want to join a harem."

"Not helping. I'm still feeling insulted," Connor muttered.

Maggie noted his tense jaw and felt sneaking sympathy. She knew from personal experience he saw only one woman at a time. He didn't go into relationships lightly. "Stop giving Connor a hard time. How did your dates go, Susan?"

"There were three that were reasonable and I put them on my list of men I'd like to meet again. I'm thinking of running a personal ad or joining one of those online dating sites. What do you think? Is that too sad?"

"Of course it isn't," Christina said. "You should let us help you vet them though. And you need to be careful. From what I've heard some of those men are weird. Julia, are you sure none of your dates are worth meeting again?"

"Positive," Julia said in a crisp voice. "I managed to get a bunch of losers."

"Did you have Connor?" Susan asked.

Connor made a protesting sound. "Still insulted here, people."

Maggie laughed. "Stop picking on Connor. You know we

love you, right?"

"You might, but I'm starting to wonder about the others," he said easily. The quick wink passed as a joke to the other girls, but Maggie knew he'd sent her a secret message. She felt the blush take over her cheeks and spread across her face. Worried the others would notice, she applied herself to opening her sandwich.

"I have a date tonight," she said, before they could continue the speed dating discussion.

Her statement stopped the discussion flat and drew their attention. Now she had a real excuse for blushing.

Christina peered over the top of her glasses. "A date?"

"How?" Susan said.

"More to the point, who?" Julia added.

"It had better not be Greg," Connor said with a trace of disgust. "You're well rid of him."

Maggie caught the trace of hurt on his face. His face blanked quickly, and she couldn't read him, despite knowing him better than she had a couple of months ago. "I met him in the elevator this morning," she said. "He asked me out for dinner, so I said yes."

Connor scowled. "You didn't tell him your address or phone number?"

"She's not stupid," Julia said. "You didn't, did you?"

Maggie rolled her eyes. "Of course I didn't. Credit me with some sense. I'm meeting him at the restaurant."

"What's he like?" Christina pushed her glasses up her nose. "Why don't I meet men in the elevator?" she added before Maggie could answer.

"I was late." Maggie's tone was dry. "That's the secret."

"In other words, meeting a man is pure luck," Susan said. "Good to know."

"I'd better head back to work," Connor said. "Catch ya later."

"Connor seems quiet," Christina said, frowning as he strode away. "He seemed a bit cranky last night too."

Julia shook her head staring after him. "I don't know. He used to drop around to see me a couple of times a week, even when he was going out with Gwen."

"I wonder if he's going out with someone else," Susan said.

"Don't look at me," Maggie said, ignoring the guilt rippling through her. Hopefully they put her flushed cheeks down to discussing her date. "I know nothing, except I need to get back to work."

"Have fun on your date. We want to know all the details tomorrow." Susan grinned. "If I can't get lucky at least you can, although I have to tell you I'm starting to get jealous."

Maggie settled back into work. The phone rang.

"Maggie, it's Greg. Can you report to my office please?" He hung up before she could ask questions. Irritated, she marched down the hall and into his office.

"Ah, Maggie. I've talked to Tanya. You're going to work with me for the rest of the month."

"But... I don't think that's a good idea. Given our personal history and how we're not together any longer, can't you get one of the other accounting officers to work with you instead of me?"

"No." Greg stood and circled his desk. He squatted by her chair and took his face between her hands. "I choose you."

"What?" She stared at him. "No, I'm dating someone else," she said. "We can see each other at work and sometimes work together because we're both adults. I'm not interested in anything else. We've broken up and I don't want to date you again." She shot to her feet. "I'll tell Tanya you changed your mind and one of the others will work with you."

Greg watched her practically run from his office. He slammed his office door and stalked around the edge of his desk.

"Damn," he muttered and kicked his chair. He cursed softly and slumped into his black leather executive chair. Somehow he had to talk Maggie into going out with him again before the partners' dinner next month. He didn't have time to find another woman to take her place before the partners voted to decide which of the junior partners would advance to senior status. Hell, his parents liked her, and she was the perfect woman to help advance his career. He wanted that promotion.

"I deserve it, dammit." Greg picked up his pen and

thumped it on his desktop. Thump. Thump. Thump.

A plan.

Think, man. There must be something you can do to get Maggie back onside and keep her there.

Connor found himself back in the IT department without remembering walking there. All he could think of was Maggie with another man. Touching her. Kissing her. Making love to her.

He shook his head, trying to shake the vision away. His throat tightened. His hands clenched to fists. Damn, he needed a plan. He'd fallen hard for Maggie and the last thing he wanted was another man to snatch her away from him.

His phone rang and he picked it up. "Grey," he said. He listened for a few minutes and hung up. He sighed, dragged a hand through his hair and stood. Damn, he'd expected this was coming, but he hated acting like a watchdog.

"Roger. Larry. One of the big bosses is coming to talk to us about private Internet usage."

"Aw, crap," Larry said. "That takes all the fun out of work."

"What time is the meeting?" Roger asked.

"In half an hour." This should be interesting. He knew for a fact a lot of the staff used the Internet for private purposes while at work. Even he'd jumped online a couple of times to check email and Maggie's blog. Cursing softly, he returned to his desk.

A plan to catch Maggie. For a moment he wished he could talk to Julia, but that was impossible. This one he'd have to handle on his own.

"Man, you have to see this blog," Larry said.

The excited light in Larry's eyes made Connor's stomach twist into a knot. *Please, not Maggie's blog.* "You're not meant to check all the links," he reminded his workmate. "You're meant to try to link employees to private Internet use."

"But the blog is called Big Bad Ass. I *had* to check it out."

It was Maggie's blog. Damn, they'd been careless reading her blog at work. He couldn't exactly tell the girls off when he was guilty of the same crime. Surely Maggie wouldn't be silly enough to do a post at work?

"Which computers have accessed this blog?" He held his breath while he waited for Larry to consult his printouts.

"At least four different computers. No, wait. It's more than that." He glanced at Connor. "This blog has been accessed from all over the place. You'd think that if it was that popular, we would have heard gossip."

Belatedly Connor remembered Julia worked all over the place, depending where her secretarial services were required. "What sort of blog is it?" He asked the question knowing Larry expected curiosity.

Larry smirked. "It's all about spanking. Bring up the URL and take a look."

Connor typed in the URL and hoped Larry didn't notice it came up automatically after he'd typed the first few letters. Maggie had posted a new entry since he'd last checked.

I've been thinking about the physical act of spanking recently. Yes, it's true. I'm driven to discover more in my thirst for knowledge. To date I hadn't considered spanking positions. I'd merely thought about the act itself and the sounds. Thunk. Crack. Thinking about the sounds gets me hot. Isn't that strange?

A shudder went through Connor. Hell, the sounds haunted him and wouldn't let go. Every time he read Maggie's blog and thought about actually spanking her, the sounds came back. *The memories.* The sharp cry from his mother when his father's fist hit her face. The crunch of a bone breaking. The grunt his father made when he struck out with his hands. And the crying. The crying haunted him most of all. His own muffled sobs as he squeezed into a corner, trying to remain out of sight. His mother's soft tears, restrained despite her pain. And his father's loud sobs that he was sorry and it would never happen again. A promise he broke again and again.

Connor concentrated on the computer screen forcing the painful memories away, the sense of helplessness and feeling that he should have done something to help. Of course, his mother and Frank had told him repeatedly it wouldn't have made a difference. As an adult he knew he hadn't had many choices. Intellectually, he knew there was nothing he could have done to change the course of events, but try telling that to his heart.

> *I came across a post in a forum I enjoy visiting. It contained a list of spanking positions. Twenty in all. Who knew? Reading through them was an eye-opener.*
>
> *All I can think of now is trying out the positions until I come back to my main problem. No man to spank me.*
>
> *Maybe I need to cast my net further afield and try dating some new guys. I'm not stupid enough to mention spanking on the first date but if we clicked and decided to take our relationship into the physical, I'd mention spanking then. No matter how embarrassed I felt. I think that's where I went wrong last time. I hesitated and second-guessed myself instead of stating my needs upfront. By the time I gathered courage I'd learned things about my lover's background that made me worry about his reaction to my request for a good spanking.*
>
> *Yeah, as much as I like this guy I'm going to pursue other men. And before you think I'm two-timing or being unfaithful, let me assure you I'm not. We have a casual agreement and have promised each other if someone else comes along, we'll let the other know. We're both adults. We knew the score before we started sleeping with each other.*

Hell, wasn't that a kick in the head. Maggie had accepted a date with this other man, and if things worked out, he was down the track. Their *friends with benefits* deal would end and he'd lose the one woman he could actually love— Nah, he needed honesty here. He loved Maggie, and that was the problem. Too many secrets and holding back on telling her how it really was with him. Damn, why was it so bloody hard?

"I'd love to meet her," Larry said. "I've read lots of the blog posts. Hell, I'd spank her if she asked me. I wonder what she looks like. Probably a dog."

"You should get back to work. The partners are expecting results on this and a report on how to stop the problem."

"Sure, Connor." Larry strode back to his desk and soon

appeared immersed in his work.

The hours passed, and Connor left work. He met Christina and Susan on the way out, but turned down their offer of drinks. He didn't feel in the mood and knew it showed. The last thing he wanted was a series of nosy questions.

He spent an hour prowling his apartment, thankful his two flatmates weren't present to witness his fall. They'd joked about him getting caught one day. It seemed they were right. Finally, unable to stand his own company for a moment longer, he grabbed his wallet and left his apartment. There was a pub down the road. He'd order a whiskey or two and try and come up with a half-decent plan to win Maggie over. And he needed to get past his aversion to spanking her. She wasn't going to change her mind, at least until she received her spanking. If he was a lucky man, she'd hate spanking and would never speak of it again. And if she enjoyed the experience, he'd face that later. Come up with a new plan.

"Connor! How are you? I haven't seen you for ages."

Connor found himself with an armful of blonde. Automatically, he wrapped his arms around her slim body and gave her a hug before stepping back. "Jenny."

He glanced up and met Maggie's enigmatic gaze. *Crap.* Did he have a sign on his back that said, *kick me*? He smiled, but she didn't return his welcome, turning her attention back to her date.

Double crap.

Ever polite, he turned his attention back to Jenny. They'd dated for about three weeks before they'd moved on with no hard feelings. "I'm good," he said. "I haven't seen you for a while. How have you been?"

"I'm engaged," Jenny said, wiggling her left fingers at him. "We're getting married next weekend."

"Congratulations. Anyone I know?"

Jenny shook her head, settling her blonde curls in motion. "I don't think so. I went home for the holiday weekend and met him again. We went to school together and hadn't seen each other for years. This time we clicked." Jenny grinned and kissed him soundly on the lips. "I'm so happy I could burst. Are you here with anyone? No? Come and meet my friends."

Jenny dragged him over to a large table at the far end of the pub and ordered two of her friends to squeeze up so they could fit in Connor. He laughed and joked with the girls, but couldn't have repeated a word they said. All he could think about was Maggie and the man she sat with on the other side of the pub.

Twenty minutes later, he watched them leave. The guy was probably close to his own height—over six feet tall. He had blond hair and looked fit. Connor wanted to jump to his feet and knock the arm the man had slung around Maggie's shoulders away. He flirted with the idea of smacking him before he shook himself. That wouldn't happen. Not unless the other man hit him first. He gazed after them scowling. Nah, that wasn't gonna happen either. No baiting. Maggie would never forgive him. He needed to fight for her fair and square.

"Do you know her?" Jenny asked. "You've been watching her ever since you arrived."

"Yeah." Connor let out a heavy sigh. "I know her."

Jenny's green eyes widened a fraction. "If I didn't know better, I'd say you feel something for her."

Connor couldn't force a word past the lump in his throat, and his silence said it all.

"I never thought I'd see the day," Jenny said. "Connor Grey has fallen for a woman."

"She doesn't think the same way about me," he said, a ball of misery curling through his gut. Damn, he needed to get out of here.

"Fight for her," one of Jenny's friends said. Connor couldn't remember her name but she was a pretty blue-eyed blonde. "A woman likes to know a man wants her."

"I don't want to talk about it," Connor said, taking a slug of beer from his bottle.

"Pooh," another of Jenny's friends said. "Don't run away. We're trying to help."

"Yeah," Jenny said. "What you need to do is give her a night she'll never forget. Plan something special. Something private that says you're thinking about her special needs."

"Oh, yes," the blue-eyed blonde said. "And make it a night you can repeat in the future on special occasions. That's after you're married. Make it really memorable."

"Married?" Connor damn near stuttered in his shock. He didn't want to marry Maggie.

The girls glanced at one another and started laughing.

"Connor, you're toast," Jenny said. "You're a fallen man. You love that girl. Now all you have to do is tell her."

Connor fired up his laptop when he arrived back at his apartment after midnight. A memorable idea. Marriage. *Right.*

Jenny and her friends' ideas flitted through his mind but none of them fit into a scenario that would work for him. He kept coming back to the memorable night and knew they were right.

He went straight to Maggie's blog, and to his surprise he found a new blog entry. That meant she'd gone home instead of indulging in hot sex with her date. He didn't think she would have posted a blog if they'd gone back to her place, either. Unless, she'd pre-scheduled the post.

Connor cursed and read the post instead of thinking about Maggie in bed with the blond man.

There's lots to think about when it comes to spanking. Positions, as I've mentioned. Spanking implements. I've also started thinking about lingerie.

As someone mentioned on my favorite forum, lingerie plays an important part in a spanking. There're all the different styles to consider. Do I want my butt cheeks on display or totally covered with material? Should it be cotton or something silky? Different lingerie. Different sensations.

One woman mentioned G-strings. She liked wearing them for a spanking because her ass cheeks were fully on display. Another woman liked plain cotton panties—the sort of panties a grandmother might wear. A third woman liked silky briefs while another preferred the square-leg boy pants. She said nothing turned her on more than when her husband put her over his knee and flipped up her skirt, spanking her a couple of times through the plain cotton boy-leg panties before dragging them down and spanking her properly.

"Jesus," Connor muttered. "Where does she get this stuff?" He couldn't get past the actual act of spanking. Maggie had thought about positions, implements and now lingerie. She'd posted about communication. Part of him was curious as to what she'd write about next.

I feel a yearning for some lingerie shopping. Maybe I'll see if my girlfriends are up for a spot of retail therapy. My current lingerie is fairly plain, and I'm due for a spending spree. I like the idea of wearing sexy lingerie while at work. Dress for work is always so conservative because management doesn't want us to frighten off the customers. At least I can express my individuality with lingerie.

I've always liked the idea of a corset. Some of them are so beautiful these days they can be worn as outerwear with a pair of trousers or a skirt or as lingerie.

What sort of lingerie do you think would work best with a spanking? I look forward to your comments.

Connor reread the end of her post about the corset, and an idea came to him. *The* idea. It was perfect and would feed into her spanking fantasy. This time he wouldn't dodge the issue because he realized if he tried that avenue again he'd lose Maggie to another man.

He felt so good about his idea he decided to email her.

Dear Bad Ass,

Why don't you ask your lover what sort of panties he'd prefer you to wear? Or better yet, why don't you tell your lover exactly what you want from him? Give him the option of saying no instead of taking the decision away without giving him a chance. Your lover might surprise you.

The worst that could happen is that he'll say no.

The truth is you'll probably surprise him. You've had more time to think about spanking than him. He might not understand why you want him to spank you. He might not like the idea because his parents raised him to admire and protect women. You might want to tell him what you think spanking will bring to your relationship, explain to him why you think spanking will improve things between you. Give him reasons. Men are used to taking the facts and acting. When you spring this on him, your man will likely feel a little confused and want answers. He might wonder how a negative activity like spanking could improve a relationship. Have those answers ready for him.

Tell your man how you feel about him, and most of all exercise patience.

Best,
Kinky Lover

Connor checked through his note and decided it said everything he wanted to know. Hit the high points. If Maggie could think about those things and have answers ready, it might help him get past the worry about hurting her.

His thoughts drifted to his father. He hadn't seen him for years and then only during supervised visits. The last time had been when he was thirteen. A typical teenager, he'd gone sullen when his father had started ordering him around. The visit hadn't gone well, and they'd fought. The fight had escalated from verbal to physical pretty quickly. He'd managed to land a few punches and had broken his father's arm before his father had overpowered him.

Not his finest hour.

And the potential for violence worried him. Connor had grown up quickly that day and worked to control his temper every day.

He looked like his father. Same build. Same good looks. Same volatile temper. If he raised a hand to Maggie once, would it become easy? Would he strike out no matter what the provocation? Would he turn into a monster?

So far he'd never hit a woman in his life.

He hoped like hell he could hold his shit together and keep it that way.

Chapter Eleven

Dear Kinky Lover,
Thanks for the great advice. It's funny because I'm not sure I can say exactly what it is about spanking that makes me want it so much. I've been thinking about it ever since I received your email.
During my research I've discovered many couples enjoy incorporating spanking into lovemaking because it deepens the intimacy. Rougher treatment stimulates some people. That doesn't make it wrong. It doesn't make it right, either—just different.
I want a man I can explore erotic boundaries with and submit to in the bedroom. That doesn't mean I'm a wimp. I think of lovemaking as stress release and a way of showing a man I care for him. I want a relationship that's full of fun, laughter and loving, a relationship that's robust with mutual trust.
I'm sure spanking will help bring this dynamic to my relationship. Don't ask me how I know—it's a gut feeling at the moment because I haven't experienced more than a swat on my butt. That felt pretty good and certainly made me hot.
But, when it comes down to it, I'll have to wait and see.
Best wishes,
Big Bad Ass

"It's a blog about spanking," the employee in front of Maggie in the lunchroom line said. "You should check it out."

Maggie leaned closer to hear. If someone else local was writing a spanking blog, she wanted to know about it.

The woman glanced at Maggie and frowned.

Oops, she'd better do something quick or she'd never learn the URL for the blog. "I'm really sorry," she said, curving her lips into her sweetest smile. "I thought I heard you mention a spanking blog. I know I'm being nosy, but it's not something that comes up every day."

"You're not wrong there," the woman said, the suspicion fading from her face. Her conspiratorial grin gave Maggie a glimpse of uneven white teeth. "The blog is called Big Bad Ass. All you need to do is do an online search and it will come up."

"Big bad ass," Maggie repeated, praying she hadn't heard right.

"Yes, that's right. Everyone is talking about it. It's worth looking at—very interesting."

"I'll look it up," Maggie said in a faint voice, trying to dredge up bright interest when she felt as if someone had kicked her feet out from beneath her. People knew. They were talking about her blog. How?

She didn't believe for a moment one of her friends had told. They'd never do that to her.

In a panic, she paid for her lunch, scanned the lunch room and found her friends. She hurried across the room and slipped into an empty chair. Thank goodness Connor wasn't present so she didn't need to confess to him.

"Everyone is talking about my blog," she whispered. "What am I gonna do?"

"None of us told," Susan said. "I don't know how they found out."

"They're only talking about the blog and the contents. They don't know it's your blog," Julia said. "If you keep your cool, no one will ever know it's yours."

"But it's not easy," Maggie muttered, shoving her sandwich away. "I can imagine what they're saying. Oh, heck, here comes Connor. Don't dare tell him it's my blog. You promised," she added when they looked as if they might argue. "I'm holding you to your pledge."

Connor grabbed an empty chair from another table and joined them.

"Have you heard about the blog everyone is talking about?"

Julia asked him.

Heck! Maggie glared at her friend. Julia stared back in complete calm and had the nerve to wink at her.

"Yeah, one of the guys in the IT department found it. Management asked us to check everyone's computer usage. They're tightening up on private Internet use."

"And you didn't think to mention this to us?" Christina asked in distinct horror. "I always check my private email at work and surf the web a bit."

"I wouldn't do it anymore if I were you," Connor said. "I shouldn't tell you this, but if there are rumors about website links, word is probably out. Management has asked for a usage report for each individual computer and details of who works on the terminal."

Maggie wilted in her chair. It could have been worse. "I've used my computer for a little private stuff. Mostly to check my email." Thank goodness she hadn't done any blogging from work. Although some of the girls must have checked her blog if word was out.

"Cripes," Susan said. "I've done a little blog hopping during office hours. How strict are they going to be?"

Julia offered Maggie an apologetic look. "I've done the same thing, Susan. I've checked a few interesting links. Are they going to sack offenders?"

Connor shook his head. "They didn't say. All I'm saying is that you should be careful and leave the Internet alone unless it's for work purposes."

"Done," Christina said. "I intend to leave soon, but on my own terms. Thanks for the warning."

"I wouldn't worry too much," Connor said. "Most people have used the computer for private purposes when they should have been working."

"They can hardly sack everyone," Julia said.

"Good to know." Maggie grabbed her sandwich again and opened it. Maybe she'd overreacted. She hadn't looked at her blog while at work, confining her blogging to home. It wouldn't matter if a few other people had looked at her blog. Interest would die gradually and life would return to normal. "What's everyone doing this weekend?"

Christina pulled off her glasses and inspected them for smears. "Work for me. I'm advising a young school leaver on a wardrobe. It should be fun since our budget is really tight."

"I don't have any plans," Julia said. "Not yet. I might have a lazy weekend and stay at home."

Connor grinned. "Say it isn't so. You always have plans."

"So I thought I'd change things up a little," Julia retorted. "No rule says I have to do things the same way all the time."

"What about you, Maggie? What are you doing?" Susan asked. "Do you have a date? I'm starting to feel a bit jealous about your love life." She wrinkled her nose, but Maggie gained the impression she wasn't entirely joking. It made her feel even guiltier about her lies to her friends.

She averted her gaze from Connor, finding her sandwich more interesting and far less threatening. "I'm not sure yet." Why couldn't she stop looking at him? Thinking about him?

It was like some sort of disease. An illness, because she couldn't resist him. Memories of their lovemaking kept flashing through her mind in a never-ending loop. The memories had kept her from kissing Kevin. She'd enjoyed spending time with him, but when it came to a goodnight kiss, she couldn't do it. She'd mumbled about it being too soon. Excuses. Yeah, she'd stuttered through quite a few.

And Kevin had asked her out again. They had a date for tomorrow night. Maggie knew she needed to move on with her life. Heck, Connor had a fixation with blondes. She's seen him in a clinch with that blonde, and the close attention he'd paid to the other women in the group he'd joined. Yes, she and Connor were casual lovers, not meant to last.

The plan took time to execute. Since the night they'd seen each other in the pub, Maggie had distanced herself. Connor rubbed his tired eyes. He hadn't slept worth a damn, lying in bed imagining all the things Maggie might be doing with her new man.

The only positive note was that she hadn't told him she wanted out of their *friends with benefits* deal. They hadn't exactly talked, either, but knowing Maggie, she'd never sleep with a new guy or continue seeing another man without letting him know. She had honor. It was only that knowledge that kept Connor going each day.

He didn't intend to lose Maggie because she wanted something he couldn't deliver. They'd get through this roadblock and come out the other end. Together. He was determined about that.

Taking a deep breath, he walked into the exclusive lingerie shop, strode up to the counter and told the woman exactly what he wanted.

Lace. Satin. Sexy yet tasteful.

A corset a woman could wear with pride and confidence. A corset that would draw a man's attention.

The question of size had stumped him until luck really smiled. A woman of Maggie's size had sauntered into the lingerie store. Kismet, he'd decided.

They needed to special order, which took time. He'd had to wait. Impatiently.

The rest of the Tight Five had questioned him, asked if he was all right or had a problem.

No, he'd told them, even though he'd wanted to pepper them with questions about Maggie, his confidence at an all-time low.

Now, almost two weeks later, he stared at the black and gold creation, nestled inside a gold box and tissue paper. He imagined Maggie wearing the corset...

"Damn," he muttered, shifting to release the stress on his cock. "Down, boy." At this rate, he'd need to have another cold shower. His flatmates were asking questions already, pulling his leg about the length of time he'd spent in there.

Connor ran the tips of his fingers over the black material, imagining it heated by Maggie's skin.

He hoped this didn't backfire on him, because he thought it might kill him if he lost Maggie.

Connor picked up a pen and chewed the end while he considered what to write on the card to accompany his gift. He stared at the pristine white card and leapt off his chair to search for paper. A draft. This note needed to be perfect. He'd practice first so he didn't stuff it up.

Dear Maggie,

Join me at the Stamford Plaza hotel on Friday 13th. I'll leave a key for you at reception. Wear the corset, and come prepared to spend the night. You won't get much sleep.

Connor

Black Friday. Hell, he hoped that wasn't a bad omen. Things were difficult enough without bad ju-ju coming into play. Connor stared at the message again and decided it said exactly what he wanted to say. After rewriting the message on the card, he tucked it into the box containing the corset. He taped it shut and picked up the phone to call a courier. If this didn't work, he was out of ideas.

Work was getting on her nerves. Maggie felt as if she were in the middle of a bad disaster movie with two out of control trains heading for a collision. She drove one train and could see the other coming. Her workmates drove the other train and were clueless. They couldn't see a thing, but that didn't stop them speculating.

"Why would someone want a man to spank them?" one of the secretaries asked. "I don't get it. We've spent years trying to gain equality, and this woman..." She trailed off, gesturing with her hands as if words failed her.

Another woman added her thoughts. "It's like this woman wants to set us all back to a time when women didn't have the vote and men ruled supreme."

"Yeah, we're a progressive country. We've had two female prime ministers. New Zealand women were the first in the world to earn the right to vote. Shouldn't that mean something?"

Maggie gritted her teeth and tried not to listen. She was not deviant. She cared about freedom and the right to vote as much as the next person. It didn't mean she was taking a step backward. What about freedom of choice?

"Don't listen to them," Julia said in a low voice. "Feel like missing lunch tomorrow and doing a spot of shopping instead? I feel like a bit of a splurge. It will cheer us both up."

"Thanks. I'm having to bite my tongue. It's hard not being

able to defend myself. Shopping sounds great. Where are the others?"

"I don't know about Connor, but the girls both have special assignments. We probably won't see them for the rest of the day."

Maggie nodded, feeling really down. The idea of spending tonight alone sent shudders through her. "Do you fancy having drinks and dinner at my place tonight?"

"Sure. Do you want me to ask the others if I see them?" Julia asked.

"Let's make it a girl's only evening then I can whine about my blog," Maggie said. "Just a little bit, I promise. I won't go on for longer than an hour."

Julia laughed. "Make that half an hour of complaining and we have a deal."

"Done." Maggie's tone was smug. "You should have negotiated harder. I would have settled for ten minutes."

"Well," Julia said, wrinkling her nose.

"Ah-ah. No renegotiation," Maggie said, and with a laugh, she left the lunch room feeling better than she had for days. Good friends were worth gold.

After work, she rushed home, going via the supermarket to grab half a dozen bottles of wine, some brie, cheddar and blue cheese, along with two loaves of bread and some hummus. She figured they could order take-out from their favorite Thai restaurant later if the girls decided they needed something more filling.

Maggie changed into jeans and a top that skimmed her upper body, showcasing her curves instead of losing them under acres of baggy material.

The doorbell went when she'd started to organize the snacks.

"Hey," she said with a grin when her three girlfriends walked in together. "I didn't think you'd be so early."

"We can go away again," Susan said.

"Oh, no you don't," Maggie said, gripping Susan's forearm firmly and propelling her inside. "Julia promised I could have half an hour of non-stop whining about people at work dissing my spanking blog. I intend to utilize every second of my half hour, and you have to listen."

Christina shook her head. "You're a bad negotiator, woman. You should have let me do it."

"I probably shouldn't tell you Maggie said she would have settled for ten minutes." Julia grinned. "I'm sorry. I blew it, but I brought a bottle of champagne in penance." She produced a bottle of Moet.

"Oh, the good French stuff," Susan said. "I love me some Moet."

"What's the occasion?" Christina asked.

The doorbell went, and Maggie frowned. "Don't tell me that's Connor. That would spoil everything. I can't whine with him here."

"I'll get the door," Julia said. "And if it's him, I'll send him on his way."

Maggie nodded and took the champagne to the kitchen. She pulled flutes from the depths of the cupboard and washed them before opening the bottle.

She heard Julia answer the door and the low sounds of a masculine voice. She felt bad about getting Julia to send Connor away, but she couldn't face him right now. Deep in her heart, she knew she had to call off their *friends with benefits* deal. Everything had become too complicated. And it wasn't as if they were communicating that well. She couldn't even find the guts to tell him what she wanted sexually. Why did she have to pick a man who'd suffered through a topsy-turvy childhood and abuse? It can't have been much fun watching his father beating his mother. Maggie understood his reluctance to spank anyone. It would bring back bad memories.

"Was Connor okay with us having a girl's night?" she asked, guilt nipping at her heels. She shoved it away with an ease that made her blink when she realized what she'd done. During the last month, she'd changed, lying without a qualm to suit herself.

"It wasn't Connor." Julia handed over a white box bearing courier labels. "Besides, I get the feeling he's seeing someone. I haven't seen as much of him recently. I think it's serious, because he hasn't mentioned her."

"Connor serious," Christina said with a roll of her eyes. "As much as I like Connor he treats women like a buffet, taking whatever appeals to him at the time."

"Christina, that's not very nice," Maggie said, indignant on Connor's behalf. She placed the box on the countertop. "He has a real gift for ending romantic relationships and remaining friends." And that was the problem. Her crush had deepened into more. If it weren't for the spanking thing and Connor's lack of enthusiasm, she'd never want to say goodbye. He was fun in bed and a giving lover who went out of his way to make sure she enjoyed herself. If only she were blonde.

"You're right," Christina said. "I'm tired and cranky after working hard on the special assignment today. And jealous. My sex life is non-existent."

"What's in the box?" Susan asked.

"I've no idea." Maggie poured the champagne and handed each of her friends a flute of the bubbly wine.

She grabbed a plate of bread and two of the dips, heading for her small lounge area. After plunking them on the coffee table, she returned for the cheese and a third dip. The women took seats and eased off shoes while she made a final trip to the kitchen to grab the package and her champagne.

In the lounge, she dropped into an empty chair, took a sip of champagne before attacking the tape on the package. "I'm not expecting anything," she said. "Any guesses?"

"Nope," Susan said. "I vote for something boring."

Maggie seconded the guess for something mundane. "It's probably from my stepmother. She's learned how to knit this year. Last time I talked to her, she mentioned scarves." She ripped off the tape and opened the box.

"It's not a scarf," Christina said.

"Oh," said Maggie. "It's beautiful." She lifted the black satin and lace confection from the delicate gold tissue paper.

"A corset," Julia said. "And matching panties."

Susan leaned closer. "Is there a card?"

It was gorgeous. Beautiful. And her size, she saw when she checked the swing tag. She rifled inside the box and found a small white envelope. A sealed envelope. She glanced up at her friends and saw them watching her with avid curiosity.

Swallowing, she looked down at her trembling hands. "I'll read the card later," she said, replacing both the corset and the card back into the box. Instinct told her either Connor or Kevin had sent her this gift. Her instincts leaned toward Connor, which meant she couldn't read the card now. She'd have to wait until later when she was alone.

"You can't do that," Susan said in a sharp voice.

"I'll put this in my bedroom," she said hurriedly.

"I agree with Susan," Christina said. "You can't leave us hanging like this."

"It's...um...private." Maggie jumped to her feet and hurried from the room, her heart pounding in alarm. Although she was certain her friends wouldn't stoop to search her room, she removed the card from the box and slipped it into her bra. The cool surface of the envelope sent prickles across her skin, and a flush of shame seeped from her cheeks down her neck.

Maybe it wasn't from Connor.

She sighed and walked back to join her friends, bracing herself for questions.

"Are you seeing a married man?" Susan asked. "I've been meaning to ask about the lover you mention in your blog. Is he married?"

"No! No, of course not," Maggie said, the color in her cheeks intensifying. How could they think that?

"Oh, God, Maggie. You should see your face," Julia said.

"Susan's right. You've talked about a lover in a couple of your posts." Christina peered at her closely. "Who is it?"

"I'm not seeing anyone apart from Kevin. We've had dinner once. That's all."

"The more you deny it, the worse you're making it," Susan said. "You might as well fess up and tell us the truth."

"Stop picking on me." Maggie grabbed her champagne and took a slug. The bubbles tickled her nose, and she sneezed. Champagne splashed over the rim of her glass and onto her jeans. "Damn." She brushed the bottom of her glass with her fingertips to stop further drips. "I am not sleeping with a married man."

"Too late," Christina said. "We're on to you. You know we're going to worm the info out of you, so you might as well tell us now."

No way was that ever going to happen. Maggie could imagine what her friends would say if they learned she and Connor were sleeping together. With a trembling hand, she picked up the plate of bread and one of the dips. She offered it to Susan. "Have something to eat."

"Maggie, honey, I know it's none of our business, but we love you. Do you think you should do this? I mean, a married man. Does he have kids?" Christina placed a hand on her arm and lightly squeezed. "Have you thought about that? It's not just you involved here. If the man is married that means there are other people who can be hurt by your actions."

A tight sensation gripped her chest. They really thought she'd come between a husband and wife? "I refuse to discuss this anymore. Can we change the subject?"

Uncomfortable silence filled the room. Maggie opened her mouth to say something. Anything. Her mind froze and she snapped her mouth shut. Damn, how had she managed to get herself in this position? She snorted inwardly. Simple.

Desire and lust.

Weak will.

Connor had asked, and she'd caved. Yep, no willpower.

She glanced up and caught the tail end of the silent messages flying between her friends. *They didn't believe her.*

And the more she argued, the guiltier she appeared. Maggie lifted her glass and offered a toast. "To friends," she said.

They stared, slow to react to her gesture of friendship. Despite the guilt buffeting her in waves, she maintained a confident smile and met their gazes. She was in too deep now. There was no way she could admit the truth and tell them she'd broken her promise about not becoming involved with Connor.

"I guess you know what you're doing," Julia said, raising her glass. "To friends."

"To friends." Christina heaved a sigh, the inherent disappointment guaranteed to raise Maggie's guilt. "Julia's right. You're an adult, and this is none of our business."

Maggie stomped on her words of explanation, her need to babble excuses. "Thanks." It was all she allowed herself to say in fear her conscience would have her adding unwanted details to raise more questions. Her fault, she thought. Her father would have started muttering about bad genes and foolishness. And he'd probably refer to Penisgate and reporters. Maggie fought horrid, embarrassing memories of the past, shoving them from her mind.

"I'm sorry," Susan said. "The others are right. We're your friends and we shouldn't judge you. But you know we're here if you need to talk, right?" She lifted her glass and smiled.

Maggie suspected Susan forced her smile, but shoved aside her misgivings and pretended everything was okay between them. Her friend tended to see things in black and white rather than gray, one of her least endearing qualities. "Anyone for more champagne?"

When she reached for the bottle, she felt the envelope tucked inside her bra like a ticking time bomb. She wondered how long her friends intended to stay, how long it would be before she learned who had sent her the sexy and decadent corset.

Julia followed Susan and Christina from Maggie's apartment. None of them spoke until they reached the street outside.

A cat yowled from the tiny balcony garden above their heads as they walked to Susan's car. She unlocked the white Mazda, and they all climbed inside.

"I didn't even realize Maggie was seeing anyone," Christina said.

"She mentioned it in a couple of her blog posts," Julia answered.

"I can't believe she's sleeping with a married man," Susan said, starting the car and merging into the traffic. "No matter what the temptation, someone always gets hurt. The only person who wins in a relationship like that is the man. And they might make promises about leaving their wives, but never do."

Julia reached into her bag and pulled out a lipstick. Using a small portable mirror, she reapplied the deep pink color adorning her mouth. Once finished, she said, "That sounds like the voice of experience. Personally, I've always steered clear of married men. More trouble than they're worth."

"And sometimes they lie," Susan said with a trace of bitterness. "Sometimes the first time the women hears the news is when she's mentioned in divorce proceedings as the other woman."

"Ouch," Christina said. "I'm sorry, sweetie. I didn't realize you'd been through something like that."

"Yeah, it was a few years ago now, before I moved to Auckland." Susan pulled up at a red traffic light. "It's made me wary and very picky, which is probably why I don't have a steady man in my life. The one experience has turned me into a cynic."

"So, what are we going to do about Maggie?" Christina asked.

"I'm concerned," Julia said, "but we're her friends, not her keepers. She needs to learn from her own mistakes." Her mouth firmed as she thought about the empty apartment waiting for her. Alone again. Who was she to talk, because her mistakes weren't teaching her much. "I think we should forget about it and be there for her if she needs us."

"I don't like it." Susan's voice was grim as she pulled up outside Julia's apartment. "She's setting herself up for a fall."

"We could always follow her," Christina said. "See where she goes, who she sees?"

"Isn't that a bit Jane Bondish?" Julia asked. "She's an adult, and she's not breaking any laws."

"Julia's right," Susan said. "I think we should leave it alone and let Maggie do things her way. She'll tell us when she's ready."

Chapter Twelve

Maggie let her breath hiss out in weary relief once the girls left. Talk about uncomfortable.

A married man.

Huh! Maggie winced at the insult all over again. Surely they didn't think so little of her? She'd never willingly come between a man and wife. *Never.*

She walked into the kitchen and grabbed a bottle of wine from the fridge. With a glass of wine in hand, she dropped into her favorite chair, retrieved the envelope from inside her bra and ripped it open.

Connor. The corset was from Connor. A slow smile crept across her lips, and yearning twisted like fast-growing ivy around her heart. Maybe things between them weren't broken. Three days to wait.

She'd missed him during the last few weeks. The long-legged blondes at the pub... Maggie cut off the thought immediately. She could hardly yell at Connor for sleeping with someone else when she'd agreed to the terms, agreed to be his fuck buddy. So why did jealousy eat at her? Why did she feel as if he'd rejected her?

An impatient sigh huffed from her, and she wrinkled her nose with a trace of disgust. She knew why, but didn't want to rehash the past and her romantic failures. The motor vehicle accident and resulting tempest in the papers when she was eighteen had not only caused pain, it had caused extreme embarrassment for both her and her former boyfriend. It had made her realize that all he'd wanted from her was sex. As he'd so cruelly told her during their last meeting, why should he settle for a chubby nobody when his looks and money left him free to choose any woman he wanted? He'd chosen a beautiful blonde model, a woman who was everything Maggie wasn't. Was it any wonder she held a prejudice against bubbly blondes with long legs and flashing smiles?

Maggie pushed aside the destructive thoughts and decided to blog. Connor had sent her the corset and wanted her to meet him in a hotel. That didn't sound like rejection. Besides, the way he'd phrased the note, couching it as an order rather than a request, made her sizzling hot all over, her pussy aching and empty. Roll on Friday evening.

I think about my first spanking often, wondering what it will be like and how it will affect me. I wonder if I'll hate it and want to forget about spanking for the rest of my life. When I start to wonder, I worry. What if I've made a big hullabaloo about nothing?

I've mentioned before the amount of reading and research I've done. Each couple is different, and I've stressed the most important thing between a consenting couple is good communication.

It surprised me to discover a good spanking experience is a learned skill. People in the spanking world say not to expect too much at first. Spanking should be good for both partners. Yes, I know all the theory, but it's going to be difficult if my lover hates spanking and I love it or vice versa. I don't believe spanking is the first step into the heavier BDSM scene, because I've learned many couples never go any further than spanking. This is enough for them. It's not even necessary to assume dominant and submissive roles, although I believe I'll feel happier and derive more pleasure from receiving the spanking. My lover doesn't seem the submissive sort and that's fine with me. What I want is the closeness that comes afterward, the freedom to let myself go and give my lover the responsibility for our pleasure.

A first spanking should be free of distractions and take place in a relaxing setting. My upcoming weekend will fulfill these requirements with lots of kisses and tender touches, careful stroking to start. I hope so anyway. I hear practice makes perfect because like anything, a good spanking is learned—much like lovemaking, a couple needs to experiment with positions, scenarios and spanking implements.

For a first spanking, the position should be one that's comfortable for both parties such as draping over knees or a chair.

Should a spanking hurt? I bet that's what most of you want to know. Yes, it will hurt, although that's not the primary aim. Erotic stimulation is the purpose of a spanking—lots of stroking, touching and rubbing. Nakedness isn't necessary. It's best to remove clothes or panties gradually, because the sensations vary from clothed to bare skin. The smacks should dance over the buttocks. The flesh should sting, the sensations building to a crescendo. A pretty blush is the aim rather than bruises.

The person doing the spanking needs to look for subtle signals such as raising hips to meet the blows, a sign the experience is enjoyable. The person receiving the spanking needs to say what they like and don't like during the experience. Around a dozen strokes are sufficient for a first spanking and definitely end the session with hugs and lovemaking.

Afterwards, it might help to discuss the spanking, what worked and what didn't.

So, there you have it—suggestions for a successful spanking. All I need to do is put the theory into practice.

How was your first spanking? Were you disappointed? Did you enjoy the experience?

The days passed slowly, and Friday found Maggie fidgety and unable to settle to anything. Fridays really did suck.

"What is wrong with you?" Susan asked. "I asked you to pass the sugar, please."

A blush suffused her face. Her entire body hummed with arousal from just thinking about the coming night with Connor. "Sorry."

"Have a hot date tonight?" Connor asked with a grin.

"You're not meeting *him* again," Susan said in clear exasperation. "You should stay at home, or better yet, come out to a movie with me."

"Who are you seeing?" Connor asked.

If she'd sat closer, she would have aimed a kick in his direction. Her pointy shoes would do a bit of damage if she aimed well enough. "None of your business."

Christina's brow furrowed in clear disapproval. "But Maggie—"

"Don't say it," Maggie said tartly. "I don't want to argue with you. Just remember that life comes in shades of gray. Let's change the subject. Do you think the All Blacks will beat the French tomorrow?" To her relief, Connor led the conversation, adroitly steering in the direction she'd sent it. The man would be the death of her. *Who was she seeing tonight?* Huh!

Maggie paid the cabbie and smoothed her coat as the driver pulled out of the hotel forecourt. Nerves danced in the pit of her stomach, cinching it tight and making the thought of food impossible. She intended to tell Connor exactly what she needed tonight, without wimping out or allowing fear to dictate her actions. They were both adults. It was time she acted like one.

Her heels clicked on the marble tiles as she strode past a dramatic arrangement of orange bird of paradise flowers and green foliage to the reception desk. Heat curled between her legs, the firm boning of the corset hugging her breasts and sending messages through her sensitized body.

They said the brain was the biggest and most powerful sexual organ. That was certainly true of her today. She'd thought about sex and Connor so much for the last few days and today in particular, it wouldn't take much for her to explode.

She waited in the short line and stepped up to the reception desk when it was her turn. "Hi, Connor Grey said he'd leave a room key here for me to collect."

"Ms. Drummond?" the young man asked.

Maggie refused to let her embarrassment show. Sex outside of marriage wasn't illegal. "That's right."

He smiled. "Room 832. Take the elevators to the eighth floor and follow the signs. Enjoy your stay."

Maybe she'd overreacted. There was nothing in his expression to suggest he was judging her morals. No, her guilty conscience stemmed from the fact she'd lied to her girlfriends and let them think she was involved with a married man. She hadn't lied, but she hadn't exactly told the truth either. Shades of gray. And if they discovered she and Connor were doing the wild thing...

Maggie forced the fear away and smiled at the receptionist, accepting the keycard. Even though she knew she shouldn't stride boldly across the foyer to catch the elevator to Connor's room, her legs kept moving. Excitement increased inside, layer upon layer until her stomach churned with both fear and exhilaration. Her fingers clenched around the handle of her leather overnight bag while the hem of her long, beige coat whispered against her stocking clad legs.

Her heart thumped in time with the beat of the canned music floating through the lobby. The elevator dinged its arrival, and she stepped inside. Two men boarded the car with her, and the audacious smiles told her she'd done a good job with her hair and make-up. Feeling confident, she returned their smiles, her alter-ego in sharp, pointy boots coming to the fore.

"Would you like to go out for a drink tonight?" one asked.

"Thanks, but I'm meeting my husband." Amazed shock froze her smile in place. Those words had come out so naturally. She hadn't realized her thoughts had headed in that direction. Surely she didn't love him? Maggie drew a sharp breath. She did.

She loved Connor.

Shaken by the realization, it took her a few seconds to notice the elevator had stopped on her floor. On trembling legs, she exited, checked the directional signs and turned to the right.

Connor had made it clear permanent wasn't for him. She nibbled her bottom lip. A sharp nip should have jolted her back to reality but now that she'd acknowledged her love, her mind wouldn't let go of the thought. Heck, if she were honest, she'd been halfway in love with him before they started their *friends with benefits* deal.

Maggie halted in front of room 832. She fidgeted, shifting her weight from foot to foot. Maybe she should leave and ignore

Connor's note. Even as the thought formed, she trashed it. Her right hand fisted until the leather strap of her overnight bag cut into her palm.

Not gonna happen.

The truth would be good. She could tell Connor she'd fallen for him and didn't like the terms of their agreement anymore. Maybe he'd change them for her? A half laugh, half sob emerged. She knew Connor pretty well. As much as she liked him, she knew when a woman showed possessiveness or wanted more, he cut her loose.

A film of tears shrouded her vision, and she blinked rapidly to dispel them. The way she saw it, she had two options. She could walk away and pine for impossibilities or she could pull off the best acting of her life.

Aware of her prevarication, she slid her card key into the lock, waited for the small green light to blink and opened the door.

Showtime.

"You're late." Connor turned away from the window and, drink in hand, stalked to the bed. He set down his drink, the glass making a faint clink when it hit the wooden bedside cabinet. "Come here."

Maggie blinked at the stern note in his voice. "I'm sorry." To her dismay, her voice broke slightly.

"No excuses." Connor sat on the end of the bed. "Come here."

Definitely stern. His dark expression sent a haze of emotions and desires swimming through her, and she struggled with the combination of apprehension and arousal. Slowly, she stepped toward him, her head swirling with doubts.

When she stopped in front of him, he stared at her. For an instant, she thought his face softened, then he spoke coldly. "You have been a very naughty girl."

One moment she stood in front of him, and the next, she lay over his lap, facing the oatmeal-colored carpet. She let out a surprised shriek so startled by this turn of events, words failed her.

"Do you know what I do with naughty girls, Maggie?"

"N-no."

"I spank them," he said, his tone no longer dark or quite as stern but conversational. Matter-of-fact. "I spank their bottoms to give them something to consider the next time they think about misbehaving."

"Oh, God," Maggie said.

"He won't help you." Connor stroked her bottom, the heat of his hand radiating right through her coat, corset and panties.

Her stomach muscles tensed, and a jolt of pleasure arced right to her pussy. She held herself tense with excitement while curiosity filled her. What would he do next?

"Nothing to say for yourself?"

"No, except I'm sorry. I'll try not to let it happen again." Liar. If this was an indication of what happened when she was a few minutes late, she intended to misbehave a lot more.

"You'll try? Oh, babe. You need to do better than that. Hmm, let me see. Six minutes late. One smack for each minute. Does that sound fair?" He caressed her bottom in a confident manner, and she had no doubt he meant it. She tightened her buttocks and, unable to help herself, lifted into his caress, loving the shimmer of heat that came with each tormenting stroke. Her vagina gave a hungry twitch, clenching on emptiness and she wet her lips. A whimper slipped free.

"Maggie?" An order to respond. "Have you been a naughty girl?"

"Yes," she whispered.

"Yes, what?"

"Yes, I've been a naughty girl."

"That's right." His hand slipped beneath the hem of her coat. He stroked his fingers along the crease where her buttock met one thigh. A shiver slipped through her, and when his fingers stilled, she knew he'd felt her reaction. He skimmed his fingers down the back of one thigh, pausing when he encountered silky stocking. "Babe, you've been very naughty coming across town, wearing nothing but sexy underwear beneath your coat."

"But you told me to wear the corset."

He chuckled. "Good try, babe. You're right. I did tell you to wear the corset. I presumed you'd wear other clothes as well."

"I wore my coat," she shot back, emboldened by his playfulness.

Connor removed his hand, and she immediately felt the lack of contact. His thighs flexed beneath her body, and she felt him tense.

Whack!

A startled cry escaped Maggie. The smack hurt, even through the layers of material. Rapidly, she catalogued the sensations. Not too bad. Each of her nerve endings fired to life and astonishment gave way to real excitement. Decadent heat.

"That's for wearing your underwear and not much else to come to meet me," Connor said.

The second blow took her equally by surprise, the smack coming from a different angle. Seconds later, Connor lifted her coat, baring the bottom half of her body to him. Her breath caught and she waited, tensing slightly.

His soft touch surprised her yet again.

"I like your ass, Maggie," he whispered. "I like your soft curves and the rounded shape. It's very sexy."

"Um, thank you." It was the first time anyone had complimented her butt. Off-balance, she wasn't sure what he would do next.

Smack!

Her eyes widened at the increased sensation. With only the thin panties between his hand and her flesh, the smack stung more than the first two. Fiery heat ran to the point of contact before seeping down to her pussy. She felt the moisture growing between her legs and swallowed.

Another two smacks in quick succession made her groan. Aimed at slightly different places on her butt, the heat danced through her, swirling and bringing a rush of conflicting emotions. Something like this shouldn't feel so good, yet it did. Her breasts pulled to hard peaks beneath the boning of the corset, the nerve endings in her buttocks firing messages to all extremities of her body. She squirmed on his lap and found herself lifting her hips, silently seeking another blow.

It didn't take long to arrive, the placement perfect, across both buttocks but low. Her pussy clenched in yearning, and she bit on her bottom lip to stem the groan of matching hunger.

"Good girl," Connor said in a thick voice. "You took your punishment well." His hand lingered on her bottom for an instant before he rose and lifted her to her feet in one smooth motion. He scrutinized her closely before he kissed her, a mere caress of lips, as tender and light as that of a child's. But the heat in his eyes when he unfastened the belt at her waist and slid the coat down her arms was pure male adult. Her coat dropped to the floor forgotten as they stared at each other.

The stroke of his fingers across her jaw was gentle, barely there. "You look beautiful, babe. My imagination didn't do you justice. Turn around so I can see you."

Bemused, she turned at his bidding, the faint tremor in her legs a reminder of the emotions pulsing in her body, the residual sting and heat.

Connor had spanked her.

How had he known that she wanted a spanking?

He drew her against his body and she felt the hard ridge of his erection pulsing against her buttocks. She sighed and pushed back against him, savoring the tender moment with his arms wrapped around her waist. Her eyes fluttered closed and her other senses kicked in working overtime to compensate for her blindness.

Connor wore aftershave, not his usual citrus scented one, but something spicier reminding her of the Far East with its hint of sandalwood. His hands rose to cup her breasts, the warmth of his fingers permeating the fabric.

"That feels good," she said without opening her eyes.

"What feels good? Tell me."

"Your hands on me." She responded to his order without hesitation. "The way you stroke my breasts. My nipples feel tender yet needy. I'd like it even more if you used a bit more pressure." Color filled her cheeks—she knew because of the heat glowing in her face—but she didn't regret her suggestion when Connor tugged on one nipple.

"Like this? Does that feel good?"

"Oh, yes. I like that." What she really wanted was for him to drag off the corset and panties and pound into her with his hard cock, but she didn't think she'd managed to verbalize her wish. Maybe slow was better. They should let the urgency build between them. Instinct told Maggie if they took their time, the lovemaking would be spectacular.

He stroked and squeezed, tugging on her sensitive nipples until sensations raced through her body. But it wasn't enough with the stiff boning of the corset between his fingers and her flesh.

One of his hands splayed across her ribs, feeling like a brand. His. She was all his. Maggie wished she had the guts to admit it to him, to tell him he fit every one of her dreams and fantasies. The ache in her pussy intensified, hot, sensual flames licking all the way from the juncture of her thighs up to her breasts.

"As much as I love this corset on you, babe, I want to touch skin. And because you're sorry about being late, I want to lick away the redness on your beautiful bottom."

Maggie smiled. She knew her ass would hurt later and didn't care.

At his direction, she stood still while he unfastened the laces tying the corset in the front. It had taken her ages to tie them but he made short work of the task. With competent hands, he peeled the material from her body, helped her remove her shoes and panties.

"Leave the stockings," he said when she went to roll them down her legs. "They're very sexy."

"Aren't you feeling overdressed?" she asked when the desire in his eyes started to make her feel vulnerable. Self-conscious.

"Are you feeling underdressed?" he countered.

"Just a tad."

"I can fix that." He peeled off his clothes and seconds later stood naked in front of her. He prowled toward her and, laughing, she backed away until the bed halted her retreat. When Connor kept coming, she toppled backward and he caged her in place on the bed. "Turn over."

When she hesitated, he repeated the order.

"Turn over for me, babe."

Their gazes met and held. His dark brows rose and his smile turned quizzical. She let her breath ease out and turned over to lie with her head resting on her arms. The silence lengthened, and she glanced over her shoulder to look at him.

He was staring at her butt.

"You have a sexy ass, babe." He smoothed his hand over one cheek, the coolness of his palm a startling contrast to the heated blush of her ass. She shuddered at his touch. "Up on your hands and knees. Spread your legs as wide as you can. I want to see your pussy bloom, all the private places you normally hide. Do I need to use a condom tonight? You've seen my test results. I haven't been with anyone except you."

"No more condoms." The frank language brought a flash of arousal, and his husky voice held truth. She trusted him implicitly when it came to her health. "I want that too. I want you." If he could speak candidly, so could she.

His hand stroked across her cheek before lifting and returning in a quick smack.

"*Ooh.*" Maggie swallowed and pushed up to her hands and knees.

The mattress depressed when he moved behind her. He slipped a hand between her legs and stroked her swollen flesh. With hot, easy glides he fingered her clit, sending jolts of pleasure skittering through her body. His touch felt so good, and she wanted more. She wanted to feel the stretch when he entered her body, hear his grunts when he thrust into her body.

As if he read her mind, he moved behind her, and she felt the glide of his cock over her flesh. He pushed inside, curving his body over hers and treating her like a treasure. He brushed a kiss over her shoulder blade and pushed her hair aside to kiss her neck. His muscles flexed as he pumped into her, increasing the friction with rapid strokes. Maggie pushed back, savoring each invading thrust.

"Faster, Connor. Please," she begged.

He seemed to agree because he increased his pace, sending ripples of pleasure surging from each stroke of his cock. He bit lightly at her neck, the jolt of pain sending her over the edge. Her sheath pulsed, clutching his cock. Connor groaned, his rapid drives forcing her up the bed. Another raw and guttural shout signaled his climax, and he stilled, his cock jerking in explosive contractions.

Her limbs gave way, and she collapsed onto the bed. Connor curled around her, making her feel loved. Their lovemaking… Fantastic. Spectacular. Amazing. The spanking. Wow! She'd expected pain and hoped it would enhance lovemaking, but hadn't realized she'd feel so close to Connor, so energized. Despite her extensive reading, the intimacy came as a surprise.

Connor moved a fraction, making her realize they were still joined and the man was interested in another session.

"Again?" she asked.

"I've missed you," he said, his voice gruff.

In answer, she pushed back against him, silently telling him she wanted more.

"I want to watch your face this time."

Connor pulled out of her and as she flopped over to her back, Maggie mourned the loss of his cock. His smile cured her straight away. Devilish and full of promises, he looked like a bad boy intent on mischief. There was nothing tentative about his kiss. He consumed her, taking and demanding her participation. He plundered until she responded and gripped his shoulders like an anchor in the emotional storm. Tongues slid together and his taste exploded through her. Urgency thrummed through her body, each touch from him igniting a reaction in her. Passion. Love.

She wished she could separate the emotions, knew she would get hurt. Inevitable. A leggy blonde would enter the picture, displacing her. A blonde like the one she'd seen in the pub. She knew it, and her heart refused to deal with reality. And no way was she going to ask shrewish questions right now and spoil her first spanking.

Enjoy the moment.

Maggie forced her mind from the future to concentrate on the present. *A sexy man who wanted to fuck her.* Yep, candid language. Blunt truths. No one could ever say her feet didn't touch the ground.

Connor swept her dark hair off her shoulder and kissed her neck. His heart bucked when he saw the faint bruises he'd made earlier. He couldn't find the energy for sorry, not when he liked the marks. A badge of ownership. *Caveman stuff.* He kissed a trail across her collarbone before moving back to her neck and sucking in the exact same place. He wanted everyone to know what they'd done together.

"Connor," she whispered, straining and rubbing against his body.

Spanking. Damn, once he'd actually managed to get past his aversion to spank Maggie, her response had made him hot. His cock had never grown so hard, his balls throbbed so much for release. Something to think about later.

"Let's go for traditional this time," he said, parting her legs with his knee. Her musky scent rose and he smiled, liking the fact he'd made her feel good. Her lips were red and swollen from his kisses, her eyes dark and heavy with passion. She was all his carnal fantasies come to life, responsive and submissive in bed, following his orders without hesitation. Yet, she held her own out of bed, doing whatever she believed was right. Brave and courageous. "Watch my eyes the entire time."

"Okay." Her husky whisper of obedience sent a jolt to his groin.

Connor moved between her legs and lined up his cock. He slipped inside her easily, savoring the tight clench of her pussy. So damned good. One hand dropped to cup her buttocks and tilt her hips up. He surged forward, pausing when balls deep, without taking his gaze off her.

Her snug channel pulsed around his shaft, her emotions shining in her eyes. She wanted this. Him. It was a heady thought.

The last couple of weeks had worried him, but it seemed they were on the same page now. He cupped a breast and rolled her nipple, withdrew and glided back inside her. He didn't feel the same urgency this time and kept the pace slow. Enough to keep her on edge. Enough to make him work at keeping his strokes easy without giving into the instincts starting to roar through him.

A pinch of her nipple made her gasp. He grinned at the narrowing of her eyes. She never looked away, accepting the soothing stroke of his fingers when they followed the pinch. A surge of wetness let him know she was enjoying their loving.

"I like fucking you. I intend to do this to you all through the night until we're both tired and sore. Sated." He pushed deep and scored the tender skin along her throat. "And when we're done, we're going to shower together, and I'm going to shave you."

"Why?"

"We talked about it before. Don't you like the idea of smooth skin, increased sensation?"

Maggie ducked her head in a quick nod.

"Good girl."

"On one condition. I will if you will."

Connor barked a laugh of surprise, giving her a series of open mouthed kisses on her neck and upper chest. "You have a deal."

Her chest rose and fell when she sucked in a deep breath. She released it as a sexy moan. The quick punch of heat clamping around his cock told him he wouldn't last much longer. His balls ached and drew high. Chills raced across his skin when he surged into her tight, wet heat again. Her eyes contained pleasure and her fingernails dug into his shoulders, a silent entreaty to hurry.

"Tighten your inner muscles on me. Yeah. Like that." It was an effort not to close his eyes to concentrate on the feel-good sensations, the fire whipping through his groin. Hell. Connor bit down on his tongue, words of love fighting to spill free. *Toast.* He was bloody toast if he uttered those words. She wouldn't believe him for one and she'd run a mile. To preserve his dignity and keep an in with Maggie, he dipped his head to kiss her breast, sucking her nipple into his mouth.

She bucked at the sensations, groaned softly, and on his next stroke shattered, spilling over into climax, her pussy clutching greedily at his cock. He held off for as long as he could, wanting to prolong the pleasure. He lasted three strokes before he lost it, spilling his seed into her and losing his heart completely.

Chapter Thirteen

I did it.
I'm officially a member of the spanking club.
Did my first experience meet my expectations? Hell, yeah. It met and surpassed them. It was such a shock too. My lover took me by surprise, punishing me because I arrived late to our rendezvous.

I'd decided I would bring up the subject of spanking, but his wonderful surprise took away the need for an embarrassing discussion. That's a bit weird, right? Kink excites me, yet I can't discuss it with my man. I guess that makes me human. We all have things that matter to us, but for one reason or another, we don't let our friends or partners know. It might be because of past experiences—I can attest to that—or we've told lies and don't want our friends to think less of us. It might be fear of change or fear of the future.

Now all I need to do is tell my lover I'd like spankings on a regular basis. I won't have a problem there—it's a case of telling him I enjoyed it the first time and would like a repeat. He's probably worked it out already because the sex was the hottest it's ever been between us. We couldn't get enough of each other, and I can't wait to do it again.

How was your first spanking? Did it leave you wanting more or did you hate the experience and never try it again?

Maggie listened to the buzz at work with half her mind, the rest centered on Connor. She'd thought about him all morning and had him to thank for the distinctly damp panties. She reached for a coffee cup and waited for her turn at the coffee machine.

"Man, did you read the latest post on the spanking blog? She did it. She let her lover spank her and enjoyed it," a man said behind her.

Maggie wasn't sure how to react, whether to turn around and glare at the man or pretend she hadn't heard.

"That is so fuckin' hot," one of his friends said. "It makes the plain old vanilla stuff my girlfriend and I do look pretty tame."

"Nothing hot about it," another scoffed. "It's sick. Why would she want a man to hit her? It's probably a game to her and the minute he does something she doesn't like she'll turn around and report him to the cops."

Maggie clenched her cup harder, biting her inner cheek to stop turning around and flaying him with her tongue. He had no right to judge her. Her bedroom activities were none of his business. Yes, he had a right to an opinion, but he shouldn't force it on everyone else. She poured her coffee, pausing to add milk before returning to her table.

None of the others had arrived for morning tea yet and she sipped her coffee, staring out the window at the Auckland harbor bridge and the moored yachts at Westhaven marina. A flock of gulls rode the air currents and the flag on the top of the bridge fluttered in the wind. She was too far away to identify the flag of the day, but it was red, yellow and green.

The conversation of the women sitting at the table next to hers finally registered. *Spanking.* Of course. Why shouldn't the girls in the secretarial department have an opinion as well?

"She's submissive," one said.

"And that's a problem because?" another one asked. "I don't know about you, but by the time I get through my day, make all the decisions for the kids, decide what to have for dinner, what to wear and the hundred other things I have to do, I don't want to take control in the bedroom as well. I like my husband to take control and order me around."

A woman laughed. "Does he spank you?"

Maggie expected the woman to deny everything strenuously. She listened while trying to appear caught up in the view.

"No, but only because he hasn't thought of it. I'm not averse to experimentation. There's nothing worse than going through the motions in bed."

"Hey," Connor said, sliding into the seat beside her. He smiled and she warmed all over. "Are you okay?" He slipped his hand over hers and squeezed lightly before letting go.

"I'm fine. More than fine," she said, instantly catapulted back to the weekend when she met his direct gaze while they made love. "Although I'm feeling bare. It's a weird sensation. I like it."

Connor chuckled. "I know the feeling. I loved touching and kissing all that pretty, soft pink skin of yours. Can you meet me tonight at my apartment? I have rugby training first and won't be home until after nine. Is that okay?"

"I can't wait," Maggie whispered, trying to tell him without words just how much she wanted to be with him again. "Everyone is talking about the spanking blog. Is that where you got the idea from?"

Connor hesitated and nodded. He started to speak, but Julia, Susan and Christina arrived to join them.

"Did you have a good weekend?" Susan asked.

Maggie swallowed, understanding from her tone Susan still had reservations about her mystery lover. She bit back her flare of irritation toward Susan, reminding herself her friend had really suffered at the hands of her previous lover. It had colored her perceptions, so maybe she should cut Susan a break. She and Connor would have to be careful or their friends would catch them out, then there would be trouble.

"Yes, I did." Keep it simple, she decided. No need to go into unnecessary details. "How about you?"

"I painted," Susan said. "Look what I found in one of the ladies magazines. I thought I'd ask your opinions. I'm not sure whether to apply or not." She handed over two loose pages for the rest of them to read.

Country Men Seek A Wife.

The Country Women's Weekly is seeking a few good women for our lovely country bachelors. Our men are farmers, raised on the land and ready to settle with an adaptable woman.

All applicants must be single and provide a recent photo. They must also agree to take part in a reality show documentary for the duration of the contest. Complete the application form by 31 August. We will contact successful applicants with relevant details prior to 30 September, ready for filming to commence on 1 October.

"Well, what do you think?" Susan demanded after a few minutes.

Julia laughed. "A reality show. I like it."

"Give me a chance to read it first," Connor said, drawing the article closer and scanning it rapidly.

"You don't like the country," Christina said. "You hate getting your hands dirty."

"It's true I'm a city girl, but that doesn't mean I can't live in the country," Susan said, her shoulders tensing in a combatant mode. 'I can do anything I set my mind to. Besides, all my speed dates were disasters. I met the last one for coffee at the weekend. I'm pretty sure he wanted a mother figure—someone to boss him around and tell him what to do and when. Not my type at all."

"I think you should go for it," Maggie said. "There's nothing in the rules to say you have to marry the guy."

"It's a chance to meet different men," Christina said. "Maybe that's what we both need. I'll enter if you will. That's if you'd like company."

Susan beamed. "Deal. I'll print out two application forms. Maybe we could get started on them tonight?"

"Come around to my place," Julia said. "I'll provide the wine."

"I have rugby training," Connor said. "If we win this week, we're going to make the quarter-finals. Coach wants an extra session."

"It was a great game on Saturday," Maggie said. "I'm going to be at the next game cheering on the team. You guys should have been there. Connor had a great game and scored a try."

"Why didn't you ring me?" Julia asked. "I would have gone with you."

Shoot. "I...um...was busy for most of Saturday. I needed some fresh air and went for a drive. I ended up at the rugby..."

Weak. The truth was Connor had dropped her off a block away and she'd walked across the park to the rugby grounds. They'd met up later at the hotel and ordered room service, not emerging from the hotel until their late checkout at midday.

"Can you come tonight?" Julia asked. "Or are you going to be busy?"

They all stared at her, the silent accusation bringing a wave of guilt. She hated this part of her relationship with Connor, the secrecy and sneaking around.

"There's some sort of family crisis about my father and stepmother's upcoming anniversary. I promised my stepsister I'd be at home at nine so she could ring me. I can stay until about half eight. Is that okay?" Lies. Not good. She was getting good at them. There was a lot of discussion about the anniversary—namely her father didn't want a big celebration and her stepmother did. She wasn't lying about that. She just wasn't telling the truth, either.

Susan smiled at her—genuine excitement lighting her face. "I'm not sure I should be quite so excited about this. I might not even get picked, but from the moment I saw the ad, I've had this feeling."

"A question," Connor said. "What's wrong with meeting a man in the normal way?"

Christina blinked and Maggie bit back a smile when Susan's mouth gaped. Julia's eyes twinkled with suppressed laughter, and Maggie waited because Connor had just dug himself a hole. He hadn't realized it yet.

"What normal ways?" Christina asked.

Maggie watched wariness creep over Connor's face, saw the minute he realized his innocent question had peeled off scabs and let bad memories run free.

"At work or at the pub." He offered a weak smile before he turned his gaze on Maggie and Julia with a silent plea for help.

"Men are pigs," Susan said. "They only want one thing, and that's to learn how quickly they can get their dick in a girl's panties. I'm tired of fending off drunken idiots who are only interested in sex. I want a man who is interested in making a future with me, having a family. Is that so much to ask?" Her voice broke toward the end of her rant and tears shone in her eyes.

Maggie swallowed, trying to rid her throat of the lump of emotion Susan's impassioned words had caused. She reached across the table for her friend's hand and squeezed it. "You deserve happiness, Susan, and we'll support you in this contest. Anything you need. We'll be there for you. Right?" She glanced at her other friends.

"Of course we will, sweetie," Julia said. "We'll drum up votes or whatever they do on those shows."

"Hell, Susan," Connor said. "I'm sorry. You're right. Men are pigs. We take longer to grow up and think playing the field is fun."

"You don't want responsibility," Christina said in a sharp voice. "We're not blind to your faults, Connor. You're not as bad as the rest of the guys, even if you do like leggy blondes."

Maggie's stomach dropped and fear settled, squeezing her lungs like a tight elastic band. She wasn't Connor's type. She knew it. She'd always known it but had agreed to act as his fuck buddy. They didn't have a future. She accepted it and while her head went with the program, her heart didn't agree. Maggie knew she was setting herself up for a fall. She perched on the edge of a precipice and the only way off was down.

"I didn't realize I'd need to write a novel to enter this contest," Christina whined.

Maggie grinned at her peeved tone. They'd met at Susan's flat after work, and now, three hours later, they were still working on completing the forms for Susan and Christina. Two empty wine bottles stood on the kitchen counter, and Julia was busy opening a third.

Papers covered the kitchen table, and Susan's pale face told Maggie she was as tired and as dispirited as Christina.

"Almost done," Maggie said. "All you need to do is write the essay saying why you want to marry a farmer and what you could bring to the partnership."

"An essay." Susan groaned. "I was terrible at essays at school."

"Me too," Christina said. "This is hard. I don't want to do it anymore."

Julia topped up their wine glasses. "Don't be wimps. Man up and write that essay."

Maggie snorted. "Is this where we start spouting sayings like, 'Save a horse. Ride a cowboy'?"

"Works for me," Susan said. "I'd love to ride a cowboy. Do they have cowboys on New Zealand farms?"

"Yeah, we're not in Kansas now," Christina said, reaching for her wine. She missed and almost knocked her glass over.

"Whoa," Maggie said with a laugh. "No more wine for the pair of you until we eat. Focus. Yes, we have cowboys in New Zealand. Haven't either of you been to a rodeo before?"

Susan shook her head. "No."

"An agricultural show?" Julia asked.

"No," Christina said.

Maggie and Julia glanced at each other and grinned.

"City girls," Maggie said. "This is gonna be so much fun. Let's work on those essays. I want you both chosen so I can watch the reality show for a long time."

"Who do you want? Susan or Christina?" Julia's eyes widened and a wicked grin spread across her face. "How about a wager to sweeten the pot?"

"Done. Dinner and a hotel room at Whites?" Maggie laughed and quickly muffled the sound with her hand.

"A romantic night with the man of my choice. Works for me." Julia's giggle set Maggie off again and they laughed so hard they clutched at each other to stand.

"I'm glad the pair of you thinks this is funny," Susan said in a stern voice.

Maggie noticed her lips twitched and Christina's mouth pursed. She looked as if she wanted to laugh but was trying not to on principle.

"I'll take Susan," Maggie said.

"Christina, we're going to beat them," Julia said, wiping the tears of laughter from her eyes. "We'll wipe the floor with them."

"There are six farmers up for grabs," Susan said. "More than enough to go around."

"Not if I'm aiming to grab two." Christina glanced at Julia. "Tell me you're a whiz at English."

"Two?" Susan asked in a faint voice.

"I'm a whiz at English," Julia said.

Christina brightened. "Really?"

"No. I barely passed, but I have a wager on the line. I respond well to a challenge."

"We're doomed," Christina muttered. "Absolutely doomed. It's all my fault. I shouldn't have been greedy and asked for two men in my Christmas stocking. I knew I was pushing it. I knew it. This is fate come back to screw with me."

Maggie glanced at Julia. Julia made a hiccupping sound and they were off again, laughing so hard they ended up on the floor.

"I need food," Susan said. "I have some lasagna in the freezer." She stood and strode to the upright freezer. A blast of cold air hit Maggie when Susan opened it.

She grabbed two containers and turned on the oven. The fan started whirring as it dispersed heat throughout the oven. Fifteen minutes later, the rich scent of herbs and meat wafted through the kitchen.

"What we need to do is use honesty," Maggie said to Susan.

"Right," Julia said. "We'll use honesty. That's the way to go. Can't go wrong if you come across as sincere and honest. Farmers like those qualities."

"You know this from experience?" Maggie asked. "How many farmers do you know?"

"I know men," Julia said in a lofty tone, waving her right hand in a dismissive move. "All men are putty in your hands if you tell them what they want to hear. If you can make that truthful all the better."

Maggie's smile died. She knew that from experience with Connor. Even though she'd had feelings for him, feelings that had grown stronger, she'd pretended differently, telling him what he'd wanted to hear. She glanced at her watch. Almost time to go. Maybe she should ring and tell Connor she couldn't be meeting with him tonight. Maybe she should stay with her friends and go back to the way things used to be with them.

"Maggie, stop looking at your watch. You're not going anywhere until my essay is done and you've eaten," Susan said.

Maggie pushed aside her qualms to concentrate on Susan. "I think you know what you need to do with your essay. Write down exactly what you want in a man and why you're entering this contest. Go for truth and honesty. Tell them you're grumpy in the mornings until you get a cup of coffee, tell them you're snappy if you get overtired. Tell them you're a loyal friend, you're not frightened of trying new things and open to new experiences. And tell them you're an awesome cook and love children."

"Christina, exactly what Maggie said," Julia said with a nod. She picked up a pen and started to jot notes. "Don't tell them you dream about two men because it sounds plain greedy. Most of us have trouble finding one."

"All of us have trouble finding one man," Maggie said with a heartfelt sigh.

Christina's bracelets jingled as she tapped her pen on the tabletop. "Yeah, you'd think in this day with all our modern conveniences finding a mate would be easy. If anything it seems harder for modern women."

Susan nodded. "I've been thinking about this a lot lately. I think it's because women are programmed to want a mate, to have children. That part of us hasn't changed. We're also programmed with ambition, told we can be anything, anyone. The Prime Minister, a lawyer, an astronaut or scientist. These things take time and it saps our femininity in the eyes of some men. At heart, they want to protect and provide for us. They don't want to stay home and look after kids, so in defense, they play the field. They sow their wild oats."

"Don't you think that's cynical? Not all men are like that," Maggie said, not liking the pessimistic picture Susan painted.

"Oh, yeah? Then why did you break up with Greg? He wanted you to stay home and play the little wife. Right?" Susan glanced at all of them before turning her attention back to her. "That's why we're all in our late twenties with not a husband in sight. There's nothing wrong with us. There are no eligible men available."

Julia shook her head, setting her blonde locks in motion with the vigorous movement. "Wow, you really have thought about this."

"Sorry," Susan said. "I didn't mean to preach, but I'm pissed because society paints us as loose women and says no wonder we can't catch husbands. I'm saying I want a husband, but the right men aren't out there. Either they're playing the field or they've married their childhood sweetheart right out of school."

"Or they're gay," Christina said. "Twenty years ago a gay man married and lived in the closet. These days they live together openly and even marry in civil unions."

"There's nothing wrong with being gay," Julia said.

"I'm not saying that." Christina sighed. "All I'm doing is agreeing with Susan and saying the men aren't available in the dating pool."

Julia flicked a lock of hair over her shoulder and shot Maggie a challenging look. "Don't worry. Maggie and I are going to help you bag a farmer. They have a shortage in the country and we have two beautiful women in the city. Easy."

Maggie grinned. "A match made in heaven."

The oven timer dinged and Susan rose to attend to the lasagna. She sliced a loaf of bread into chunky bits and pulled a salad out of the fridge.

As they settled down to eat, Susan's words echoed through Maggie's mind. Her arrangement with Connor was a casual one, temporary by nature. Maybe she should tell him she'd found someone she wanted to spend time with and they couldn't continue any longer. She wondered about signing up for the chance of meeting a farmer. She wanted marriage and children. Listening to Susan and Christina had forced herself to look at exactly what she wanted. But the thought of cutting Connor loose made her stomach hurt.

"Maybe you should fill out the forms as well, Julia," Christina said.

"I know myself well enough to know I'd never survive in the country. I'd make a man plain miserable," Julia said. "Susan, I love this lasagna. It's delicious."

"What about you, Maggie?" Susan asked. "You're not dating anyone."

"Don't forget about her secret spanking partner," Julia said.

"Yeah, after lecturing me, I can't believe you forgot. " Maggie softened her words with a cheeky grin. *Attack. Divert!* She didn't want to lie to them again. "I'm happy as I am," she added, hoping that would suffice.

"Leave Maggie alone," Julia said, coming to her defense. "She'll tell us when she's ready."

Maggie concentrated on her lasagna, shoving a piece from one side of her plate to another because her stomach churned so much she knew she'd never get another bite down. She'd never tell them because she'd made a mistake in agreeing to Connor's scheme. If her mistake ever came to light, she'd lose her friends because she'd done the one thing they'd agreed they'd never do—hit on Connor.

Chapter Fourteen

Maggie almost didn't go to meet with Connor. She left Susan's flat at quarter to nine and dithered. She went home and rang her father to say hello, to ease her guilty conscience.

"Hi, Dad. It's Maggie."

"I thought you were going to ring during the weekend."

Maggie only just caught her sigh. It was always the same, and it didn't matter what she said or did, she couldn't do anything right where her father and stepmother were concerned. "I'm sorry." She didn't bother making excuses.

"I see *your* mother is in the magazines again."

"Oh?" Good grief, what had her mother done now?

"You haven't seen the Woman's Weekly?"

"No."

"She has a new lover." Her father snorted, and she knew if they were standing in the same room his cheeks would blaze with anger, and that fury would echo in his eyes. "Some rugby player," he added with disgust.

As usual, Maggie didn't know what to say, planted firmly in the middle of her parents.

"A younger rugby player. He's your age!"

"Oh." Maggie wondered what Susan would say about an older woman whisking another eligible bachelor out of the dating pool.

"It's disgusting the way that woman flaunts herself."

"Dad, I rang to see how you are. I'm meant to meet a friend—"

"At this time of night? You don't get that from me."

Maggie's hand clenched around the phone. "I'd better go. I'll ring you next week. Give everyone my love." And she hung up before her father could wind up for another volley of complaints about her mother's morals and bad blood passing on to her. She stomped around her apartment in an attempt to disperse her anger at both her parents. They were as bad as each other.

Half a dozen times, she picked up the phone to ring Connor, only to put it down again. If she hurried, she could leave a message.

Cowardly.

Finally, she dialed and waited for the answer machine to pick up. One of Connor's flatmates answered.

"Connor's here. Just a sec." He was gone and hollering for Connor before she could say she'd leave a message, that it wasn't important. Her heart thumped while she waited for him. She could hang up but his flatmate knew it was her on the phone. Connor would ring back and start asking questions. Questions she didn't want to answer.

"Maggie?"

"I'm running late," she said. "I'm still at home."

"I'll come over. Be there soon."

"I—okay." *Weak. So bloody weak. Why couldn't she tell him it was over?* Maggie hung up, took a deep breath and let it ease out. Truth stared her in the face. She didn't want to end things between them. That was why she couldn't tell him.

Sad. So sad.

Sighing, she went to tidy her bedroom before taking a quick shower. She knew exactly where Connor's visit would end.

Greg hadn't counted on rugby training going for so long. He'd thought about giving the sport away, but the partners liked knowing he played rugby, and he'd take every edge he could. He deserved a full partnership. He'd earned it.

He pulled up outside Maggie's apartment, cursing when there were no parking spaces out front. He drove past, finally finding a space two blocks down. With any luck Maggie would get over her snit and let him stay the night. A man needed sex, and while he could have slept with someone else, he hadn't,

183

wanting Maggie.

A man jogged across the road in front of him, and Greg cursed.

Bloody Connor Grey. What the fuck did the man want with Maggie at this time of the night?

He knew they were friends and resented their closeness. He wasn't stupid enough to let her know, but after they married, he'd push Grey out of Maggie's life. Let him know Maggie didn't want him hanging around.

Greg hesitated, not wanting Connor to see him. They'd had their usual niggles on the rugby field tonight and Greg had decked him. Connor had a fat lip in the changing rooms after practice. It would look worse tomorrow at work, Greg thought gleefully. Bastard had it coming. Way Greg saw it, he still had a few free shots coming as payback for his black eye.

Connor entered the apartment building, and Greg decided to go for a coffee down the road. He'd grab a takeout and come back to wait for Connor to leave. Maggie would probably send him on his way. She liked to have early nights during the week and was usually in bed by ten.

Fifteen minutes later, Greg returned. Connor's car was still parked outside. Greg sipped his coffee and watched the lights in Maggie's lounge on the second floor. They flicked off and he straightened, moving into the shadows so Connor didn't see him when he left. Maggie's bedroom light flicked on, and he saw her wander over to pull the curtains. Another shadow walked up behind her, and the two blended into one.

Greg blinked, unsure if he'd imagined that or not. The next instant the curtains shut off his view. What the hell?

Were Maggie and Grey involved? Nah. He shook his head and glanced at the window again. He waited for an hour, his fury increasing with every passing minute.

Connor didn't come out again.

"What's wrong, babe?" Connor had thought he might find an excuse to spank her again, because he'd kinda enjoyed it last time. One look at her face made him change his mind. "Are you okay?" The words came out sounding a little weird because of his fat lip.

"I should be the one asking that. What happened to your lip?"

"A tackle at training," he said easily, making light of the truth. Greg had punched him on purpose. Not that he intended to tell tales. They'd work it out between the two of them, either on the field or off.

"And you had your face in the wrong place."

Her teasing note made him smile. That sounded better. When she'd first opened the door she'd looked like a whipped puppy. "Yeah, something like that."

"I'm tired," Maggie said.

"So am I." His ribs hurt like hell. Greg had managed a couple of good shots before the rest of their team mates had separated them. Connor wasn't about to involve Maggie in the middle of their petty squabble. "Can I sleep here the night? Hold you?"

"I thought we were about sex."

"We're friends." He hated the note of vulnerability in her voice. It made his chest ache. "Maggie, what's the problem?"

"I have a guilty conscience."

"Why?" Connor caught her hand and tugged her to him. "Tell me."

"We're sneaking around behind our friends' backs. Lying to them."

"Babe, our private arrangement is none of their business, but we can tell the girls if it makes you feel better."

"We can't do that."

"Why?"

"Never mind. I'm going to bed."

"Am I staying tonight?"

She shrugged and turned away. "Whatever."

Connor stood, indecisive for a few seconds. Women. They confused the hell out of him at times. But one thing was clear. If he walked away now, she might not let him back into her life. He didn't intend to walk away. Soon, he'd start pushing for more. She was so damn skittish, reminding him of the wild deer that used to graze on his grandfather's land when he was a kid. He followed and wondered why she didn't want to tell the others about him. Didn't she think it would last between them? Granted he didn't have a good track record with women, but it was different with Maggie. She was a friend first. They knew each other, their strengths and weaknesses.

Damn, why did this have to be so difficult?

He walked up behind her as she drew the curtains, pulling her against his chest. At first she stiffened, but she relaxed into him quickly enough to mollify his sense of pique. He curved his hands around her waist, enjoying her warmth, her softness. Her old-fashioned lavender scent.

"Come to bed," he whispered. His cock started to fill and he dredged up every bad, embarrassing and cold memory he could to will his erection away.

She turned in his arms, stretched up to plant a chaste kiss on his lips and pulled away. Her robe slipped down her shoulders, and naked, she crawled between the sheets.

"Goodnight, Connor." She turned away onto her side.

Connor's eyes narrowed, his temper rising. Hell, how did he fix this if she wouldn't tell him what the problem was?

He stripped off his clothes, leaving his jeans, T-shirt and underwear in an untidy pile on the floor. After flicking off the light, he crawled into her bed, thankful for the first time that it was a double rather than one of the larger sizes. It gave him an excuse to touch her. He swallowed the curse trembling on his lips, thinking it instead. Fuck, what happened if he couldn't fix whatever was wrong between them?

Connor woke slowly, his arms full of delectable woman. Sometime during the night they'd gravitated toward each other, seeking warmth and touch. He let himself drift, content to enjoy the moment of tenderness until his body started to react to her presence.

Maggie stirred, stretching like a cat, her body brushing his erection. Connor couldn't help the involuntary jerk of his hips. He watched her face, the flicker of her eyes as she came awake.

"Connor."

"Morning, babe." He drew her closer and kissed her, signaling his intentions clearly. He wanted to make love to her. He mightn't be able to tell her he loved her, but he could show her with his body, his actions.

"I need to clean my teeth," she muttered.

"No," he said, instinctively knowing she'd start to think too hard if she left the bed. He slid her mouth over her silky cheek, taking nibbles out of her neck. He slid his hands down her body in a long, luxurious stroke. Damn, he wanted to wake like this every day. His hand halted at the dip of her waist, and he kissed his way down her body, sliding a leg between hers. She softened beneath him, her relaxation giving implicit permission to continue. *Thank you.* He touched. Stroked. Kissed until sensation roared through him.

Chills rippled across his flesh when he entered her, contrasting sharply with the heat surrounding his dick. Man that felt really good. Amazing. He rocked into her, taking it slowly at first, using every bit of his expertise until she shuddered against him, cried out.

Pushing deeply, he let go, giving in to a sweet orgasm. Afterward, he held her closely and wondered how he should play this. How did he demolish the wall he sensed between them? He wanted forever, and she wanted only what they had now. Connor recalled one of his ex-girlfriends crying when he'd broken things off with her because he hadn't wanted serious and she did.

One day, she'd said. You'll find a woman you want. I hope she doesn't want you back because then you'll know how it feels.

Connor knew how it felt. It felt like a kick in the guts.

Sex is good. Spanking is fun and makes me hot. Sometimes variety helps spice things up and gives our lovemaking a new edge.

I've been reading about bedtime stories. No, not the run-of-the-mill kids' ones like Goldilocks and the Three Bears. That would be plain weird. I've been thinking about stories for grownups.

Imagine reading a story together. You and your partner are both naked. The book is open in front of you. There are pictures—explicit ones—and the words are even better, stimulating the imagination.

You're in a private Turkish bath. The scent of fragrant oil lingers on the air. The air is moist and you lie on your stomach, sweat trickling down your face, your chest, between your breasts. Patiently, you wait for your massage, mind drifting away with the soft notes of birdsong, piped through an invisible sound system.

A door opens.

Footsteps pad closer.

Strong hands begin to work your back. Stroking and gliding across moist skin. Slowly, they move down your body, kneading and pushing your buttocks. A hand snakes between your legs, spreading them. The hand works even lower, tickling across the root of your balls. The hand slips lower, massaging and teasing until your penis fills with blood and becomes erect.

I'm sure you get the picture. Adult bedtime stories can be a lot of fun and are a novel way of building desire—a form of foreplay, if you will.

Another method of foreplay I wanted to mention is role-playing. We role-play when we're kids, pretending we're bus drivers, nurses or shopkeepers. It's a fun way of playing, involving imagination and sometime props. Think about it. Extend the idea into the adult arena. I'm sure you've seen or talked about some of the corny porn movies available for viewing. There's a reason doctors and nurses or teacher and the naughty schoolgirl scenario are popular.

What? You think we're all sick in the head?

I hate to break it to you, but if you're reading my blog now, you're probably on the same page. You like things a bit different. Role-playing falls into kink for some people. I guess it depends how far you want to take it, but role-playing is great for spanking foreplay.

Get costumes. Dress as a school girl, a nurse, a disobedient servant or geisha girl. Have your lover dress as his or her chosen character, improvise a script and have fun together. As always, have a safe word in case things go a little far. Agree beforehand what's acceptable, what strays out of bounds and use a pre-agreed safe word if boundaries are crossed. Play time should be enjoyable and not stray into torture.

And just so you know, I have an old school uniform that still fits me. Guess what I'll be wearing for my next spanking...

Connor stared at the screen, shifting uncomfortably in his chair. Damn, that was hot. His Maggie had hidden storytelling talents. He wanted her to read a Turkish bath story to him, tell him how it ended and, even better, show him.

Of course, he'd return the favor and tell her a story guaranteed to make her squirm. A story to make her hot and desperate for him. His brow wrinkled as he considered the possibilities. This weekend. After his game, they'd shoot away for the rest of the weekend. Waiheke Island, he decided. Close but not too close to home. They could walk on the beach, visit the World War Two gun placements and dine at the vineyards. And when they weren't doing all that, they could make love. Some adult storytelling. A spanking for a manufactured infraction. Some traditional sex to balance things out. Yeah, he thought. A great plan. And if he could find out what was troubling her so much the better.

He grabbed his cell phone off the kitchen counter and hit speed dial. Maggie answered almost straight away. "How do you feel about a gym session?"

"Sounds good. We haven't been for a few days. I'd arranged to meet the girls, but I'll ring them and let them know I'm going to be a bit late."

"I'll pick you up in ten minutes." Smiling, Connor put the phone beside his laptop. He hit a search engine and a few minutes later had picked out a good place to stay.

Leaping to his feet, he jogged to his bedroom, changed for the gym and grabbed his car keys. He arrived at Maggie's apartment just as she walked outside.

"Great timing," she said, opening the passenger door.

"Do you have plans for the weekend?" he asked.

"Apart from going to rugby? No."

"Would you like to go to Waiheke? After the game."

"Just the two of us?"

He nodded, pulling up at a red traffic light. "Just us," he confirmed.

"I'd love to."

Connor let his breath ease out, a smile unfurling. He'd

thought he'd have to persuade her to go away with him. All he'd needed to do was ask.

He thought about asking her to bring her old school uniform, but wimped out. He was good at improvisation. Hell, it was hard-wired into all Kiwis. It was a well-known fact New Zealanders thought outside the box, and as a good, red-blooded Kiwi male, he fit the profile.

Bring on the weekend.

Chapter Fifteen

"Damn, where is she?" Christina paced a corridor in Auckland hospital and slammed the cell phone closed.

The disinfectant scent made Susan's head ache, while worry for Julia had her stomach roiling like the Hauraki Gulf during a storm. She opened her cell and dialed Connor. Nothing. His phone wasn't turned on.

Christina stalked back to her, her runners squeaking on the faded tiles when she executed an abrupt turn.

"Stop pacing. It's driving me nuts," Susan snapped.

"Julia looked so pale. You don't think she's taken drugs, do you? They wouldn't tell me anything because I'm not family."

"It was lucky we went round to her flat," Susan said. "At least we contacted her father. He said he'd be here as soon as he could get a flight from LA."

Christina frowned. "Both Connor and Maggie were at rugby. That's the last time I saw them."

"Well, neither of them is answering their phones. I've rung them at home. Connor's flatmate said he was away for the weekend with some woman."

Christina's frown deepened. "Do you think they're together?"

Susan laughed. "Romantically?"

"Yeah. They've both been acting a bit strange recently."

"Don't be silly. Maggie isn't Connor's type. She's not blonde, for a start. They're friends, that's all. Besides, we have a pact. We all promised not to become involved with Connor. Heck, the pact was Maggie's idea. Remember?"

Christina started her pacing again, and Susan had to bite her lip to stop snapping at her. They were both worried about Julia. They didn't need to snarl at each other.

"I guess you're right." Susan bounded to her feet when she saw the doctor. "Let's see if we can find out anything. Doctor, how is Julia?"

"Your friend is lucky you found her before it was too late. She's lost a lot of blood, and unfortunately, she's lost the baby, but she'll be okay."

Susan stopped listening when the doctor said baby.

"Baby?" Christina blurted. "I didn't even know she was pregnant."

Susan knew exactly how Christina felt. "How far along was she, Doctor?"

"About two months," the doctor said.

"But she was drinking," Susan said. "How could she? Why didn't she tell us?"

"I can't help you with that," the doctor said.

"At least she's going to be okay," Christina said. "Now if only we could reach Maggie and Connor. They'll know what to do. Connor and Julia are close. Maybe he knew about the baby."

A nurse bustled out. "You can go in and see her for a moment. No longer than five minutes. She's awake, but needs to rest."

They hurried into the hospital room and up to the bed.

"Man, I hate the smell of hospitals," Susan muttered.

A hoarse laugh came from the bed. "Me too."

"Julia, how are you feeling?" Christina smoothed the tangled hair from Julia's face.

"Like I've been run over by a bus." A tear tracked down her cheek.

Susan swallowed. Although she'd known Julia for several years, she'd never seen the other woman cry. She was all about good times and parties, popular with men and sometimes a bit aloof with other women. Susan had held reservations about Julia at first, but once she'd come to know the other woman, she'd realized what a big heart she had. She'd do anything for her friends.

"Can we call anyone for you?" she asked, knowing their five minutes were almost up.

"Connor. I want Connor," she said and started crying in earnest.

The nurse bustled into the room, her pale blue uniform rustling with each brisk step. She made shooing motions with her hands.

"We'll pop in and visit you after work tomorrow," Christina said.

Susan sent Julia a bright smile and followed Christina from the hospital room. Neither of them spoke until they were inside the elevator.

"Do you think Connor is the father?"

Susan shook her head. "I don't know, but why else would she want Connor?"

"I don't know. We'd better keep trying to contact him," Christina said. "You saw how upset she was."

"I wonder if Greg knows where Maggie is. I've tried everywhere else." As she spoke, Susan pulled out her cell phone and rang directory service. A few minutes later, her call connected.

"Greg, it's Susan," she said and explained the circumstances. "Is Maggie with you?"

"No. Try Connor," he said and disconnected abruptly.

Susan frowned, her confusion giving way to anger.

"What did he say?"

"He told me to try Connor. I don't understand what's going on," Susan snapped.

"Don't snarl at me." Christina stomped out of the hospital entrance and made for her car.

"Well, something's going on. I don't know what Maggie and Julia are playing at, but it's clear there's something stinky here. What happened to trust? And what about our pact?"

"Don't jump to conclusions. It might be nothing."

"Huh! You know it takes a fire to make smoke, right? What we have here is lots of smoke, so I know there's a fire there somewhere. I just can't see it yet."

Maggie cuddled up to Connor. Her bottom smarted, but she'd never felt so close to another person before. Intimate. That was the word for it. There was a new intimacy and trust between them that hadn't been present before.

"How did you know I'd like a good spanking?"

Connor's breath tickled her neck, and she pressed even closer so it didn't distract her quite as much.

"You know the blog everyone is talking about at work?"

"Yes," Maggie said, suddenly glad her back was pressed to his chest and he couldn't see her guilty face.

"I guess you could say the blog gave me the idea."

"Oh. I thought you'd want to stay away from anything like that because of what happened with your mother."

"It did worry me," he said gruffly. "Which is why I want you to tell me exactly how far you want me to go. I never want to hurt you. *Never*."

Maggie pulled away and turned to face him. She cupped his face, his jaw bristly beneath her fingertips. "I feel safe with you. In all the time I've known you, you've hardly ever lost your temper. Please don't tell me you're worried you might take after your father?"

"His blood runs through my veins," Connor said. "I worry."

Maggie smiled. "You've been brought up to respect women. I bet you take after your stepfather, Frank. I've never seen you brawl at the pub or get into a fist fight at rugby. Oh, apart from you and Greg. What's up with you two?"

"Greg and I didn't hit it off the first time we met. There's no love lost between us, and that hasn't changed."

"I trust you. I feel safe with you, but I know how you feel. My mother—my real one—is Elle Walker."

"Elle—the one dating the rugby player?"

"The same. My father is convinced I take after her and is always lecturing me on proper behavior."

Connor stroked his hand over her cheek and the corners of his mouth kicked up in a faint smile. "You have nothing to worry about, babe. Your behavior is exemplary."

Maggie let out a loud huff that came close to a snort. "My

spanking blog isn't the worst of it. I have a worse sin. When I was twenty, I ran with a fast crowd. They were the sons and daughters of my father's workmates. I thought I was so special, going out with one of the most popular guys. There were eight of us and we'd decided to spend the weekend at the beach. We stopped at a pub for lunch and I drank quite a bit. I got...um...a bit frisky." Maggie paused to draw a breath, her face heating with shame. So many times she'd wished she had refused Jason. She'd liked him so much and wanted to belong to the crowd of popular kids. "Oh, heck. This is so embarrassing." She hid her face in her hands before peeking at Connor.

"You don't have to tell me," he said.

"But I do. You were honest with me about your past, and I want to do the same." No matter what he thought about the subject. In this, at least, she intended honesty.

"We all have history, babe. You can tell me anything. I won't judge you."

She swallowed, started to talk and swallowed again, concentrating on her clenched hands. This was harder than she'd imagined. "I...Jason asked me to suck him off while he was driving. It was okay for a while, until he drove off the road and went into a ditch. I bit him," she muttered, talking faster and faster to get out the story. "He had to go to hospital and have surgery." Maggie risked a glance at Connor. His face contorted in a weird expression. Disgust, she thought. *Figured.* Her father and stepmother had borne similar expressions on their faces.

A muffled snort sounded, and she gaped at him. "You're laughing at me."

He roared then, laughing so hard tears streamed down his face. Anger stiffened Maggie's spine and she jumped to her feet. He grabbed her hand and hauled her right back. She glared at him while he attempted to control his hilarity.

"I'm sorry, babe," he said, wiping his eyes with his free hand. The other banded her wrist, halting her escape. "Tell me what happened."

"So you have more to laugh about?"

"No, so I can understand." This time sincerity emblazoned his face, and some of her pique faded.

"The press got hold of the story and some of my so-called friends leaked my identity. Everyone was talking about Penisgate. They made my life hell. They made my family's life hell, and my father lost his job over it because he worked with the same firm as Jason's father."

"And?" Connor prompted.

"Isn't that enough? My father blamed me. He said if I'd managed to control my sinful urges, none of it would have happened. He said I took after my mother and I seek attention to make myself feel better."

"Bullshit," Connor said. "None of that is true. You were young. You made a mistake. Hell, we all make mistakes. It's part of learning and growing up." He crushed her to his chest, hugging her so tight she could scarcely breathe. Then his mouth settled on hers, his hands touching her everywhere until all she could think about was his next touch. He nuzzled the hollow at her throat and pulled away, caressing every part of her with his gaze.

"We're a pair," he said. "Neither of us takes after our parents. Okay?"

She smiled, warmed by his acceptance. "Okay." At least Connor really understood her feelings because of his family situation.

He ran his lips down her neck, gently biting, tormenting her until she clung to him, her heart thudding in an erratic manner, her fingers entwined in his dark hair. He pulled away, his blue eyes twinkling down at her.

"Are you tired?"

"Of you? Never," she said, and she pushed at his chest.

Confusion covered his face until she shoved him back on the bed and straddled his chest.

"It's my turn to play," she said.

"I'm ticklish."

"Only when it suits you," she said tartly. "Man up and deal with it."

He chuckled. "Do your worst. Let me prove I can take it—like a man."

Maggie grinned and splayed a hand over his chest. She

could feel the rapid beat of his heart and knew he wanted her. Heck, his cock prodding her backside gave her a big clue.

Her finger lightly circled a flat masculine nipple. Fascinated, she watched it harden and leaned over to repeat the move with the slow slide of her tongue. A faint saltiness hit her taste buds.

Gradually, she moved down his body, lingering over hard pectoral muscles, tracing her fingers over his biceps, his ribs. He didn't say a word or try to take control, letting her explore at will. Violent? Connor Grey? She didn't think so. At the moment, the man was like a big pussy cat.

"Are you going to get to the good stuff any time soon?" he asked.

Maggie glanced up at him and winked. "Still charting unknown territory."

"You've been with men before."

"Yeah, but none of them ever let me explore like this. It's fun with you." She traced around his belly button with her tongue and paused to grin at him again. The flare of desire in his eyes sent an arrow of heat through her. Like a wave, it rushed over her skin, pulling her nipples tight and tingling its way to her pussy.

She loved him so much.

The words trembled on her lips. Aware that friends who were lovers didn't cross into this forbidden territory, she bit the words back and concentrated on giving him pleasure. If she couldn't say the words, at least she could show him and say them in her heart.

"Making love is fun with you too," Connor said in a husky voice. "Different. Exciting."

"I excite you?"

"Yeah." A hiss escaped him when she wriggled her ass against his erection and did a sexy little shimmy.

"You know knowledge is power, right?"

"Yeah?"

"That's right." And she lifted up and moved farther down his body. Without taking her gaze off him, she used a finger pad to remove a pearl of pre-come from the head of his cock. Raising her finger to her mouth, she licked it away.

His dark groan sent a thrill through her.

"I could torture you with the things I'm learning about you."

"Newsflash, babe. You're torturing me now."

"Oh, no," Maggie said. "I haven't even started with you yet." She lowered her head and took the head of his cock into her mouth, smiling faintly at his sharp intake of breath. This time she tasted the spicy tang of arousal and was fiercely glad she could do this to him. Taking a little more of him into her mouth, she licked and sucked and used her hands to massage the rest of his shaft. His hips jerked when she pumped his cock. He grew harder inside her mouth, his balls drawing up tightly when she continued to tease him. Her cheeks hollowed as she sucked harder, each wet rasp of her tongue making him shake, his muscles bunch and tense.

She'd done this before, but had never ached to give a man pleasure or play the seductress. Teasing was a double-edged sword, she discovered, because desire, liquid and molten, pulsed through her body to settle at the juncture of her thighs.

"If you keep that up, I'm going to come," he said in a gruff voice and, lucky for him, he didn't mention danger, her teeth, or the possibility of accidents.

"Precisely my idea," she said after pulling away. She reclaimed his cock and licked him with the same attention she gave to a cone of her favorite hokey-pokey ice cream.

"But wouldn't it be better if I came inside you? Or you could turn around so I could give you pleasure at the same time?"

His suggestion snared her attention. She lifted her head again. "Really?"

"Turn around and back up so I can reach."

"But you'll see my butt."

"I like your ass. Besides, I've seen it before. Turn around. *Now.*"

Somehow, Maggie found herself straddling his body and facing his groin and jutting cock. How did he do that? The minute he spoke in that tone, she seemed to obey automatically.

The wet rasp of his tongue ran the length of her slit, and she froze at the jolt of pleasure. Okay. Maybe this was a good idea. The muscles of her stomach quivered when he repeated the move.

Maggie turned her attention to his cock, but froze when quick flicks of his tongue distracted her.

"Jesus, Maggie. Watch the teeth."

"Oops, sorry. It's hard to concentrate when you do that." Inside her confidence took a beating. She should know better! Maggie waited for him to mention her confession but he didn't bring up the subject. Relaxing, she sucked him hard and laved the underside in silent apology.

"Do it again and I'll spank you. If I want a piercing, I'll have a professional do it."

Maggie bit back a relieved grin. "Okay." She ran her tongue down the prominent vein on the underside of his shaft before taking him into her mouth again.

He used his fingers and mouth, each flick and lick of his tongue like a strong intoxicant. Intense bursts of heat swirled through her, and she found it hard to focus under his delicious assault. Her thighs clamped together around his head, and all she could think of was the pleasure.

"Right, that does it," Connor said. "I don't feel safe with those teeth of yours."

"Did I bite you?"

"I bet I have teeth marks," he muttered, but his eyes glowed with humor.

Her heart started to beat faster. Did that mean he was going to spank her again? She hadn't meant to bite him. She really hadn't. But it wasn't a bad result. It sort of made her want to misbehave whenever she was with him.

Grabbing her hips, he lifted and repositioned her so she faced him again. "Ride me," he said gruffly.

"But don't you want me to kiss it better?"

He snorted a laugh. "Minx. Consider yourself on a warning. One spanking sometime this week for endangering my manhood after I specifically told you to take care."

"Yes, sir. Sorry, sir," she said, even though her grin said

the exact opposite. Maggie lifted up and guided him to her entrance, sinking down slowly until he filled her completely. "Does that feel better?"

"Much. I love the feel of your tight pussy squeezing my cock."

"How does it feel?" she asked, falling into an easy rhythm. "Describe it for me."

"Imagine sliding a sword into a scabbard. You feel snug like that but the heat is incredible. I want to go as deep as I can. The drag of the tip of my cock against your inner tissues starts to feel real good. My balls tighten and draw up and I start to feel like I'm going to explode."

"Do you feel like that now?" she moved a fraction faster, tightening her inner muscles in the way she'd already noticed drove him crazy.

"Yes," he gritted out.

"Then come," she said. "Don't hold back."

"But what about you?"

"I'm feeling really good, but this isn't a competition you know. We don't both have to come at the same time or in the same session."

"You're a treasure, Maggie Drummond."

Maggie's heart twisted, and she closed her eyes, pretending she wanted to enjoy this and concentrate when inside her heart was breaking. This was as close to heaven as she'd ever come. She loved him, and he thought she was a treasure.

Connor let out a hoarse shout, and she felt the splash of seed deep inside her. She ground down hard, and a shard of pleasure pierced her. Rhythmic pulses shot through her pussy, and she squeezed her eyes shut tight, throwing her head back as climax transported her.

Maggie Drummond was a treasure.

Maybe they could write that on her epitaph.

Maggie picked up the phone at her place with a smile at Connor.

"Back to normal," he said, pressing a kiss to her cheek.

"Are you there?" a harsh feminine voice demanded.

"Susan? What's wrong?"

"I've been trying to get you since Saturday night. Where have you been?"

"I went to visit my father," Maggie lied. "Problem?"

"Julia's in hospital. Christina and I went around to her place and found her collapsed on the floor."

"Is she okay?"

"She's asking for Connor. Do you know where he is? I haven't been able to reach him, either."

"He picked me up...uh...from the airport. He's here. I'll get him."

"Julia's in hospital," she murmured, handing him the phone.

"Susan, it's Connor. What's wrong with Julia?" He froze, a scowl furrowing his brow. "A baby. Shit. Okay. Maggie and I will come now." He hung up.

"Did I hear right? A baby?"

"Yeah, Susan said Julia is asking for me and got really upset."

Maggie's mind made the leap. "Is it yours?" she whispered, trying to keep her hurt balled up inside.

Connor took her by the shoulders and turned her to face him. The playfulness of the weekend faded, leaving a stranger. "Julia is like a sister to me. It's true we've spent a lot of time together in the past, but I have never, ever slept with her. Never."

The hurt seeped away under his intent gaze. Truth shone on his face and in his voice.

"Okay," Maggie said. "I'm sorry for doubting you."

"You know what happens to doubters?" Connor asked.

"They get spanked?"

No," he said. "They get sent to bed with no supper."

"I'll lose my beautiful curvy shape."

Connor grabbed her hand and gave her a swift kiss. "That would be a disaster. We'd better go. It must be fairly serious if they're keeping Julia in hospital. I'll drive."

They walked into the hospital room together to find Susan and Christina already present.

"We've been trying to ring you all day," Christina said.

"Susan said. I've been away for the weekend and turned off my phone."

"Connor?"

"I'm here, babe." Connor moved closer to the bed and took her hand. Maggie had never seen Julia without her make-up. Her face was pale, and huge purple circles beneath her eyes made her seem very fragile.

Maggie watched them, working to maintain a passive face. She couldn't let the surge of jealousy choking her inside free, couldn't let the others see it.

"I lost the baby, Connor. I really wanted this baby." She started to cry, and Connor dragged her into his arms, holding her and whispering soothing words to her.

Maggie swallowed, figuring Julia would like some time alone. "We'll be in the canteen grabbing a coffee," she said softly.

Susan and Christina followed her from the room.

"What do you think that's about?" Susan asked.

"I don't know," Maggie said.

"How could Julia go behind our backs and sleep with Connor?" Christina muttered. "She promised."

Cripes. "I don't think this is the time to hash it out now," Maggie said. "We don't know what happened. I didn't even know Julia was pregnant."

Susan scowled. "I wonder if Connor knew."

"About our agreement?" Maggie knew he didn't know a thing about the promises they'd made regarding him.

"That and the baby," Christina said.

"Discussing it now won't help," Maggie said. "It's more important for Julia to recover. I've never seen her look so fragile. I've noticed she's been quieter than normal. She still smiles, but she's not the same party gal."

"You don't think we should worry that Julia has broken her promise? What sort of friend does that make her?" Susan asked, a tart note in her voice.

"Susan!" Maggie stared at her two friends in shock. How would they react if they learned about her and Connor? "Don't you think she needs our support and understanding right now? Isn't friendship about forgiving?"

"Friendship is also about trust," Christina said. "Something you don't know much about if you're seeing a married man."

Maggie jerked, feeling as if the blow were physical rather than verbal. "That's enough. I know you're both upset and worried about Julia, but you're out of line. I don't think I'll bother with coffee," she said, proud of herself for keeping her voice even. "Tell Connor I'll see him tomorrow at work."

Maggie stalked away without looking back, her shoulders and neck tense, her hands curled into fists at her side. According to Connor, he and Julia had never slept together. Julia didn't deserve their bitter words.

She did.

It was true Susan and Christina could be a little judgmental at times. She knew and accepted their flaws because they had so many other good qualities. Susan volunteered at a women's shelter and worked tirelessly in raising funds for them. The women there loved her, while Christina was enthusiastic and optimistic. She was resourceful, and Maggie knew she'd done free makeovers for some of the women at the shelter. Everyone had a few character faults. She wasn't exactly Ms. Perfect. Once they realized how meanly they'd behaved, Maggie was sure they'd apologize. Besides, she wasn't entirely blameless. Maybe she should do what her conscience bid her, both to protect her heart and maintain her friendships.

Walk away from Connor.

Easier said than done. Maggie sighed when she stepped outside into the growing darkness. She heaved another sigh and crossed the road to wait at the bus shelters.

Why was love so bloody difficult?

Chapter Sixteen

"Don't you think you were a bit rough on Maggie?" Susan asked. "Bottom line, we're friends. We should support each other."

"But she's seeing a married man," Christina said. "People will get hurt, especially if he has children. Surely Maggie knows that?"

"Yeah, but are we sure Maggie and Connor aren't together? They've both been disappearing a lot during the last month."

"Greg did tell us to try Connor. Maybe we should ask Greg if he knows what's going on."

Susan shook her head. "I'm not asking Greg. I never liked the man when Maggie was going out with him. You ask him."

Christina laughed and wrinkled her nose. "*Ah-ah*! Not me. We're a pair of yellow-livered cowards."

"Speak for yourself." Susan tossed her head and sprang toward a vacant table, sliding into the seat seconds before two men.

"Coffee or tea or a cold drink?" Christina asked.

"I feel like a ginger beer."

"Is there just the two of you?" the man asked. "Would you mind if we shared?" He was tall, dark and had a dimple when he smiled.

Never one to let a chance pass by, Susan returned his smile. "Sure. Grab a seat."

His blond friend returned and grinned at Susan. "Thanks for sharing with us. It's busy in here." He slipped his arm around his friend's waist as he spoke, and the dimpled cutie leaned into him. Gay. Susan almost groaned out loud. It was true. All the good men were married or gay. Even if she made it through the initial rounds of the *Farmer Wants a Wife* competition, there was no guarantee the men would meet her expectations. "Do you mind if I ask you a question?" she asked the men.

"Sure." The man with the dimple ripped open a pack of sugar and stirred it into his coffee, knocking the teaspoon against the edge of the thick white china cup before he put it aside.

"Where do I find a man?"

"You're asking us?" Blondie's blue eyes narrowed as if he thought Susan was playing a game at his expense.

Christina arrived in time to hear Susan's question. "We're asking everyone," she said. "Good men are hard to find. You both look happy. Where did you meet?"

"We went to school together," Blondie said.

"We're doomed," Christina said in a dramatic voice. "No hope for us at all."

"That guy's checking you out," Dimples said.

Connor. Susan frowned, wondering if Maggie was right and they were overreacting.

"That's our friend, Connor," Christina said, waving. "We're here to visit one of our other friends."

Connor strode over to them, ignoring the women who stared after him. Dressed in jeans faded in interesting places and a tight shirt, with dark hair and dazzling blue eyes, the man was a major hottie. It hadn't gone to his head. Susan had always liked that about Connor.

"Where's Maggie?" he asked, glancing around the crowded canteen.

"She went home. Said she'd see us all at work tomorrow."

"I thought she'd want a ride home," Connor said, frowning. "Julia was upset, and the nurse gave her something to help her sleep. I might go home too." He lifted a hand and turned for the door. "See you tomorrow."

"Bye, Connor," Susan said.

"See you tomorrow," Christina said.

"What's wrong with him?" Dimples asked. "He looks straight."

"He's a friend. We have two other female friends and we all made a pact not to hook up with Connor," Christina answered.

"Not that Connor has ever shown interest in any of us. He goes for tall blondes." Susan grinned. "Female tall blondes."

"Why did you make an agreement like that?" Dimples asked.

Christina fiddled with her bracelets. "Because he offers a male opinion and is always truthful. We didn't want to spoil that. Besides, we love Connor. The last thing we want is jealousy between us."

Dimples and Blondie finished their drinks and left to visit Blondie's brother before visiting hours finished.

"We might as well go home," Susan said. "There's no point visiting Julia again if she's asleep."

Susan fell into step beside Christina as they walked down the corridor to the elevators. "I keep thinking about what you said about jealousy and Connor. Were we acting like jealous bitches before with Maggie?"

"I don't know. Maybe. What pisses me off more than anything is secrecy. None of us are talking to each other anymore. It's felt weird lately, like there are undercurrents."

"I want to know one way or the other," Susan said.

"And how are we going to do that if everyone keeps denying it?"

"I think we should follow either Maggie or Connor and see where they go, who they meet. That will tell us what we need to know."

"And Julia and the baby?" Christina unlocked the car doors and climbed behind the wheel. "Don't you think that would be a bit underhanded?"

"Let's eliminate one thing at a time and go from there."

"Okay," Christina said, merging with the traffic. "We might be making a big mistake, but at least we'll learn why everyone is behaving so strangely."

"Hey, babe. I missed you last night." Maggie wiped the sleep from her eyes and smiled, his husky words coming down the telephone line working better magic than a morning cup of coffee.

"I missed you too." It hadn't taken long to become used to Connor sleeping with his arms wrapped around her. "It was cold last night."

Connor laughed. "I didn't wake up with cold feet on me. I'm going to be busy today and probably won't leave my office, but do you want to meet me after work tonight? I have a project in mind. Can you meet me at Botany Town Center? I figure no one we know will see us there, and the pub there does good meals."

"It's a date." Maggie cringed the minute the words left her mouth. Friends with Benefits didn't date. They had sex. That's all. "I'll meet you at Whitcoulls," she suggested, naming her favorite bookstore and stationer.

"Make it six to be on the safe side," Connor said. "And make sure you take your cell phone so I can ring if I'm running late."

"See you then," Maggie said, hanging up with a smile. At least she had something to look forward to today.

The morning dragged at a pace slower than a snail's. Things were uncomfortable in the lunch room with Christina and Susan, although, to their credit, they tried to act normally.

Susan pulled a magazine from her handbag, and Maggie glanced at it with disinterest until she noticed the cover—the issue with her mother and the rugby player.

"It isn't fair. Look at Elle Walker. She clicks her fingers and men swarm around her," Susan said, glaring at the cover.

Maggie winced, thankful her mother had reverted to her maiden name after the divorce.

"Who's the rugby player?" Christina asked.

Susan flicked the pages of the magazine until she came to the story and color photos. They all stared at them, Maggie unwillingly.

Christina glanced up at Maggie. "You know, you look a bit like her."

"Me?" Horror laced the word. "I'm nothing like her."

Susan and Christina both look surprised at her vehemence.

"It's your features. Your eyes are the same color, and you have similar shaped noses and faces."

"I can't see it," Maggie said, wanting to change the subject and knowing her abruptness and harsh tone was attracting their interest rather than repelling it. She wished Connor and Julia were here. Right now, without the buffer and with the harsh words between them, it was hard. Add a guilty conscience and the constant speculation about her blog and Maggie couldn't wait for the work day to end.

"Do you know what time visiting hours are tonight at the hospital?" she asked.

"Seven to nine, I think. Are you going to visit Julia?"

"Yes. I have a couple of things to do first, but I should manage to get there before nine." Maggie stood and forced a smile. "I might see you there."

Greg stopped her in the passage outside his office. "I want to talk to you."

"Now? Can't it wait?"

"No." He grasped her arm and dragged her into his office, closing the door behind them.

She yanked away and glared at him. "Stop manhandling me."

"What's going on between you and Connor?"

"Nothing." She saw by his face he didn't believe her.

"I saw you the other night. Connor stayed the night."

"You're spying on me?"

"You admit it, then."

Maggie backed away until a chair stood between them. "My private life is none of your business."

"None of my— Of course it is. We're on a break, that's all. I thought you understood that. I intend to marry you."

Maggie wanted to scream. "Did you ever think of asking me?"

He broke into a broad grin. "Will you marry me?"

A snort escaped Maggie. "No, I don't love you, and I know you don't love me. I'm convenient, that's all. Leave me alone or I'll report you to management for sexual harassment." Before he could reply, she stormed from his office and slammed the door after her.

In her office, she fell into her chair, anger pulsing through her and making her hand tremble noticeably when she picked up her pen. Jerk! What did she ever see in him?

The afternoon dragged too, and Maggie didn't start relaxing until she reached Botany Town Center.

"Hi, gorgeous." The familiar husky voice stopped her by the mall center stage.

"Connor!" She flung herself at him, and he caught her, grinning and, seconds later, kissing her as if they hadn't seen each other for weeks. Her hands crept around his neck and she held on, enjoying the strength of him, his taste and the feel of his lips beneath hers.

Gradually, he pulled back. "Wow, I like saying hello to you."

Maggie slipped her hand in his and winked. "What sort of project brings you all the way out here? I'm curious."

"You know curiosity killed the cat?"

Maggie wrinkled her nose. "I'm not a cat."

"But it could earn you a spanking." He tweaked her nose with the tip of his finger. "No threat." He lowered his voice. "That's a promise."

A soft blush suffused her cheeks, if the heat in her face was any indication. She ducked her head before peeking up at him again. "A promise?"

"Yeah. You need to be on your best behavior, otherwise you'll end up with a punishment."

"So I can't ask where we're going?"

"Nope, it's a surprise." He grasped her hand and tugged her past three shops. He stopped in front of a lingerie shop. "In here."

A surprised laugh erupted from her. "A lingerie shop? I don't believe you. Most men run a mile when it comes to women's undergarments."

He dragged her inside. "I'm not most men." He leaned down to whisper in her ear. "We're going to buy you some lacey bits of nothing. Special panties for spankings."

Her heart stalled before kicking into a racy beat. "Spanking lingerie?"

"That's right." He stopped by a stand with boy-leg panties in a range of colors and fingered the navy blue cotton of the nearest pair. "So if I email or ring you and say wear the navy blue ones, it means you should wear a short skirt that I can flip up easily to spank your ass."

Maggie blinked, fire swarming through her body to settle low between her legs. "And if I wore a silky pair like this?"

"If you were wearing those ones, I'll leave them on. They're thin and you'll feel every swat through the material."

"And these ones?" She pointed to a pair of granny pants in a delicate pink.

"I think those would be perfect to wear under a school uniform."

"Some role-playing?" she whispered, because one of the assistants was heading their way.

"Yeah, what do you think? We could spice things up a little. I enjoyed the story telling we did while we were on Waiheke."

Her every fantasy coming true. That's what she thought. "You're the boss."

"Does that worry you?" he asked, his blue eyes full of questions.

"I'm not doing anything I don't want to do."

The shop assistant strutted up to them. "Can I help you?" Her eyes scanned Maggie before zeroing in on Connor. "I'd be happy to show you some of our latest arrivals."

"Thanks, but we're good." Connor waited until she walked away before turning his attention to Maggie. "Do you see anything you like?"

Maggie didn't hesitate. "You choose for me and I'll pick the sizes."

"Done deal," Connor said. "I've never been in a lingerie shop before. Do I get to watch you try them on? I've heard rumors about people doing it in the changing rooms." He waggled his eyebrows, watching her closely.

Maggie giggled. "With eagle-eye shop assistant watching us? Listening? I don't think so."

"So you've never considered letting someone watch you?"

"Have you?" Maggie stroked the silk of an almost

transparent pair of violet panties and glanced over her shoulder. "You've done it," she said flatly, disappointment surging through her because she wanted to be the one who experienced firsts with him. Ridiculous, really, since she knew there were lots of women before her. Neither of them was inexperienced when it came to sex.

"I went to a party with some friends a few years ago. We drank a lot. The party lasted the entire weekend, and there was lots of sex." He didn't try to evade the silent questions in her eyes.

Her eyes teared up and, blinking, she turned away to concentrate on the matching violet bra. If she didn't quit with her possessiveness, she'd lose him, what tenuous ties they had with their fuck buddy arrangement.

Connor grabbed several items and said to the shop assistant, "We'll try these on."

"Call me if you require any help," the woman said.

With a curt nod, he grabbed Maggie by the hand and dragged her toward the changing rooms. A grandmother-type eyed them before firmly shutting the door on her cubicle. Not exactly private, but it would have to do. Connor opened the door of the end cubicle and pushed Maggie inside. He followed, closing the door on both of them and locking it. Setting the lingerie aside, he dragged Maggie into his arms and held her quivering body. He ached to tell her how he felt, but he didn't think she was ready for the truth yet, not with so many half-truths between them.

He gave her another half-truth. "I'm not seeing anyone apart from you, Maggie. I haven't found anyone who matches up to you." She was the only one for him. Not even her need for a little kink scared him off now.

"But I'm not blonde. I'm not even tall," she mumbled.

"You're intelligent and caring. And you have the sexiest curves this side of the Bombay Hills."

"You have to say that. I'm your friend."

"Friends don't lie to each other. They're the ones who can tell the truth."

Her face closed up again, and he cursed. Damn. Wrong thing to say. When was he going to get this right? "We could tell the girls we're seeing each other."

"No."

"Why not?"

"I don't think our arrangement is anyone's business except ours."

Connor nodded, not agreeing, but deciding not to push her right here. But it was obvious he needed to push up his romancing. The last thing he wanted was to lose her to another man.

"Try these on first," he said, handing her the violet lingerie paused to study earlier.

"I don't know, Connor. I need hold and lift, otherwise I'm going to sag badly in my old age."

"Try it on anyway," he said.

She glanced at the labels, her mouth dropping open for an instant. "How did you know what size I needed? I thought we agreed I'd choose sizes."

"I did my research before I came."

"How?"

His grin brought a flush to her face, and he wanted to follow the blush to see where it ended. "I have powerful skills of observation."

Maggie moaned out loud. "Do not tell me you scoped out my lingerie drawer."

"I scoped out your lingerie drawer."

"I have granny pants in there."

"Granny pants have their own particular charms."

"Not if they have a granny in them," she muttered.

There was a startled moment of silence before he snickered. "Thank God I haven't thought of that before. Try these on," he said. "I'll be right back."

Grinning widely, Connor backed out of the changing room, shaking his head when he heard the bolt shoot home. He headed for the shop assistant who was standing behind the counter.

"I'd like a selection of panties in different colors and styles. Twelve pairs, please."

"G-strings as well?"

"Please." He shot a glance toward the changing rooms. "And a couple of full pairs." He should have felt out of his comfort zone in this women's domain. He didn't, and knew it was Maggie's influence. He followed the sales assistant around, and she sought his approval of each style and color before she added it to a gift box she'd retrieved from beneath the counter.

"Perfect," he said. "I'll check on my girlfriend and we'll probably add a couple of more sets before I pay."

"Take your time," the woman said.

Connor strode to into the changing room. "Maggie, open the door." He'd suspected she'd refuse to open it. She surprised him, opening it immediately.

"Wow, you look amazing." The violet lingerie really did things for her. Him too. He slipped into the changing room and let his gaze slide across her breasts and down across her belly. He caught the faint shadow of her sex. Lifting one hand, he stroked the tip of one breast. She gasped, and he watched with satisfaction when her nipple pulled to a tight point. "How does it feel?"

"Surprisingly comfortable."

"Should we take them?"

"Yes. I was pretty sure I wanted them, so I broke the rules and tried them on without my own panties underneath."

"Okay." He cupped her ass and kneaded it, loving her swift intake of breath. He liked keeping her off-balance, so she never knew when to expect a swift swat on the butt. He didn't mind it when she did something outrageous as an excuse to earn a spanking, but today he had in mind something a bit different. "I'm going to spank you when we get back to your apartment."

Her eyes rounded. "Why? I haven't done anything."

"Do I need a reason?"

"N-no."

"Expect a spanking, then."

Connor left the changing room with the set of violet lingerie and a grin on his face. For a man who'd hesitated about hitting a woman, he thought he was doing well. He never felt as if he was spanking her in a bad way. If he ever did it in anger, he'd cross a line. This way, the way that Maggie wanted, made for some hot loving. And afterward, when they cuddled or made love, he'd never felt so close to a woman. The crazy thing was, he could imagine a future with her.

He paid for the lingerie, and Maggie joined him.

"Ready for dinner?"

"I thought you'd changed your mind and we were going home."

"Not yet. Anticipation is a good thing, babe. What you're going to do is sit, eat your dinner and anticipate the coming night." He stopped her outside the pub and placed his mouth on hers. A slow set of nibbles and licks that drew a groan from her. Maggie gripped his shoulders, and he took the kiss deeper until a childish giggle reminded him they were in a public place. Even so, he pulled away slowly. "Anticipate," he reminded her as he opened the door and ushered her inside the English-style pub.

"Did you see that?" Christina asked with a trace of shock in her voice.

"Maggie and Connor… How could she? She denied everything. She stuck up for Julia…"

Together they watched the couple enter the pub, Connor's hand dropping to rest on Maggie's butt.

"They've been doing this for a while. Look how comfortable they are with touching each other," Christina said.

"She promised. She lied to us! Now I know why things have been weird between the five of us recently," Susan snapped, taking three steps toward the pub.

Christina yanked her to a stop. "Not now, when we're angry. Tomorrow."

Chapter Seventeen

I have a question for you. What do you think about your bottom? Do you like it or hate it? Or vacillate between the two?

I'm curvy, which means my ass is curvy, as well. Curvy. It's such a lovely word. I like saying it. I haven't always liked my body, but being with my lover has helped me come to terms with my shape.

After a good spanking, my ass hurts. It's not always easy to sit, which means each spanking lasts long after the event. It's hot. It's arousing. It's also disconcerting thinking about spanking and the resulting lovemaking while I'm at work.

Sometimes my lover bruises me—not intentionally, but it happens. He doesn't spank me every night or each time we make love, because that would be overkill. Spanking would lose some of its attractiveness for both of us.

I like to keep my skin smooth, and my gym sessions help keep my backside firm. Squats. That's the secret to a taut bum. I hate doing them, but they work.

I use a loofah and my favorite moisturizer from the Body Shop to keep my skin smooth and supple. Sometimes my lover will give me a massage, taking special care with my bottom. There is nothing better than the feel of my lover's hands stroking my buttocks.

Is it any wonder I feel the urge to let loose and misbehave? A spanking and later a massage, a cuddle. Hot sex. Works for me.

Connor shut the front door of Maggie's apartment and locked the door. As they moved into her small lounge, he turned to her. "Maggie, go into your bedroom and undress, then come back out here. I'll wait for you."

Maggie tried to hide her quick flash of pleasure and suspected she failed. "Aren't we going to talk about Julia and discuss how much better she looks? How she refuses to talk about the baby or anything that's related?"

"Nope, this is where anticipation tips over into reality." Connor winked at her. Her pulse jumped at the flare of desire in his eyes. "Don't make me wait too long."

"You're enjoying this entirely too much.

"I know." His voice had a smoky quality that had her breathless with excitement. "It's a surprise to me. I didn't realize what a turn-on it would be to smack your beautiful ass."

Her mouth went dry as he prowled toward her. The contrast between the fire in his eyes and his languid, lazy pace had her turning and fleeing to the bedroom. His soft laughter made her heart thud, her fingers tremble when she unfastened the buttons on her fitted shirt.

Somehow, she kicked off her boots and undressed, leaving her clothes in a heap on the floor. With a thumping heart and a fleeting thought for her naked vulnerability, she returned to the lounge and Connor.

"Good girl. Come here."

"Why do I feel like wagging my tail?" she muttered dryly.

He offered her a cool smile. "Wagging isn't what I want from you right now."

Oh, yes. He was getting very good at this. It was as if they'd been together for a long time and reminded her of their agreement. The casual basis of their relationship. "What do you want?"

"Curiosity killed the cat, babe." He tapped the tip of her nose with one finger. "I want you to lean over the back of the couch and wait for me."

A surge of excitement thumped her in the gut as she stared after him.

"Clock's ticking, babe," he called over his shoulder.

The excitement intensified, and she felt the surge of wetness between her thighs. Gulping, she walked toward her couch. It was the perfect height, she realized. Licking her bottom lip, she leaned over, pressing her breasts against the textured fabric. Her breathing quickened while she waited for Connor's return. The agonizing wait about killed her. First she thought about the feelings and sensations roaring through her body. Then she thought about the way she'd look to him, her buttocks raised, her legs slightly apart with her lady parts on display. She immediately shifted her stance, primly drawing her legs together.

"Put them back the way they were," Connor said.

A surge of heat flooded her face. "How long have you been standing there?"

"Long enough to appreciate the view." He walked around the front of the couch so she could see him. He carried her wooden hairbrush in his right hand. Mesmerized, she watched him tap it against his thigh several times. A shudder rocked her body.

Tap. Tap. Tap.

Her breasts prickled. She wanted to tell him to hurry, to swat her butt already, but didn't. The wait held its own sweetness, her imagination, the situation feeling like the best foreplay.

"Do you know how beautiful you look?" Connor circled the couch and studied her from all angles.

He'd removed his leather jacket, his boots and socks, and padded around her in bare feet. His black T-shirt stretched across his chest while his jeans clung to his butt and muscular thighs. Even his bare feet looked sexy. She sucked in an excited breath and waited while he did another circuit. Hunger etched on his face, and she let out a strangled moan.

"Maggie?"

"Yes?" With another deep breath, she waited, putting herself totally in his power. Maggie didn't hesitate, because she trusted him implicitly.

"If you want me to stop at any time, say television."

"Television." She swallowed. "Okay."

He ran his hand over her bare bottom, kneading her cheeks. He dipped a finger into her pussy until she squirmed a little. Without warning, he struck her on one cheek. She'd barely processed the jolt of pain when he smacked her again. Another blow followed swiftly afterward until her bottom smarted. Yet she wanted more, arching up and silently seeking another smack.

"Do you like that, Maggie?"

"Yes," she said with a tiny gasp.

"So you don't want me to stop and strip?" He cupped his hand over one buttock to feel the heat generated by his smacks.

"Yes."

"Which would you prefer?"

"You're asking me?"

"Yeah, babe. Multi choice. Do you want me to smack you again or do you want me to stop and strip?"

Maggie laughed, despite her vulnerable position. "Gee, that's a tricky one."

"Okay, time's up." Connor smoothed his hand over her ass and smacked her again. The jolt of pain smoothed out into a blast of pleasure. She felt the wet lap of his tongue over a hot spot and groaned when his hand slipped between her legs. His finger lightly circled her clit. He guided her feet apart a fraction more, and she felt the slow slide of his tongue down her slit.

She heard the rasp of a zipper, then felt the throbbing hardness of his cock poised at her entrance. With a single thrust, he slid deep, making her gasp. Fully impaled, he held still. He throbbed deep inside her. Connor dropped his hands to cup her breasts and tease her nipples to hard points.

Every part of her body was aware of him. He filled her, surrounded her. Mastered her, and she'd never felt so needed. So loved.

At last he started to move, talking to her in his husky voice the entire time.

"You feel so good wrapped around my cock. Tight. Wet. Your pussy is like hot silk surrounding me and your beautiful ass is still glowing from where I smacked you. God, Maggie. I had no idea how much I'd like doing this with you. No idea." He punctuated his words with even thrusts. Unhurried. Deep.

The pleasure built while his masculine scent surrounded her. He pressed kisses to her spine, her shoulders, and bared her neck biting down on the fleshy part of her neck where neck and shoulder met. The frissons of excitement came faster. She floated, coasting along and wondering how a body could feel so good.

His hand tangled in her hair, and he pulled until she lifted her head. Once he knew he had her attention, he increased the pace of his strokes, flesh slapping against flesh. His teeth scraped over the pulse at her neck, and she shattered, a series of tiny explosions that seemed to go on for ages.

Connor's hips jerked and he plunged into her with rapid thrusts that made the couch skitter forward. His fingers branded her flesh as she lay pliant, still awash in the aftershocks.

With a harsh groan, he stilled, his cock twitching. He released her hair and leaned forward, drawing her body against his sweaty chest. His heart thundered against her back, his breathing ragged.

"Maggie," he whispered.

Even though she kept wishing for words of love, words that would build a future, she couldn't find disappointment this time. He invested a wealth of silent meaning into her name, making her feel special.

That was enough for now.

The next morning, after arriving to stake out Maggie's apartment just before seven, Susan and Christina watched Connor leave and drive away.

"Everything has changed," Susan muttered, staring after Connor's car. "Things started to change when Maggie started her spanking blog. She's different. I don't know her anymore. The old Maggie would never have behaved this way, breaking her promise to us."

"Let's go," Christina said. "We'll see what Maggie says."

Susan snorted and climbed out of Christina's car. "What can she say? We've caught her red-handed in a lie." Memories of her past, her fiancé walking off with her best friend, rose up to taunt her. Although Maggie's betrayal wasn't quite on the same level, it made her wonder how far Maggie would go, whether she valued friendship and loyalty at all. Her mouth firmed as she fought to control the fear and anger writhing inside her. She tried to tell herself Maggie was their friend—she shouldn't judge her so harshly, but hideous memories kept shouting in her ear until she wanted to scream her pain out loud. All she could think of was how much she wanted someone special to love, a family...

They rang Maggie's doorbell and waited. Almost instantly, her voice floated through the intercom.

"It's Susan and Christina."

"Is it Julia? Wait, come on up." Maggie buzzed them inside and met them at the door in her robe. The scent of her favorite lavender shower gel wafted from her, indicating they'd interrupted her morning routine.

"What's up? Is something wrong with Julia? Has she taken a turn for the worse? She seemed okay last night when I dropped in to see her. She said they were discharging her today."

"Julia's fine," Christina said.

"Good. Come into the kitchen and we can talk while I make coffee." She sauntered away before either of them could reply, leaving Christina to close the front door.

"We want to talk to you about something else," Susan said, her gaze raking Maggie's face as she went through the motions of making coffee. It was obvious how she'd spent her night. Her mouth looked swollen, her eyes sparkling with life, despite the faint shadows beneath them. She looked beautiful. Happy.

Susan hardened her heart, shoving aside the envy threatening to break through, the wish she could find someone. "We know about you and Connor. We know you're lovers."

Maggie paled and swayed before gripping the edge of the kitchen counter to right her balance.

"You broke your promise," Christina said.

"You lied to us," Susan said, the past thumping into her like a man wielding a stick. All she could think about was the betrayal, the breaking of promises, the lack of loyalty. Her past bled into the present, and anger hardened her face into a scowl.

"But I—"

"No excuses," Susan snapped. "We all agreed Connor was out of bounds. You've changed, Maggie. I don't know you anymore."

"I don't believe it," Christina said. "You'd risk our friendship in exchange for a few weeks of him in your bed? You know what Connor's like. His relationships don't last. I can't believe you'd betray us all so you had someone to spank you."

"This is not about spanking," Maggie retorted, squaring her shoulders. "It's not like that."

"It looks like it to us." Susan ignored the sheen of tears in Maggie's eyes because if she looked too hard, the anguish she felt inside would spill out and she'd bawl.

"No, Maggie is right. This isn't about spanking. It's about friendship and trust. You made a promise and you broke it," Christina said. "Now you have to live with the consequences."

Susan knew Christina had feelings for Connor but had done nothing because of their pact. Susan watched a tear roll down Maggie's cheek and hardened her heart. Georgina had cried too, said she hadn't meant to fall in love with Susan's fiancé and begged forgiveness. Susan swallowed rapidly, the sting of tears and ache in her throat echoing her inner turmoil. Yeah, her luck with men sucked, but she'd thought she'd had a wealth of friends. Just showed what she knew.

"Wait! Let me explain," Maggie pleaded.

"I'm so angry I can't talk now," Christina snapped. "All I can think about is the lies."

"Come on, Christina," Susan said. Now wasn't the time to discuss Maggie and Connor rationally. She wanted time to regain her equilibrium. "We might as well go." Christina wasn't the only one who was angry; besides, talking to Maggie wouldn't achieve a thing. The damage was already done.

You won't last.

The words echoed through Maggie's head like an audio on a continuous loop during the entire trip to work. Tears leaked from her eyes, and she dabbed at them surreptitiously, ignoring the other commuters on the bus. One hanky became so wet she had to fumble in her purse for another. She came up with a napkin from the pub she and Connor had visited the previous night. That started her off again.

The bus came to a stop, and a teenage girl thrust a packet

of travel tissues at her when she exited the bus. "Men are pigs," she muttered as she stomped down the back steps and walked away.

Embarrassed, Maggie tried to stem her tears. Christina and Susan hadn't said anything she hadn't already thought herself. She was nothing like Connor's usual girlfriends. The fact had always worried her, yet she'd gone ahead and slept with him anyway. They'd had fun, but maybe it was time to end their agreement before she really got hurt. Aw, hell. Who was she trying to kid?

She loved him. Walking away, breaking up with him, would feel like a kick in the guts. But she had to do it. In her heart she knew they didn't have a future together. He'd already cost her friends, and somehow, she didn't think Susan and Christina were in a forgiving mood. Once they talked to Julia, she'd lose her last remaining friend.

She needed to end things with Connor before she got hurt even worse.

The bus neared her stop, and she gathered her bag, ready to spring to her feet and push her way to the exit. She stared out the window, watching a beautiful blonde woman kiss her lover. Her arms wound around his neck and he, in turn, held her tight, his hands resting on her butt.

They pulled apart and walked past the bus.

Maggie let out a pained cry of horror.

Connor.

That was Connor. How long had he been seeing her?

The bus left them behind, pulling in at Maggie's stop. In a daze, she pushed her way down the crowded aisle and stepped off the bus.

The doubt demons in her mind stood up and shouted at her. *It wouldn't last.*

Like an automaton, she made her way into the accounting offices of Barker & Johnson, catching the elevator to her floor. In the privacy of her cubicle, she went through the motions. Answering the phone. Coding bank statements. Analyzing accounts. She worked through her morning tea break, emerging only when her stomach started gnawing at her backbone.

In the lunchroom, the first people she saw were Susan and

Christina. They saw her and looked away in a measured snub. Her cheeks heated and tears prickled at her eyes. Obviously, they weren't ready to talk. Swallowing, she paid for her sandwich and left the building, deciding a walk about the Viaduct Basin might help.

People crowded the waterfront, a school group spilling from a bus into the Martine Museum. The pubs and restaurants overlooking the boats moored at the Viaduct were full with the lunchtime crowd. A raucous seagull perched on a railing, squawking at a rival.

"Maggie, wait!" Connor ran to catch up with her, a brilliant smile lighting his blue eyes.

"Connor," she said, feeling dead inside.

He frowned. "Are you okay?"

"Not really." Her heart raced while she struggled to find the words to sever their relationship. Insecurity tore at her, robbing her of speech. She couldn't believe he'd made love to her so sweetly and there'd been someone else. *Fool.*

"Maggie?" He stopped her and placed his hands on both shoulders, surveying her face closely.

"I saw you kissing a blonde this morning. You should have told me there was someone else." Her hands trembled and she clasped them tightly to hide the shake. "I think it's best if we end our agreement."

"This morning?" His frown magically cleared. "Oh, that was my cousin."

A tight sensation in her throat forced her to swallow before she could answer. "A kissing cousin, I take it?" The intended quip didn't quite come off.

"She really is my cousin."

"Since our agreement, this is the s-second blonde. The one in the pub and this c-cousin." Maggie hiccupped. "I don't kiss my cousins like that. I can't talk now. I have stuff to do." She turned away and started walking. Tears ran freely down her face, but she ignored them, intent on escape. *Please. Please, don't let him follow me.*

She rounded a corner and ducked into a busy pub she'd visited several times with her friends, and headed for the restrooms. For the first time today, luck was with her and she walked into an empty stall, locking the door after her. She grabbed a handful of toilet tissue and dabbed at her damp eyes.

He hadn't followed her.

The thought dragged a sob from deep in her chest. She knew breaking up with him was the right thing to do. The right thing for her, even if it didn't feel like it today. The lies and half-truths needed to stop.

Maggie grabbed more tissues and held them to her eyes, willing the tears to stop. At this rate, she was going to be late back to work. And the only good thing that could be said about that was that none of the others worked in the same department as her. She could avoid everyone without any trouble.

Half an hour later, feeling much calmer, she exited the stall and did a double take at her face. She looked terrible and didn't have any makeup with her to fix the damage. She wiped away the raccoon eyes and did the best she could before heading back to work.

She passed a group of the young lawyers from the law office next door and overheard them talking about her spanking blog. Maybe Susan and Christina were right and all the trouble she found herself in started with her blog.

"It's interesting," a young woman said. "It makes me want to try it out."

"I'd spank you anytime," one of the men said. "Name the date and time."

"Ew," the woman said. "I don't think so."

Everyone laughed, their hilarity and comments following Maggie into the sanctum of Baker & Johnson.

To her relief, Maggie made her cubicle without meeting anyone she knew. Sighing, she picked up her pen and started work. This day couldn't end soon enough.

Her phone rang around an hour later.

"Maggie, report to my office, please. Immediately." Greg hung up abruptly before she could reply.

"Great," she muttered, standing and striding down the corridor to Greg's office. Things couldn't get much worse. She'd talk to Greg, accept whatever assignment he wanted to give her and return to her cubicle. One hour at a time.

She tapped on Greg's door and entered.

"Shut the door behind you and take a seat." His terse tone made her look at him in surprise.

"Is there a problem?"

"The blog that everyone has been talking about for the last couple of weeks."

Oh, heck. "Yes?" A note of caution entered her voice.

"You are the author."

"No," she lied.

"No? 'By the time we arrived at the Italian restaurant on Nelson Street, my temper simmered. This particular restaurant specializes in great food and for entertainment; they have budding opera singers performing several live segments during the evening. Not only did I have to spend time with Mr. X, I had to put up with his friends and the opera. So shoot me. I like rock and pop. I can even listen to country when the mood takes me. Opera, not so much. It makes my head hurt'."

He read the paragraph from her blog before he looked at her again.

"Are you sure it doesn't sound familiar? I could have sworn I've lived through an experience very similar to that. Doesn't it sound like Toto to you?"

Maggie raised her head and glared at him. "I don't think so. There must be hundreds of restaurants in Auckland."

"Then what about this part? 'If I wanted you to look at my breasts, I'd take off my clothes. Give you a good look at them. I'd even supply a tape measure so you could see if they measure up.' Do you recognize that part?"

Maggie didn't answer, merely glared at him. He knew she'd written it. She wasn't about to make things worse by giving him more ammunition.

"You will stop writing your blog. Not only will you stop writing your blog, but you're going to delete the posts you've already written."

"No." Maggie was tired people pushing her around today. "You can't make me delete my blog."

"Thank you for admitting the blog is yours."

Bother. She firmed her mouth and said nothing else.

"Maggie, you will delete your blog when you go home tonight. I'll expect your blog to be history by the time you arrive at work tomorrow." He picked up his phone and started punching in numbers. "That is all. You can go now."

Chapter Eighteen

If there's one thing that pisses me off, it's censorship. People who try to restrict others from offering their opinions or saying what they think are worse than dirt.

My blog is private. Yes, others are free to read it. They're free to comment on each post. I don't expect them to agree with me, but I do expect sensible comments—something more than "you're stupid" and "your blog sucks".

Today, someone I know well informed me I need to delete my blog or else. Sorry. Not gonna happen. I'm not doing anything illegal. I have never mentioned names, and don't believe I have caused harm to anyone. I've never blogged at work or used work computers to read my comments. My blog has nothing to do with work. It's personal.

That is all I'm going to say on the matter. Tomorrow, it's back to spanking.

Connor read Maggie's post with concern. He knew it wasn't him. Was that why she'd run off without letting him explain?

He read the post again, none the wiser. He'd tried to call her, but she wasn't answering her phone, letting the calls go through to voice mail. When he'd tried to confront her at her apartment, there had been no reply. Connor wasn't sure if she was there or not. Frustration simmered through his gut at his lack of success.

At least he had one way of contacting her.

Dear Bad Ass,

It sounds as if you had a shitty day. You're right to stick up for yourself and refuse to delete your blog. It's private and doesn't have anything to do with your job.

If you blog at work or use work time to do your posts, then an employer might have a case against you, but from what you've said, your blog is strictly a private one.

How are things going in your spanking world? Has spanking met your expectations or has the reality disappointed you?

Connor hoped she'd give her honest reaction to spanking. Maggie had said she'd enjoyed it, and he thought she'd relished the times he'd smacked her curvy bottom. When he thought about it now, he couldn't believe how wrong he'd been to hesitate. It was wrong to close himself to new experiences without considering different angles. His encounter with Maggie had shown him that. He didn't think he'd ever get into the BDSM scene and didn't want a true submissive, but having Maggie under his control in the bedroom made him hot. The resulting sex was some of the best he'd ever had, the closeness and intense satisfaction after the event living with him still.

But Maggie thought he'd lied to her about his cousin. She was avoiding him at work. Damn Sylvie and her impish sense of humor. He intended to wring her neck the next time he saw her. He cursed under his breath. Hell, he'd admire the adroit way Maggie shunned him, if it wasn't so bloody frustrating.

And something was up with the rest of the girls. None of them were talking to each other. Julia was home now. He'd picked her up after work and driven her home. She'd obviously wanted to tell him something, but had stopped at the last moment, bursting into tears instead. He'd done the only thing he could—holding her and murmuring soft words of nonsense until she'd cried herself dry.

Although he'd offered to stay with her, she'd said she wanted some time alone. Hell, when had things become so screwed up that none of them were talking to each other? They were best friends. While his mates might rib him for hanging out with chicks, he'd known they were envious of his relationship with the women. At the start, a couple of them had accused him of being gay, but over the years, the parade of girlfriends through his life had set them straight.

Cursing softly, he returned his attention to his email.

I love spanking a woman, hearing her soft cries when I give her a surprise swat. I like seeing the marks I've made on her butt. I always thought I'd feel terrible guilt.

The first time, I was horrified and worried I balanced on a slippery slope. I imagined I could turn into a violent man. It hasn't happened. I love touching and kissing a woman's bottom. It's so curvy and plain sexy.

It's a way of connecting with a woman, one I would have missed if I hadn't explored and tried new things.

Kinky Lover

Connor reread his email and hit send, watching the email flash off the screen. Damn, he had it bad. He'd never had another woman get to him like Maggie. She wasn't even his type.

He considered that thought for a moment and smirked. Nah, Maggie was his type. It was the blondes who were cast in the wrong part.

He waited in case Maggie replied, but after ten minutes, he decided to power down his laptop and have a couple of drinks with his flatmates before hitting the sheets.

Maggie slept fitfully, tossing and turning, finally dragging herself out of bed just shy of six. Another Friday. At least she'd have the weekend to regroup. Her top lip curled. *Mope.* She showered and dressed for work. Ready way too early, she decided to check her blog and email before going out for breakfast.

She smiled when she noticed an email from Kinky Lover. After reading his email, she composed one of her own.

Dear Kinky Lover,

Thanks for the support. Yesterday was a shitty day, but hopefully today will be a better one.

As you can see, my blog is fully intact and I'm not caving into demands to delete it. I believe asking me to delete my blog is an infringement of my rights.

Ever since I read the erotic romance about spanking, I was intrigued. Now that I've investigated the real world of spanking and learned more, there's no way I'm going back to vanilla. I don't have a partner at the moment. When I do hook up with another man, it will be with openness. I'll tell him straight up that I'm into spanking. I'm not interested in a relationship that doesn't include a bit of kink. I intend to make my needs clear right from the start.

Having said all that, I know it won't be easy. Finding my first partner was difficult. Ah, but the rewards. Yeah, it hurts, but after a while the pain transports into a sort of euphoria that's hard to explain. The trust and closeness—I guess you'd call it intimacy—is incredible.

Bottom line (ha-ha, no pun intended) is spanking does it for me, enhances a relationship and makes it special. I'm a true believer.

Big Bad Ass

Half an hour later, Maggie sat in a café near work, watching the ferries come and go on the harbor. She picked up a piece of toast and replaced it on her plate. Eating was the last thing she felt like at present. Instead, she sipped her coffee. People-watched. Most hurried, their coats wrapped around them to ward off the winter chills. Maggie thought they looked like a flock of dull blackbirds or whatever sets blackbirds hung out in together. They had their heads down and none of them appeared happy about going to work. A few school children blended in with dark-colored uniforms, but it was the tourists who stood out with their bulky backpacks and bright T-shirts and coats.

She glanced down at her short black skirt and matching jacket. When she'd changed her wardrobe, she'd gone with a lot of black, since it suited her, but maybe she'd invest in a few colors. A winter's day in Auckland was gray enough without her adding more black.

Sighing, she stood and left the café for work. Friends were like bright colors. They made everything fun and the day full of laughter.

Maggie settled into the routine of work with relief. Today she was ready to input the accounting codes into the computer. It was easy work, although she needed to concentrate, and the morning passed quickly. She debated skipping morning tea before deciding that was plain childish.

Susan and Christina sat at their normal table with a couple of guys she didn't know. She grabbed a coffee and asked if she could join another group who had an empty seat at their table.

Maggie slipped into the seat and almost jumped up again when she found the animated chatter she'd noticed earlier was about her blog.

"Did you read the spanking blog today? The woman is in trouble at work because of her blog."

"I'm not surprised," a woman said. "It's not the sort of stuff a business wants their employees mixed up with. It's not normal."

"What's not normal?" Maggie asked with a clear snap in her voice. "Who are we to judge what's normal and what's not?"

A woman she recognized as an accounting clerk from one of the other sections leaned forward, her eyes as round as coffee mug. "You mean you'd let a man spank you?"

Maggie shrugged. "I guess it depends on the man and how much I trusted him. It would depend on the circumstances."

Her comments started a lively debate. Maggie concentrated on her coffee, tired of the discussion. She didn't care what other people thought about the subject. Her opinion mattered. Period.

"Ms. Drummond." Greg's stern voice cut through the chatter, and she straightened from her slouch, her spine hitting the back of the chair.

"Yes?"

"My office, when you've finished your break." He strode off, and she pulled a face at his back. Several of the women giggled. Maggie rolled her eyes. What was this? School all over again? Unable to face another mouthful of coffee, she stood and followed Greg.

"Close the door behind you."

Maggie followed his orders and shut the door with a faint click.

"Have you deleted your blog?"

Maggie's chin jerked upward. Her eyes narrowed. He hadn't even looked at her, instead concentrating on his computer screen. "No."

"Do you intend to delete your blog?"

"No."

Greg nodded slowly, finally switching his attention to her. "I'm sorry to do this, but you're not the woman I thought you were. Skulking around with Grey, and writing scandalous blogs. Using the Internet during work hours for private matters. I've given you every opportunity to follow my orders. Stop by your desk to pick up your personal belongings. I'll have a security guard escort you from the building."

"What?" She stared at him dumbly, shock roaring through her.

"You're fired. I don't want to see you again. Shut the door on your way out."

On trembling legs, Maggie staggered from Greg's office. She slammed the door so hard the inner walls shook and two people popped their heads from their offices to see what was happening. On the plus side, it seemed as if Greg didn't intend to pursue her any longer.

A uniformed security guard stood by her desk, waiting for her arrival. Workers arriving back at their cubicles after morning tea stared. The whispering started.

Refusing to cry, Maggie bit down on her bottom lip, collected her handbag and a couple of personal items from her desk. The security guard watched with an eagle eye. Maggie wanted to tell him she wasn't interested in stealing her hole punch or a box of pens.

"I'll leave the stapler," she said in a sweet voice.

He stared at her, his face impassive.

"I'm done," she said a few minutes later. With her shoulders back and her head held high, she stalked down the corridor, the security guard following her like a bad smell.

Now wasn't the time to fall apart. She could do that later when she was alone.

Damn. *Fridays really sucked.*

I said I wasn't going to mention censorship and work again, but reality intruded in my life today. One of the associate partners fired me for refusing to delete my blog. He asked me if I'd deleted my blog or intended deleting it. When I said no, he told me to collect my personal belongings and leave.

He fired me.

I'm in shock right now. I'm not even sure they can do that. My head has whirred in circles ever since I arrived home. I didn't use my computer to look at my blog comments or do a post, but I have used it for other personal stuff. I'm not alone. A lot of my fellow employees did the same thing. Personal use of work computers was the reason people noticed my blog. Or at least that's what I surmise. I know they were investigating usage, because we had a memo come around about personal use.

I thought about consulting a lawyer who specializes in wrongful dismissal. The truth is I just want to forget the whole sorry mess. Maybe a fresh start is a good idea. I shouldn't have any trouble getting a new job since there are plenty of administration and office jobs around. I can probably get a job at another accounting firm without too many problems.

Chapter Nineteen

No reference. No job.

It was as simple as that.

Maggie scanned the situations vacant section of the *Herald* and circled the various accountancy related jobs she could apply for. Three weeks of job hunting and ringing around recruitment agencies had made Maggie consider the realities.

She didn't have enough money to pay the rent due next week.

Barker & Johnson wouldn't give her a reference.

No, not quite right. They'd give her a reference, but one stating the period she'd worked for them. That was all.

So far, prospective employers had taken one look at the damning sentence and started asking pointed questions. There was no point lying, because all they needed to do was ring Barker & Johnson. Despite the privacy act, they were able to do this because she'd completed a form to say they could ask for information.

A vicious circle. She was screwed no matter what she did.

Maggie clicked her pen then started tapping it on the newspaper, each rap louder than the last. Maybe she should try something else. Huh! No maybe about it. With one hundred dollars in her check account and a rent payment due, she couldn't afford to be picky.

Maggie studied the rest of the jobs, ones she wouldn't have considered in the past. She circled several. Shop assistants. Jobs in cafes. Waitressing. She had experience with most of them after working during her student days. Maybe they wouldn't mind the lack of a reference, especially if she could round up some character references to prove her honesty and reliability.

Sighing, she picked up the phone and started ringing for appointments. Several required email applications, and she followed the instructions in each particular advertisement.

The phone rang and her heart leapt. Connor? He'd rung a lot during the first week, but she'd ignored his calls and thumps on her door, leaving her apartment only when she knew he wasn't outside. Now, she was feeling her solitary state and had thought about ringing him, giving him a chance to explain.

"Hello."

"Ms. Drummond, this is Max Lynn from the National Bank. I'm ringing to talk to you about your check account. It's gone into overdraft."

"No. No, I have just over one hundred dollars in there. One hundred and twelve dollars to be precise."

"You are two hundred and four dollars in OD." The clipped voice rang with truth and her gut roiled. "You need to bring the account back into credit. When is your next paycheck due?"

"I...I'm not working at the moment."

"I see."

Maggie swallowed. What did he see? She wanted to ask, but didn't think smart-ass questions were appropriate right now. "I'm looking for another job and have several interviews this afternoon. Is it possible to arrange a short-term overdraft facility?"

"We can discuss your situation," he said, although Maggie heard the silent doubt in his voice. "Can you come into the branch tomorrow at ten-thirty?"

"I have job interviews for most of the morning. I could come in around two."

"I will see you then." He hung up, leaving Maggie gripping the phone so hard it left an imprint on her palm. Unshed tears shrouded her vision. She blinked and one trickled slowly down her cheek. Her hand shook when she set the phone back on the charger.

A sob tore free. Everything had gone so wrong. And she was lonely with no one to talk to. She missed Connor more than she cared to admit, her heart aching with the loss.

A glance around her apartment brought memories she didn't want. Her naked, stretched over the back of the couch. A quiet drink with Connor. Down and dirty laughter and off-color jokes with her girlfriends.

Loneliness gnawed at her, underlining her current position.

She had to pay her rent. And tomorrow she had to get a job, no matter what it was. She could always keep looking for something better once she was back on her feet.

A second glance around the room brought an idea. She had to sell some of her stuff to at least to make the next rent payment. Without friends, she hardly needed furniture.

With a new sense of purpose, she wandered around her apartment and made a list of things to sell. She'd list them on the Internet auction site, *Trade Me*. That would bring her some cash, and once she'd paid her rent, she'd clear her overdraft.

It felt good to have a plan.

Friends. It's funny you don't realize how important they are until you lose them.

I had four really good friends who I met through work. I'm not going to go into details, but life has sucked recently. As you know, I lost my job, and I don't see my friends these days. I miss them. I miss their teasing and the way they knew my good points yet weren't above giving me a hard time for stepping out of line.

Friends are there for you through the good and bad. They don't judge. They support. They're honest with you and worthy of trust. They tell you if your skirt is tucked into your pantyhose before you leave the restrooms or if there's part of your lunch stuck between your teeth.

They're the first people you turn to when you're down and when it comes time to celebrate, friends are the ones you ring to share exciting news. It's never a contest with friends. It's about support and encouragement, bolstering each other up in the bad times. Celebrating the good times, and lots of laughter in between.

That's the thing about friends. They love you for who you are not who you should be. True friends are like gold. Treasure them.

Connor read Maggie's blog post, his throat thickening with emotion. Men didn't cry, but dammit, he wanted to bawl. He could read between the lines. None of them had treated her very well. None of them were talking to each other. Susan and Christina avoided him at work. He and Julia saw each other every few days, but they didn't really talk. Since her hospital release, she'd become distant, a shadow of her former carefree self, and she refused to talk about the baby or its father.

She hadn't returned to work, although physically, he thought she was okay. Losing the baby had leeched away her laughter and joy in life. He wished he knew who the baby's father was, because he'd love to punch him in the nose hard enough to make it bleed.

Dear Bad Ass,
If I was there with you, I'd take you into my arms and hold you. It sounds like you need a hug.
Kinky Lover

A reply jumped into his inbox almost immediately, surprising the hell out of him.

Dear Kinky Lover,
I need more than a hug. I'm thinking a good spanking followed by a bout of hot, sweaty sex might be the only thing that will work. It's not gonna happen, but a girl can dream.
Bad Ass

A slow grin spread across Connor's face. He might not be in the same room, but he had an idea. It might work out if he played Maggie exactly right.

Dear Bad Ass,
If I were there with you, I'd walk into the room and take your hand. Without saying a word, I'd lead you to your bedroom, put you over my knee. Imagine my hand smoothing over your bottom. You're laughing, squirming a little. Enough to bring my cock to attention. I lift my hand and strike your buttocks. You still have

your clothes on, a short little skirt and a shirt that skims all your curves without looking slutty. I swat you again and your entire body jerks, but you're still laughing.

"This is serious," I tell you. "You've misbehaved and must be punished so you'll never do it again."

You giggle and shoot me a saucy wink when you look at me over your shoulder. "I like misbehaving."

I know this. I know you misbehave on purpose so I'll give you a spanking. You play the brat, and I play the stern disciplinarian, ready to do my duty.

The truth is I enjoy the spanking sessions as much as you do. We both play our parts and the spanking acts as great foreplay.

I lift up your skirt, baring a pair of plain cotton panties. They look surprisingly staid under your sexy black skirt and not what I was expecting because I can see you're wearing a lacy bra. The lace has played peek-a-boo with me all day.

I cup part of your buttock with my hand, feeling your body heat through the cotton. You groan softly and I know if I slipped my fingers between your legs, I'd find you ready for my cock. My body knows this too, blood speeding south to my shaft. I ignore the prickle of pleasure, knowing it will become better, more urgent, if I build the tension between us.

Without any warning, I smack you again. A series of slaps across your butt cheeks, varying the angle and the intensity. I pull down your cotton panties and take a minute to touch your silky skin. I love your ass—looking at it, touching and kissing it.

I feel the heat generated by my hand, but your bottom is only faintly pink.

"Do you want a good spanking?"

"I've been very naughty," you say. "Santa crossed me off his list yesterday."

I grin. I can't help it, because you're so irreverent sometimes. I can imagine what you were like as a child—always with your hand in the cookie jar and an innocent smile on your pretty face.

I think about it and give you three swift smacks. The crack of my hand on your flesh is loud in the bedroom, the sound sweetened by your soft cries, your words of apology. I know you're sorry right now. I know that. Tomorrow, that's a whole *different story.*

I feel the heat of your skin. It's a pretty pink blush with a few red overtones. I take a moment to appreciate your beautiful ass, leaning over to kiss you. This close I can smell your excitement and can't resist touching you intimately. I part your legs a fraction and see the spanking has worked its magic. The lips of your labia are pouty and swollen, glistening with your juices. I slide a finger along your slit and lift it to my mouth.

"Turn your head," I say. You turn your head, your eyes widening when I lick your juices off my finger.

"Get off my knees and unfasten my jeans." I couch it as an order because I know it makes you hot. Your hands fumble with my belt buckle, and your brow furrows in a cute little frown. Finally you manage to pull down my jeans and scoop my erection out of my boxer-briefs. You stare at the swollen crown and slowly lick your lips.

"Lick me," I say because that's what I want too—your greedy hands and mouth on my cock.

You lick me carefully, teasing my slit and letting your tongue cruise around the rim, your fingers holding me firmly. It feels so good, I know I could let go and come right now. The part of my brain that is still thinking decides it could be better yet. You could straddle me, take my cock deep into your pussy. We could kiss, touch. Tease each other until neither of us can stand it for a second longer.

Soon we're doing everything I've thought about. With our clothes cast aside, you're straddling my legs. You lift up, guiding my cock to your entrance. Then you sink down slowly, so slowly I feel your inner tissues parting—the incredible pleasure of being inside your snug pussy. You set a slow pace, lifting and falling on my cock while I yank at your buttons and scoop one breast from the cup of your lacy bra. I take your nipple into my mouth and suck, your taste and scent swirling around me.

You lean into me and nip the sinews of my neck, the muscles of my shoulders. The need rises between us and you start to move faster. Short, choppy jerks that almost make you fall off my knees. I grab your hips to steady you. My balls are tight, the cries of pleasure coming from you driving me closer to climax.

You're close too. Your eyes are closed. Your breath is coming *in quick gasps. I pinch your nipple and you throw your head back, grinding your clit against the root of my cock. With one of your hands, you touch yourself, desperate for release, and it's so damned sexy. A real turn on for me.*

I pinch your nipple again, and suddenly you're shuddering, squeezing my cock with your inner muscles, the ripples of pleasure sweeping you away.

I grab your hips and surge into you, a series of fast thrusts that feel great. My balls lift, their tightness feels bloody good. Then I shoot. It's fantastic.

You collapse against my chest, both of us breathing hard. I lift you up and remove the rest of your clothes. After putting you on my bed, I strip properly and lie beside you, our naked bodies sticky and smelling of sex.

I draw you into my arms and glance at your ass. It's still a pretty pink. I smile because this game between us is better than good. It's magnificent.

Kinky Lover

The phone rang.

"Do you want me to get that?" Sylvie, his cousin, shouted from the lounge.

"Yeah." He was in no condition to appear in front of Sylvie. Although they were cousins, they weren't related by blood, a fact Sylvie liked to reiterate on a regular basis. He wished she'd go home. In fact, he was pretty close to chucking her out. They didn't have room for her at the flat, and as far as he was concerned, she'd outstayed her welcome. Connor read his email through and shifted in his chair, yanking at his jeans to accommodate his cock. Damn, he wished Maggie were here in his bedroom instead of across the city in another suburb. And he wished she'd answer his calls or return his messages. He hit send and let his breath ease out while he waited for developments. He'd either never hear from her again or he'd get a reply.

He knew which option he preferred.

And if this didn't work, he'd try something else.

Failure wasn't an option.

"You've got the job. Can you start tonight?" The elderly proprietor of Medieval Times looked like a benevolent grandfather. She knew it was all an act, because she'd heard him putting a supplier in his place a few minutes earlier.

Maggie smiled when what she really wanted to do was hoop and holler. "Tonight is fine."

"Good. See Eva and she'll give you a uniform." His gaze drifted to her breasts and back to her face. "You'll make a good wench."

"Thanks." As long as he didn't think he could make free with the wench's boobs. She was so relieved to get a job, even if it was in a theme restaurant that relied heavily on the waitresses' assets.

At this stage, she couldn't afford to be fussy, and the pay was good. Even better, the job came with a meal, something more substantial than the rice and pasta she'd existed on for the last month.

Maggie collected her uniform from Eva and returned to her apartment. A free afternoon loomed, one where she could actually relax instead of job hunt and watch the bids on the possessions she'd put up on *Trade Me*.

After ringing Connor the other day, she'd officially given up on him. The woman who'd answered had giggled when she'd said she was Connor's cousin.

"I'm not really his cousin," she'd confessed, giggling again. "That's just what we tell people for simplicity and to avoid explanations."

"So what are you?" Maggie had demanded.

"What do you think?" the woman cooed.

Maggie had snapped out a naughty word and slammed the phone down. If Connor intended to lie to her then she still didn't want to talk to him.

An hour later, Maggie perched on a stool at her kitchen counter, her laptop powering up. She signed into her email account. An email from *Kinky Lover*.

Grinning, she opened it, a sense of real anticipation fluttering through her stomach. Since flipping him an email saying she'd prefer sex, that's what he'd given her. Raunchy cyber sex.

She couldn't wait to read what he'd written this time.

Mindless sex is good sometimes. I like a good no-strings fuck as much as the next guy, with no expectations on either side. I know there are women out there who like the same thing—the professional women who are too busy to deal with the nuances of a relationship, the careful building and romance.

Engaging the mind brings a new element to the sexual act.

Find a quiet place. I want you to feel comfortable. Strip off all your clothes. No, don't hurry. Remove them slowly, one at a time. Today I'm going to engage your mind, play your body like a musical instrument...

Maggie continued reading, her breathing becoming faster, louder. Kinky Lover had a way with words that really got to her. Made her hot. Made her shiver. Made her want to know what he looked like.

He was the one bright spot in her day.

At first, she'd worried about it. Now she went with the flow. Took pleasure in following his instructions.

Stand in front of a mirror and watch the reactions of your body while you touch it. Run your fingers down your chest, skimming over your breasts until your nipples pull tight. Take one finger and circle your nipple. Do you feel that? Finger your nipple. Give it a sharp tug. Think of how it would feel if it were my fingers doing the same thing. I'd fondle your nipples until they darkened in color, then I'd start to use my tongue and fingers, all the time telling you how beautiful you are, how much I want to fuck you.

I'll touch you everywhere: your breasts, your arms, drift my fingers across your ribs, your collarbone. I'll lick around your belly button, run my fingers up and down your legs. Even sucking your toes would make me happy.

Touch yourself, and imagine that I'm there with you, standing behind you. You can see my hands in the mirror, darker against your pale skin, while I touch you. You shiver as my hand drifts down to your pubic bone, your eyes glittering. A sharp inhalation. A soft sigh. I hear them both when my fingers skin across your folds. I want to taste you, but first I indulge my other senses. My sight because you look so beautiful as arousal claims your body. Your breathing is quicker, your eyes darker while a flush stains your cheeks. And of course touch. I like the creamy smoothness of your skin, your soft, shiny hair and the coarser hair guarding your secrets.

Maggie swallowed, pausing to fan her face. She felt the heat in her cheeks, the edgy prickle and flip of her stomach as she read his words.

A magical seduction.

The man was a maestro, adept at his craft.

She skimmed the rest of the page, closing her eyes briefly when she reached the part about touching herself intimately and smoothing her juices over her clit. She groaned softly, checked her watch and walked into her bedroom. It held nothing but her bed and an old wall mirror, her clothes sitting in neat piles along the wall where her dresser had once stood.

Maggie removed her clothes, carefully folding each item of apparel before she removed the next. Fully naked, she went to stand by the mirror, studying her body closely.

A combination of exercise and lack of money for food had slimmed her body down. Still curvy with big breasts, she would never be waif-thin, but Maggie thought she looked pretty good. And after following Kinky Lover's instructions, she'd feel better too.

Sex, the wonder drug.

She watched herself in the mirror, palming her breasts and squeezing the soft globes. A ripple of pleasure pulsed through her, sharp enough to bring a gasp. She stroked and tugged until her nipple burned, the hint of pain burgeoning into sharp arousal. When she widened her stance, she could see the juices gleaming on her sex, the sharp tang of arousal rising in the air.

Fascinated, she studied her body. The changes in it. The deep sparkle in her eyes, the flush of her cheeks. Her elevated breathing.

Her legs trembled as arousal shimmered through her. For the first time in weeks, she felt alive. Sexy.

All she lacked was a good man.

Chapter Twenty

Connor walked into the lunchroom and saw Julia, Christina and Susan sitting together. None of them were talking to each other. They were ignoring him too.

Bloody ridiculous.

Maggie wasn't there, either. Plain wrong. He picked up an empty coffee mug, squeezing his hand around it until his knuckles whitened.

With a coffee in hand, he strode toward the table where the girls sat, still in silence.

"How are you?" His lips curled in self-derision. *Nothing like the polite niceties to get started.*

"Connor!" Christina seemed startled by his presence. Heck, they all did.

"For fuck's sake," he muttered, knowing the swearing would piss them off. "Did you think I wouldn't talk to you? I'd like to think we're still friends. The reason I like hanging out with you all was because you never pulled this girly shit."

The three women glanced at each other before looking back at him.

"Have you seen Maggie?" Julia asked.

"No, she said she didn't want to see me again." Connor wouldn't say it out loud, but Julia looked like shit. Sad. Fragile.

"Why?" Susan asked.

"That's private," Connor said. "Maggie might be refusing to see me or take my calls, but I love her, and I want her back. You're all going to help me."

They stared at him, their reactions varied but all containing varying degrees of shock.

Christina shut her gaping mouth before saying, "You're really serious about her?"

"Yes." *Serious enough to want her permanently.* He hated his empty bed and missed her like hell. Their emails were the highlight of his day. Not even the upcoming final against the North Shore Raiders was enough to excite him.

"You can't help who you love," Julia said, a hitch in her voice.

Connor's heart ached when he saw the sheen of tears in her eyes. He spoke quickly in the hope of staving off an uncomfortable bout of crying. Every time he offered to listen, she started crying. In the end, he'd decided to wait. She could keep her secrets. Julia would talk when she was ready. "I've loved Maggie for a long time."

"You love her? What about the parade of blondes?" Christina demanded.

"Yeah! What she said." Susan shot him a challenging look, her brows arching up in emphasis. "If you love Maggie, why so many blondes?"

Connor glared back at them. "I don't kiss and tell. You'll have to take my word on it. Maggie is the one I love, the one I want." He'd finally gotten rid of Sylvie by making her face the truth. He was in love with another woman. Then he'd introduced her to some of his rugby teammates and she'd moved into her own flat. Now it looked as if she might hook up with his flatmate.

"Why all the sneaking around?" Susan demanded.

"Susan, you know why—" Christina cut off abruptly, her eyes widening behind the lenses of her glasses.

"Spill," Connor said in a tight voice. He'd guessed there was something else going on with the women.

"In hindsight, it wasn't such a good idea. After we met you, we decided we liked having you around, your male input and the way you never hit on any of us. You treated us like friends, almost like sisters. We liked that and didn't want to screw things up. We decided we'd make a pact and promised we'd never hit on you or go out with you in a romantic way." Julia shrugged, her discomfort doing nothing to halt the burning anger inside Connor.

"And Maggie broke the pact," Connor said, his voice rough around the edges. "So you pushed her away when she needed you most."

"We didn't exactly push, but we weren't nice either." Christina scowled. "You don't have to glare. We are sorry. You've made your point."

"It's weird without Maggie around," Julia said.

"The next time you see her, you're going to act friendly instead of snubbing her," Connor ordered. "She needs her friends now."

"She's not answering her phone," Julia said. "I rang her a couple of days ago to thank her for the flowers she sent me."

"Has anyone seen her?" Connor asked.

"No," Susan said.

"You know Greg sacked her because of the blog," Connor said.

"The official story is it's because she used the Internet during work hours," Susan said.

"Bullshit." Connor picked up his coffee, took a sip and discarded it. Cold. "Maggie hardly ever used the computer for personal stuff. There were other worse offenders who should have been made an example of before Maggie."

"Greg is a prick," Julia said.

"Pompous," Christina agreed. "And it's not fair. Maggie should take a case to the employment tribunal."

"She won't do that," Connor said, thinking about her mother and father and her past. She wouldn't want people gossiping about her or the publicity.

"Greg wasn't right for Maggie. You're much better," Susan said. "We all noticed her growing confidence, but didn't know why."

"What if Maggie doesn't want to get back together with you?" Christina asked.

Connor stared at her in shock, his gut lurching with a jolt of fear. He didn't want to consider that possibility. Instead, he'd focus on his plan. "If that's what Maggie wants, I'll walk away." He forced out the words while inside his mind screamed at him.

The words were a lie. He'd do anything to change Maggie's mind.

Undress and lie on your bed. Close your eyes.

You hear me open a drawer and know I've pulled out our favorite rope. It's soft so it won't scratch your delicate skin. Imagine me straddling your body, dragging the end of that soft rope over your shoulders and lower across your breasts. I use it as a massager, a mere scrape of fibers across your skin, and sometimes I change the pressure so it digs into your muscles, the sensation almost painful.

I awake your nerve endings until they sing and your sex tingles. Every one of my touches zaps its way there until your tissues are damp and your juices run from your pussy.

I start to use my mouth, kissing parts of your body that don't normally receive that type of attention, and gradually I tie you. I loop the rope around your legs, tying them apart so your pussy flowers and blooms for me. I imagine the cool air feels good on your swollen tissues, the contrast another layer of sensation.

Soon your arms are secure and you can't move. You're totally at my mercy. I kiss your lips, and you groan. You want me to fuck you, but I know it can be better, the need more urgent yet.

I suck at your neck, nipping then laving your flesh. You like being helpless and at my mercy. I like having you that way. It's a real turn-on for me, seeing your swollen lips, your taut muscles as you strain toward me, desperate to end the ache coalescing in your pussy.

You beg me to take you, to ram my cock deep until the pleasure takes us both.

Laughing, I say no. I flick your tight nipples, licking around the areola. I tease them, tightening my fingers until the blood rushes there, the pain an echo of pleasure in your sex. You arch upward, attempting to push me, make me lose control.

"Don't move," I say. The words are an order, and you know it. I haven't finished with you yet. I touch and tease you from head to foot until you are a quivering mass of desire, desperate for release. Desperate for me.

Your lips are swollen, your eyes glazed, yet I have never seen a woman look more beautiful. I love looking at you, knowing

I have the power to create this sort of reaction in you.

Without a word, I untie the ropes holding you captive. You're confused. Nervous. I can see it in the way you look at me and the fine tremor of your body.

"Turn over," I order.

You send me another uncertain look before you slowly turn over to lie on your stomach. Quickly I tie you again. You are my captive, mine to do with what I will.

I know you're unsure. It's a turn-on for me knowing you still trust me enough to follow my orders blindly. I smooth my hand over your ass. You start, your surprise a sharp intake of breath. I tap my hand down on one cheek and quickly wind up into a spanking. You gasp. I know I've surprised you. You adjust quickly.

From where I'm sitting I can see your pink folds and the way your juices glisten. Along with the bite of pain comes a wash of pleasure. Your butt is a delightful pink, a shade deeper than your sex. Your clit is a hard button protruding from its hood.

Finally, I stop spanking you, about to explode. I move up behind you and leaning on my elbows, I guide my cock into your tight sheath. There is nothing sexier than watching my cock disappear into your body, hearing your encouraging cries and feeling the tight squeeze of your cunt.

"Please," you beg.

I push into you, halting when I'm balls deep to enjoy the pulsing feel of you surrounding me. Then I can't wait any longer. I draw back and thrust into you. It's hard and almost brutal. We're both grunting, but I can feel you lifting up into my thrusts. You're encouraging me, reaching for the orgasm I know is swelling through you, because it's starting to tingle in my balls too. I can feel it, and it's so good.

You explode, a scream ripping from deep in your throat. Seconds later I follow as the pulses of your pussy milk me to completion...

Maggie groaned, her clothes feeling heavy on her sensitive skin. She ached, each step toward her bedroom almost killing her. The emails from Kinky Lover were becoming hotter. More explicit.

"Who the heck are you? Are you a pervert, or someone I should get to know?" she muttered, ripping her clothes from her body and tossing them aside. She fell onto the bed, her hand stroking between her legs almost before she hit the mattress.

It didn't take much. A pinch of her nipple. A stroke of her finger, the liquid squelch bringing a rush of embarrassment to her cheeks. She came with an orgasmic rush, the tight coil in her belly unraveling until she drifted down.

Maggie laid there, heart pounding while she analyzed her reaction. She was obsessed with Kinky Lover, whoever he was. She raced home from work to check her email and checked it before she left for work. Hooked by cybersex.

At least she wouldn't catch any nasty diseases.

Maggie glanced at her watch and realized she needed to move or she'd be late for the job interview she had scheduled. She couldn't blow it off, because she needed a second job at the local pub to subsidize her wages. Hopefully, another job meant she could work on a nest egg, because she never wanted to go through the same financial trauma again.

Two nights later, Maggie stared at her most recent email from Kinky Lover.

We have great email sex. I keep thinking what it could be like if circumstances were different. I want to meet you in person. What do you say?

Maggie read the short email again, nerves jumping at the thought. Immediately, Connor jumped into her mind. She missed him, even though she was having torrid cybersex with another man. Thoughts of Connor still filled her mind at odd times of the day. A lost cause. She admitted the truth, but it didn't stop her thinking about what might have been, if he hadn't been so obsessed with blonde women, if she had been enough for him.

She missed the others as well, catching herself thinking about describing a particular customer at the theme restaurant to them before she remembered they'd washed their hands of her.

A pang of loneliness hit her as she realized the last person she'd talked to was the man at the bar where she'd gone for an interview. She hadn't talked to another person since. At the gym she put on her ear phones and ignored everyone. She'd taken her phone off the hook and ignored the doorbell.

"Damn, this isolation has got to change." She couldn't keep going on like this. It wasn't healthy.

She glanced at the email again and wondered. Maybe she should take a chance on Kinky Lover. He wrote great emails and was into spanking. Other kink, too, judging by the addition of ropes.

She started to type a response, then stopped. Perhaps she'd better think about it first before she committed herself to anything with a man she didn't know. Instead, she wrote a blog entry.

For those of you who are reluctant to participate in a spanking or can't understand why anyone would enjoy a good spanking, I thought I'd give you ten reasons why I think spanking is great.

It's a great method of stress relief.

It can be a good way of opening communication, since spanking requires talking and discussion.

Spanking doesn't require special tools—a hand or a hairbrush will work.

It can bring a new buzz to a relationship.

Most bottoms are well-padded and careful swats won't do any damage.

The closeness that comes after a spanking is magical.

It's great for foreplay and sex after a spanking is hot.

It's fun trying out different positions and scenarios.

Role-playing and dress-up can be a lot of fun.

An alpha man administering a spanking is plain sexy.

Let me know if you think of other reasons to add to my list. I'm all about learning when it comes to spanking.

An hour later, Maggie worked the bar during the regular barman's break, smiled and joked with two male customers while keeping an eye on the rest of the customers. Just gone five, it was still quiet. Another hour and the place would rock. She wriggled her toes in her black flats. Thank goodness for comfortable shoes.

A young couple walked up to the bar. Automatically, she scanned their faces and decided they were legal. She poured a vodka RTD, one of the popular ready-to-drink mixes, and a beer, taking their money with a smile.

From the corner of her eye, she noted some new arrivals, and when she'd finished, she turned. Her welcome smile died a rapid death when she came face-to-face with Susan and Christina.

The pub doors opened, and Julia walked in.

Maggie's heart stuttered before kicking into its normal beat. She forced her smile back to her lips. "Hello. What can I get you to drink?"

"Maggie, I didn't realize you worked here," Julia said. "We thought we'd try a new pub. This one hasn't been open for that long."

"I needed the money." Wasn't that obvious? Why else would she work every possible hour management offered her?

Christina offered a quiet smile. "I was sorry about you losing your job."

"Ancient history," Maggie said. "If you haven't decided on what to drink do you mind if I serve those guys?" She turned away without waiting for their reply. Why did they have to pick this bar?

When she turned back, the three women lined up at the bar like birds sitting on power lines and looked as if they'd roosted for the night.

"We'll take a bottle of the house Sauvignon Blanc," Susan said.

"And some peanuts," Julia added. "I missed lunch."

Maggie nodded. "We have a bar menu. The snacks are pretty good if you'd like something more substantial." Her voice emerged stiff and robot-like. She paused to draw a sharp breath and told herself to calm down. This job was important. Her new boss had emphasized customer service. She couldn't afford to lose the job for scaring off customers.

"How long have you been working here?" Christina asked.

"I started yesterday. I have another job at a theme restaurant. You know the medieval one?"

Julia chuckled, although it wasn't with her normal gusto. Maggie thought she looked sad. "That's the one with the wenches with big boobs."

"Yep," Maggie said, handing over the opened bottle of wine. "Case in point," she added, gesturing at her breasts. "I was perfectly qualified."

"Oh," Susan said, wrinkling her nose. "Isn't that a bit degrading?"

"I needed a job." Nothing less than the truth. Jobs were in short supply if a person lacked references. "It's not so bad if you keep your wits about you. I have a good reason to keep going to the gym."

Christina nodded, her eyes holding sympathy. "You look great. Have you lost weight?"

"A bit." Money shortages had a way of making a person focus on the important things in life. She realized she'd let go of her anger toward the three women. Secrets. They weren't necessarily a good thing between friends. And lying. That was where she'd gone wrong. "I'm really sorry I lied to you about Connor. It was wrong of me to break my promise."

Maggie walked away to serve more customers.

The head barman returned from his break. "I want you to stay working this bar tonight," he said. "You're efficient and doing a great job."

"Thanks," Maggie said, appreciating the kind words. It would keep her busy so she had an excuse to steer clear of the women. She'd missed them so much. Heck, she missed Connor. But things were different now. She couldn't go back to the way it was before. All she could do was go forward. She'd apologized and meant it. She was sorry for lying to her friends, but it didn't make things right.

Susan waved her over. "We'll take an order of fries, some spring rolls and—"

"We need something healthy," Christina interrupted.

"And the vegetable crudités and hot spinach dip," Susan finished. "Is that healthy enough for you?"

The Bottom Line

"Gotta have the five plus vegetables a day," Julia quipped. "They tell us all the time on television."

"Since when did you follow the rules?" Susan asked.

Julia's smile faded. "People change. Things don't stay the same."

Maggie felt her pain and wondered at the secrets emblazoned across Julia's face. Losing the baby had hurt her. It was funny because Julia was the last one out of all of them she'd expect to get pregnant or embrace motherhood. "I'll take the order through to the kitchen. It won't take long."

When she returned a group of young guys had joined them. Rugby players she discovered when she overheard them talking.

Julia gestured for another bottle of wine, and Maggie hustled to serve both her and the new arrivals.

"How are you doing, Julia?" she asked in an undertone.

Julia shrugged. "Good days. Bad days. How about you?"

Obviously Julia wasn't willing to talk specifics yet. "About the same as you. I don't think I'm relationship material. Every one of them ends the same way, with me ending up alone. I think I'm doing okay, then things get mucked up and everything ends badly." The words burst from Maggie, making her realize how badly she'd needed to talk.

Julia gave a sharp bark of laughter, one that held little humor. "You and me both. What say we give up on men and have a raging affair with each other?"

"Julia!" Christina said in clear shock. "Did you just proposition Maggie?"

"Why not?" Julia winked at her, but made sure Christina didn't see. "We're both off men, but like sex. I'm sure I could spank you, Maggie. Let's talk."

Susan started to splutter, while one of the young rugby players picked up on a pertinent word.

"Spanking?" he asked. "Which one of you is into spanking? There's a great spanking blog that one of the other guys in my team put me on to. I thought it would be strange and kinky, but it's really interesting."

Susan blurted, "That's Mag—"

"That's great," Maggie cut through Susan's words, shouting

loudly, and her friend clapped a hand over her mouth, her eyes full of apology. "You sound very open-minded." A pity he was too young for her.

In that moment, she knew she was going to meet up with her cyber lover. He pushed every one of her buttons and already knew she liked spanking.

"Where do you play rugby?" Christina asked, diverting the conversation.

Susan wasn't so easily diverted, her speculative gaze going from Maggie to Julia and back. Maggie felt Susan's gaze follow her down the bar while she served several beers and mixed drinks. It was another hour before things calmed down enough for her to check on her friends.

At least the initial stiffness had faded, although Maggie wasn't fool enough to think their friendship would continue as if nothing had happened.

"Susan thinks we're interested in each other. Connor would have a good laugh about that. He's always said two chicks together are hot," Julia said.

"Susan is gullible." Maggie didn't want to talk about Connor. She hadn't seen him, not even at the gym. She hoped they didn't mention she was working here. The last thing she wanted was to see him with his new blonde. She didn't think she could cope with that. A sudden tight sensation behind her eyes told her she was far from over him.

Betrayal hurt—from both sides, which made her want to work to repair the rift with her friends.

"I've really missed you. I haven't been going out much. Just work and Susan and Christina dragged me out tonight. I'm sorry I didn't make more of an effort to see you," Julia said in a low voice. "I really am sorry. You're a good friend and you deserve better."

"It's okay," Maggie murmured.

"It's not, but thank you. Are you seeing anyone else?" Julia asked.

"Not really. Sort of," she amended. Cripes, she was having regular cybersex.

"So, which is it?"

"I've been having some pretty torrid cybersex with someone

I met through my blog."

Julia's eyes widened. "Really?"

Maggie moved away to serve some more customers, noting the crowd had thinned out. Some had left for home while others had moved to the adjoining restaurant.

When she returned to her friends, the rugby players had left. She gathered up the glasses, stacked them into the glass machine and switched it on.

"You can't leave me hanging like that," Julia said. "Spill." She turned to the others and whispered, "Maggie's having cybersex with some guy."

"Maggie!" Susan said. "Sorry, I didn't mean to sound so critical. What I meant is that cybersex could be dangerous."

"I intend to be careful," Maggie said.

"For goodness sake, tell Maggie cybersex is dangerous," Susan said.

"Susan, you sound like my mother when she discovered I knew about the birds and the bees," Julia said. "Maggie's having safe sex. What's wrong with that?"

"There are all sorts of weird people online," Susan said. "You're having sex with one? I don't believe it. You don't know anything about him. How do you even know it's a him? It could be a woman."

"Or a horny underage teenager," Christina added.

Maggie thought about Kinky Lover's posts. "No," she said slowly. "I don't think it's an underage male. This man knows his way around a woman's body. He knows what makes us tick."

"He could be married," Julia said.

"See," Susan said with concern. "Even Julia agrees. There has to be something wrong with him if he has to have cybersex. What's wrong with the real thing? Why can't he go out and find a date like most men do? Aw, hell, I don't mean to sound critical. It's a safety issue."

"It's not always so easy to meet people," Maggie retorted. "I know. Heck, Susan. You know too. That's why you've applied to a reality show."

Susan nodded with a wry smile. "Touché."

"We got in," Christina said, bouncing up and down on her

barstool.

Maggie noticed a new arrival. "Hold that thought," she ordered, moving down the bar to serve the elderly couple.

When she returned, the three were in deep conversation. Maggie used the time to remove some empty glasses and wipe down the bar. She chopped up a lemon and restocked the beer fridge.

"You can take a break now," the head barman said.

"Is it okay if I sit with my friends while I'm on my break?"

"Sure. Don't be late back."

With a nod, she walked around the bar.

"Are you on a break?" Christina asked. "Or are you finished for the night?"

"I wish. My feet are sore from standing. No, it's a break. I have another two hours for this shift."

"Let's sit over there at the table," Susan said.

They moved over to the table, Maggie clearing it off and taking the glasses to the bar before she rejoined her friends.

Susan stood and hugged her. "I'm sorry I was such a bitch about Connor. I have no excuses, but I'll try not to repeat it ever again," she whispered fiercely.

Christina embraced her, too, a tight squeeze that said more than words. Maggie blinked rapidly to control the surge of emotion gripping her chest.

"Don't look at me," Julia said with a wink. "I don't want to hug you and start spreading rumors about our hot lesbian affair."

Maggie laughed and pulled out a chair. "So tell me about the reality show," she said. "What happens next? Do you get filmed the entire time?"

"Christina and I have to go to another elimination round next weekend. We get to meet the farmers. From what they said, they allocate each farmer with a group of women. We get to talk to him together as a group and alone. At the end of the day, the farmer whittles us down to his chosen eight."

"Sounds scary," Maggie said. "What are you wearing?"

"We can talk about that later," Julia said. "I want to hear about the cybersex. Where does this guy live? How do you even know this guy is from New Zealand?"

"That's true," Susan said. "You don't know anything about this guy."

Christina smirked. "Apart from the fact he's good at sex."

"Yeah, well," Julia said. "You don't even know that. He might talk the walk, but can he walk the talk?"

"Huh?" Susan said. "What does that mean?"

Maggie laughed. "It might mean he's all mouth and no trousers."

Julia groaned.

Susan's confusion cleared. "Oh, you mean he might not be able to get it up. They have pills for that these days."

"Gullible," Julia mouthed in Maggie's direction and they both started laughing. "Seriously, though," Julia said when the laughter stopped. "Has he said where he lives or where he wants to meet? If you decide to follow through and actually meet him, you need to be careful. Take safety precautions."

"I suppose it would work if you met him for coffee somewhere or maybe a meal in a public place," Christina said. "One thing you shouldn't do is meet in a hotel room. Even though you know him online, you need to get to know him on a personal level."

Julia wrinkled her nose, the wine she'd drunk during the evening putting a flush in her cheeks. "Yeah, if he's short with bad teeth and no hair, you need an escape route."

"So you think I should meet with him?" Maggie asked.

Susan ran her finger around the rim of her wine glass. "I'm not convinced it's a great idea, but you're the best one to judge from the emails. I take it you don't want to share?"

"No," Maggie said quickly, unable to halt the race of color across her face.

"Just out of interest, have you been emailing him back with suggestive replies?" Christina asked.

"No," Maggie said, but she couldn't look at any of them. "Oh, okay," she muttered. "I can't lie to you guys. I have, and no, you're not looking at my replies either."

"Why don't you arrange to meet at a restaurant?" Julia asked. "Tell us the time and place and we'll book a table there too. That way, we can check him out and give you our opinions. And if there's any trouble, we'll be right there with you. Your mystery man won't even need to know we're your friends. As far as he's concerned, we'd be diners."

Susan nodded. "That's not a bad idea."

"I'll think about it and let you know," Maggie said, after studying each of their faces. "I need to get back to work."

Julia grabbed her arm. "Don't you dare meet this guy without telling us, Maggie. We care about you and don't want to see anything happen to you."

With a knot of emotion blocking her throat, she nodded before hurrying off to the bar, feeling better than she had in days. While the old easy camaraderie wasn't present again, she hoped they would actually talk soon and drag out the monsters hiding in the closets. Like all people, they each had their hot buttons from the past. Maggie poured a beer and admitted to herself if she had her time over, she'd make most of the same decisions. Sometimes a person just had to follow their gut instincts and hope for the best.

Chapter Twenty-one

"What if she doesn't come?" Connor asked.

"Stop being such a wimp," Julia said. "She'll be here. You didn't see her face when she was talking about her cyber lover."

Connor's eyes narrowed as he entered the restaurant. "She didn't tell you about the emails, what was in them?"

"Relax," Julia said. "She refused to tell us a thing."

"Other than very general things," Susan said. "I want to know why you didn't just pick up a phone and call her."

"I did call her. Constantly. I tried to see her in person, but she refused to answer her door." Connor glanced at the door, struggling to hide his nerves. "She needed time. If I'd pushed her any harder, she would have run or at least reported me to the cops as a stalker. She doesn't believe I want her."

"And maybe the blonde parade had something to do with that," Julia said in a tart voice.

"I haven't dated a single blonde since I started seeing Maggie. I'm not interested in anyone other than her."

"That's not what I heard," Christina said. "Besides, I saw you with a blonde the other day. She was draped all over you."

Connor frowned. "Oh, you mean Sylvie. Believe it or not, Sylvie *is* my cousin, and she's now dating one of my flatmates. She's putting on a surprise birthday party for him. We were talking about the arrangements."

"Are you sure?" Christina asked. "Because from where I stood, it looked as if she was interested in you and would give your flatmate the flick without a second thought."

"When did you see me with her?"

"A couple of weeks ago," Christina said.

"Did Maggie see you with her?" Julia asked. "Do you think that's why she pushed you away?"

"Yes, she saw us. That's why we broke up." Connor shrugged. "She didn't believe me, and refused to discuss it. I never go out with two women at a time," he said. "Never. It's a rule. I never look at another woman while I'm dating someone else."

"Does Maggie know that?" Julia asked. "Because I didn't know that."

"Hell." Connor dragged his hand through his hair and glared at the women. "I can't believe you'd think so little of me. Yes, I told Maggie our *friends with benefits* deal was open and we could see other people, but I never did. I didn't look at another woman after Maggie and I hooked up. And I haven't since," he added. "I don't know how many times I have to tell you. I'm not interested in any woman apart from Maggie."

Susan sighed. "That's so romantic."

"You didn't tell us it started out as a *friends with benefits* thing," Julia said.

"I couldn't think of any other way to get together with Maggie. She took a bit of persuading. And yeah, it might be romantic, but if I can't convince Maggie to change her mind about me, it doesn't mean a thing."

"You'd better take your seat before Maggie catches us together," Julia said. She grasped his hand and drew him into a tight hug. "Good luck. You and Maggie are my favorite people. You deserve a little happiness." She kissed him lightly on the lips and drew back. "Oops, you definitely don't need to wear my badge."

Connor wiped his mouth and the women announced him lipstick-free. He crossed the restaurant and took a seat at his allocated table, more nervous than he could ever remember.

Nerves skittered through her belly as she walked down the street toward the bustling seafood restaurant. Although she wasn't worried about safety because the restaurant was a busy one, she figured she wouldn't be human if she wasn't nervous. Kinky Lover made her feel good. She felt as if she could tell him anything and would receive a thoughtful and insightful reply. Plus the sex was hot. She couldn't help but wonder what it would be like in person.

What did he look like?

That worried her. As the girls said, he could be any age. Photos. Why hadn't she asked him to send her a photo? Damn, her inexperience showed. Sex and men, she decided, were like a many-headed monster. Lop off one head and another appeared in its place.

The Friday night traffic seemed heavier than normal. Maggie waited at the crossing for the lights to change and the green man to appear. She inhaled. In. Out. Probably not the best idea while standing in the middle of all that traffic.

An old Holden carrying several young teens passed. The driver tooted the horn. "Show us your tits!" one hollered.

Maggie glared after them. They'd die of shock if she actually lifted her top and flashed them.

At long last, the lights turned and she crossed the street. A thin film of perspiration coated her skin, and her bottom lip ached. Too much nibbling. She'd been doing it all day, letting nerves get the better of her. Her clothes clung to her body, and her panties felt embarrassingly damp.

A couple exited the restaurant, the man holding the door for her. She couldn't prevaricate a moment more.

"Thanks," she murmured, walking inside.

A wave of chatter and the clink of cutlery hit her along with the aroma of food and spices. Her stomach let out a rumble of protest. Maggie slammed the flat of her hand against her belly, heat rising in her cheeks. The last thing she needed was a rumbling stomach. That would create a great impression.

She stopped at the hostess desk, stated her name and said she was here to meet David.

Her stomach roiled when the hostess smiled and told her to follow. He was here.

Maggie spotted the girls sitting at a table toward the back of the restaurant, in the direction the hostess was leading her.

"Good luck, Maggie," Julia whispered when she passed. "We'll be here if you need us."

Maggie nodded, unable to muster a smile this time.

The hammer of her heart echoed in her ears. Her fists clenched and unclenched.

"Here you go," the hostess said, indicating a fairly private booth. She could see the back of a man's head. He had short, dark hair and broad shoulders. *Turn around*, she thought. *Turn around so I can see you.*

The man noticed the hostess and stood. Maggie held her breath, nibbled her bottom lip.

"Connor?" she squeaked. Her legs trembled violently, and she grabbed the top of the table to stabilize her balance.

They'd tricked her. Tears filled her eyes as she blindly turned away. God, she just didn't learn.

"No, wait." Connor caught her shoulder and pulled her to a stop.

"Is everything all right?" the hostess asked.

"It's fine," Connor said. "Please, Maggie. I want to talk to you. If you want to go after I've talked, that's fine. I'll let you go."

Maggie shook her head and swiped a tear from her eyes with the back of her hand. She saw Julia stand, blinked as her traitorous friend walked over to her.

"Please, stay and talk to Connor. He really cares about you. It's not easy to find love." Her face clouded and she swallowed. "When you find it you should fight for it, not walk away without a second thought. Just give Connor a chance to try to explain. Please."

"Please," Connor added his plea.

Finally, aware they were the center of attention, Maggie allowed Connor to lead her back to the table. She sat, glad to take the weight off her unsteady limbs.

"I'm meeting someone," Maggie said.

"I'm Kinky Lover," Connor said, watching her closely.

"You?"

"Yeah." He stopped and dragged a hand through his hair, making her realize he wasn't as confident as he appeared. "I've gone about this the wrong way. I should have been honest from the start."

"About the blonde. Yeah, you should have," Maggie spat.

Connor frowned. "You mean Sylvie."

"I saw you with the blonde. She had her hands all over you. You kissed her. And there was the one in the pub too."

"Sylvie is my cousin. You know Frank is my stepfather. Sylvie is my cousin via his side of the family. She thought we'd be good together and took some persuading otherwise. Jenny was the woman in the pub. It's true I used to date her, but she was there celebrating her engagement. Jenny and her friends suggested I do something special for you, something memorable, and that's when I came up with the idea for the corset. Our meeting was totally innocent."

"I rang your flat to talk to you, and this Sylvie answered. She said she wasn't your cousin," Maggie accused.

"You rang me?" The realization brought both relief, and anger at Sylvie. "She misled you on purpose. I'd be happy to give you my mother's phone number right now. You can ring and ask both my mother and Frank about Sylvie. Do you want me to ring them? Sylvie is dating one of my flatmates now. I could ring her so she can apologize to you. If I have my way she's going to say sorry whether she likes it or not." Connor grimaced. "Part of this is my fault. I should have told you straight off that I was interested in you and no one else. I love you. I've thought about you as more than a friend for ages. You seemed so cautious and wary I decided to do the *friends with benefits* thing. I couldn't think of any other way to romance you."

"But the blog. I remember getting an email from you almost straight away. You mean you knew all along?"

"Julia told me," he said. "She told me I couldn't say anything so I emailed you under a false name."

The waiter approached. "Can I get you a drink? Are you ready to order?"

"I'll have a Steinlager beer and the lady will have a glass of Shingle Peak Sauvignon Blanc," Connor said without consulting her. "We're not ready to order yet."

"Very good, sir." The waiter bustled off.

"But I don't understand," Maggie said. "Why did you take so long to spank me?"

"I was frightened I'd muck everything up between us. You

know about my father. Hell, your own background isn't dissimilar. Surely you understand?"

Maggie glanced at him and blushed. "You've never hurt me."

"I know I've told you before, but the intensity of the spanking is incredible. I feel really close to you." Connor reached across the table to grasp her hand. "I love you. I don't want to lose you."

"But you always go out with blondes," Maggie said.

"That was until a particular brunette seized my heart. Maggie, there's no one but you. I haven't looked at another woman, let alone had sex with one, since our first time together at the beach. You're the color in my life, babe. Everyone else is black and white."

"Really?"

"Really. I want to marry you. Will you marry me?"

She closed her eyes briefly before opening them to stare at him. "Yes," she blurted.

He laughed and leaned over the table to cup her face with her hands. Maggie leaned even closer and kissed him, trying to put everything she felt into that one kiss. It went on and on because she had a lot to say.

She was vaguely aware of applause, and when she and Connor pulled apart, she found everyone staring at them. Most were grinning.

"Way to go, Maggie," Julia shouted.

"Oh, heck," Maggie muttered. "I can't believe I did that in front of everyone."

"Yeah, you've been a naughty girl. You know what happens to naughty girls, don't you?"

Maggie's throat went dry. She opened and closed her mouth, licked her lips.

"Maggie?"

"They get spanked?"

"That's right," Connor said. "It will be a long spanking, because I have a lot of time to make up."

"I don't know. You're pretty good at cybersex."

"But it's not the same, babe. I couldn't touch you. I couldn't kiss your beautiful breasts or spank your bottom." Under the table, she felt the glide of his hands over her knees and up her thigh.

"Here in the restaurant?" she asked with a cheeky grin. "Haven't we given them enough of a show already?"

Connor opened his wallet and tossed some money on the table. He stood and walked around to her side of the table, stretching out a hand. When Maggie took his hand, he tugged her to her feet.

"No, not here, Maggie. I have a room in the hotel next door."

"Oh," she said.

He grinned, his beautiful eyes glowing with love. "Yeah, oh," he said, and without another word he swept her up into his arms and carried her through the crowded room to the exit.

The chatter in the room ceased as everyone turned to stare.

"Is she going to marry you?" Susan called out.

Connor grinned down at her but kept walking. "What do you think?" he asked in a loud voice.

The applause started.

"Way to go, Connor!" Christina shouted and stood, clapping.

Maggie hid her face when the rest of the restaurant patrons and her friends followed suit.

They exited the restaurant with the ovation thundering in their ears. Maggie couldn't believe it.

Connor loved her.

In the quiet of the hotel room, they faced each other with honesty and love. The gorgeous view of the distant harbor and Rangitoto Island went ignored as they disrobed. Connor wrapped his arms around her and kissed her lips firmly. Seconds later, she let out a shriek of surprise when she found herself draped face down over his lap.

"You will never leave me like that again," Connor ordered, paddling her backside with something she thought might be a special spanking paddle. "You will always give me an opportunity to explain if we have a disagreement."

"Yes! I promise." The sting made her cry out, dancing across her butt cheek and rushing to her clit. Her heart warmed in the knowledge of the care and preparation he'd gone through to declare his love and ask for a second chance. Each successive spank pushed her harder until her bottom stung and she felt a distinct bloom of juices surging between her legs.

"You like that, don't you?"

"Yes."

"And you're going to marry me very soon? This month?"

Maggie didn't have to think about it. "I'd like that."

"Good," he said, swatting her for a final time.

He rolled her off his knees and kissed her hard. Her bottom felt as if it were on fire, but she'd never felt so loved before.

"I love you." Connor placed her gently in the middle of the bed. Without taking his gaze off her, he removed his clothes, tossing them to the floor. He came down on the bed and kissed her again, this time tender. Slow. The brush of his lips brought tears to her eyes, the emotion pressing against her chest and threatening to make her explode.

"Don't make me wait," she whispered. "I don't need foreplay. I need you."

Connor brushed another kiss on her lips and pulled away to guide his cock to her entrance. He pushed inside her pussy, filling her, taking her with so much love on his face.

They rocked together, urgency overtaking them, the feelings rushing through them true and fierce until Maggie shattered in an explosion of pleasure.

"I love you, Maggie."

"I love you too," she said, smiling because there was no other man for her. She'd gone into this adventure wanting to learn about spanking, her reasons half-formed. Now she knew exactly why she wanted Connor to spank her. She needed to act true to herself, to explore her desires and find a man who respected her, one who accepted her despite her past, and a man who not only let her explore, but who confidently blazed trails at her side. A man who saw the real her, warts and all, and still loved her without trying to make her change. That man was Connor. Perhaps they could even continue the blog adventure together as a couple.

Yes, Connor was her lover, the love of her life. Connor Grey was her bottom line.

About the Author

To learn more about Shelley Munro, please visit www.shelleymunro.com Send an email to Shelley Munro at shelleymunro@gmail.com or join her Yahoo! group to participate in the chatter and fun with Shelley and other readers. groups.yahoo.com/group/romancebookmark

Lies and secrets have a way of returning to bite a girl in the butt...

Tea for Two
© 2008 Shelley Munro

Hayley Williams thought she was past the screwing-up stage of her life. These days, she wears her good girl persona well—except when she moonlights as a gypsy tea leaf reader in order to earn money to buy her own home. There's something about Sam Norville, though, that prods her inner imp back to life. A chance meeting, a margarita...okay, two...a stolen kiss, and suddenly she's back in hot water.

Sam, a successful businessman, doesn't believe in love at first sight. Not anymore. For him, involvement with any woman means risking a run-in with the tabloid press. But his mysterious gypsy lover keeps him coming back, keeps him prodding her for more...like the truth. Of course it's not love. No, sir. Sam only does lust.

Hayley knows she shouldn't want Sam, especially since she lied to him. The right thing to do? Shove that naughty imp off her shoulder and come clean. But at pesky imp just won't budge...

Warning: There be lies and secrets ahead, wrapped in pretty bows with margaritas, a one-night stand, fortune telling and a gypsy. Oh, and tea. Lots and lots of pots of tea.

Available now in ebook and print from Samhain Publishing.

The only way to keep what he has…is to surrender everything.

Taking Chloe
© *2009 Anne Rainey*
The Vaughn Series, Book 3…

Merrick Vaughn couldn't be happier with this life. His business is jumping and his marriage to the love of his life is about as good as it gets. At least, that's what he thinks…until Chloe announces she wants to separate.

Stunned doesn't begin to cover it, but it quickly becomes clear that's she's dead serious. And if he doesn't take action, as in now, he's going to lose the only woman he's over loved.

The last thing Chloe wants is a divorce, but she can't go on living with a virtual stranger who spends all his time—and hers—behind a desk. It's tearing her apart, and taking a break to sort out her thoughts seems her only recourse.

Then Merrick offers a wicked proposition: go to Hawaii with him for one week's vacation. After that, if he hasn't successfully changed her mind, he'll let her go. No questions asked. There's only one caveat. She must agree to give him complete control.

Chloe's intrigued and scared. One week in paradise might bring them closer—or be their ultimate undoing.

Warning: This story contains graphic language, a touch of voyeurism, anal sex, and husband-and-wife lovin' in lots of sinful positions. Have your significant other handy!

Available now in ebook from Samhain Publishing.

HOT STUFF

Discover Samhain!

THE HOTTEST NEW PUBLISHER ON THE PLANET

Romance, fantasy, mystery, thriller, mainstream and more—Samhain has more selection, hotter authors, and everything's available in ebook.

Pick your favorite, sit back, and enjoy the ride! Hot stuff indeed.

SAMHAIN
PUBLISHING

WWW.SAMHAINPUBLISHING.COM

GREAT CHEAP FUN

Discover eBooks!

THE FASTEST WAY TO GET THE HOTTEST NAMES

Get your favorite authors on your favorite reader, long before they're out in print! Ebooks from Samhain go wherever you go, and work with whatever you carry—Palm, PDF, Mobi, Kindle, nook, and more.

SAMHAIN PUBLISHING

WWW.SAMHAINPUBLISHING.COM

CPSIA information can be obtained at www.ICGtesting.com
Printed in the USA
235817LV00003B/33/P